Moira Orfei in Aigues-Mortes

Moira Orfei in Aigues-Mortes

a novel
by

Wayne Koestenbaum

Soft Skull Press
Brooklyn, NY | 2004

© Wayne Koestenbaum, 2004

Author photograph by Steven Marchetti

Published by Soft Skull Press
71 Bond Street, Brooklyn, NY 11217

Distributed by Publishers Group West
www.pgw.com · 1.800.788.3123

Printed in Canada

Koestenbaum, Wayne.
  Moira Orfei in Aigues-Mortes : a novel / by Wayne Koestenbaum.
    p. cm.
  ISBN 1-932360-53-0 (alk. paper)
  1. Pianists—Fiction. 2. Sex addicts—Fiction. 3. Bisexual men—Fiction.
  4. New York (State)—Fiction. 5. Circus performers—Fiction.
  6. Americans—France—Fiction. 7. Diaries—Authorship—Fiction.
  8. Aigues-Mortes (France)—Fiction. I. Title.

PS3561.O349M65 2004
813'.5—dc22

                              2004019383

for Steven Marchetti

PART ONE
The Situation

Notebook One

Thirty-five years ago I lost my red beanie cap. I accidentally left it in the unheated third-grade classroom. The fickle hat never reappeared. Pigeons alighting on a dung-splattered Roman Catholic church (I see it out my bedroom window) are more important than my cheap cap, worn once.

*

I live in East Kill, a tiny, insignificant, unlovely, never-discussed town to the north of the Heraclite River, and divided by a tributary known as East Kill. In New York State parlance, a "kill" is a stream. The word comes from the Dutch *kil*. I learned in first grade from grey-haired Mrs. Spence (who tied my hands behind my back because I sucked my thumb) that "kill" is Gaelic for a hermit's cell. East Kill takes pride in having neither proximity nor relation to overvisited West Kill. A pesticide factory, hidden in the foothills, clouds our air with chemical screens, producing lurid sunsets. Because of our flexible penal code (according to my mother, who follows crime), we have more artistic types per capita than any other small town in New York State, though we lack tourist appeal. We may never be an international music center, a Siena, an Aix-en-Provence, but our reputation is growing. We have surpassed Elmira, Troy, and Ancram—our nearest rivals.

My mother, Alma, claims our Mechanical Street house as her legal residence but spends much of the year performing, as pianist, to great acclaim, in Buenos Aires, where she owns a glassy penthouse apartment north of Plaza Palermo Viejo. Bougainvillea and jasmine crawl up the building's face. Her movement from East Kill to Buenos Aires is so rapid and serendipitous that when I wake, in my puritanically underfurnished bedroom, I can't remember whether she is there or here.

*

Alma insisted that if I write every day in these private notebooks, by the end of the year I will have explained our family to the nation. She understands congenital inarticulateness (she received a dose from her father, Ricardo Guadalquivar). Notebooks are the best way out of the morass. She knows every detail of my private life, musicianship, marriage, breakdowns, and ambitions. She carefully supervised my early education; I starred in her imaginary tableau, "Theo's Education," a construction superior, aesthetically, to my actual stumbling apprenticeship. She remembers the time I plagiarized my term paper on the human eye: I stole the descriptions, verbatim, from *Encyclopedia Britannica*.

In accordance with her designs, I am keeping private notebooks. We call them "books of nothing." She says, "Honey, your books of nothing are also *my* books of nothing." Their subject is *nada*—inanition that envelops me when I play piano. I have bought twenty-five blank notebooks, from the *conservatoire* supply store; I plan, over the next six months, to fill them with random, spontaneous jottings, in fountain pen. The notebooks' subject will be my comeback. I propose to return to the European stage, this May. The entertainment office in Aigues-Mortes, a tiny village in southmost France, has invited me to perform, and I have accepted. The honorarium will barely pay my expenses.

Today is November first. Snowfall blankets East Kill, covers my car. Mechanical Street, where I live, with my mother, sister, and wife, is impassable. Constance Antrim, ABC weather forecaster, predicted the harshest winter in three decades.

*

Five years of breakdown separate my last piano recital in Europe—a fainting fit at the Montepulciano festival, while playing Liszt's "Bénédiction de Dieu dans la solitude"—from my planned comeback in Aigues-Mortes, a town known for sea salt, and surrounded by intact medieval walls and flat lugubrious marshes. Guidebooks call Aigues-

Mortes the "town of dead water." I will boost its musical reputation. My European agent, Alfonso Reyes, says that the Aigues-Mortes entertainment office hopes that the return of Theo Mangrove will draw cognoscenti from across the Camargue. For five years, since my final breakdown in Montepulciano, I received no European invitations to perform. In earlier years, Europe was my mainstay: Ferrara, Toulon, Marseilles... Until now, I never stooped to perform in a village as insignificant as Aigues-Mortes. A comeback should be modest. The Aigues-Mortes spring season brochure already includes my name. Alfonso, optimist, says there is advance "buzz." I should bring a collaborator—singer, violinist, flutist, dancer, speaker, clown? I may hazard a waltz program, with Scriabin's tiny "Quasi-Valse" as centerpiece—to celebrate the partial, the flawed, the almost, the not quite.

American tongues stumble over the French name "Aigues-Mortes." Our closest equivalent: "Egg Mort."

*

After onstage amnesia, delirium, hyperventilation, fainting, seizures, convulsions, staggering, palpitations, I endured a five-year forced retirement. When I was first hospitalized, in Viterbo, the mental-health staff separated me from the piano for two months. My sight clouded and I suffered perceptual shifts that my mother later complimented by calling "psychotic," an honorific. I saw the nurse's face split in half (a blur to the right of her lips formed a cloud of unknowing); stepping into the bathroom for respite from the hallucination, I thought the mirror had a memory and a mouth, and that it, like fellatio, was swallowing me. I told my reflection, "That's the devouring scene, right?"—as if the looking-glass were not merely the cannibal, but a commentary on cannibalism, a monologue I could join. In Viterbo, I was kept forcibly away from every source of pleasure and conflict. I received a few visitors, though no family was allowed. My mother Alma and my sister Tanaquil telephoned once a week. My wife Anita telephoned daily. Usually I refused her calls. I never refused Alma's calls, though they depressed me. To Tanaquil's calls, I was indifferent. She couldn't undo the fellatio hallucination in the Viterbo bathroom mirror.

*

I was born between two miscarriages. My mother, a more celebrated pianist than I will ever be, conversationally dwells on these misfirings: "The pain during the first miscarriage was almost worse than what I felt, delivering you." After my father's death, she dedicated a recital to his memory, in East Kill: that night she performed in black, like Clara Schumann post-Robert. For the next concert, not a memorial, in Troy, she wore a gown the color of salmon roe. Her full name is Alma Guadalquivar Mangrove; she has no living rival. Her career and physical appearance beggar my verbal powers. Because she might be the only person ever to read these notebooks, describing her is pointless. She insists I call her "Alma," never "Mother." We pity women whose prospects motherhood circumscribes. Our conversations are endless, circular, orphic, psychic, and telephonic, since she spends most of the year in Buenos Aires, and I never leave East Kill. The day my sciatica acted up, her sciatica acted up. Our bodies are in sync, like sisters whose menstrual cycles match.

Her mother's name is Gertrude Guadalquivar. My current doctor, Dr. Crick, contraindicates contact with the tempestuous Guadalquivars: whenever I see them, my immune system falls apart. (One other Guadalquivar lives in the United States: my aunt Matilda.) Guadalquivars lack the wealth of my father's clan, the Mangroves, but my late maternal grandfather, Ricardo, achieved distinction as a minor composer of piano preludes, waltzes, inventions, impromptus, improvisations, and caprices, some published. He locked his daughters in their rooms at night. My mother ran away when she was six, to the grocery store, and asked for the butcher to hide her. He called Ricardo, who came to take her home.

*

Last summer, at a garden party, a benefit for East Kill Conservatory, I saw again, for the first time in two decades, my greatest piano teacher, Xenia Lamont, a domineering, temperamental woman with a history of nervous breakdowns. She called herself my "therapist" and charged me for our "sessions"—heavy-duty sex combined with musical instruction. (She disliked the name Xenia: it reminded her of Queen Victoria.

Sometimes she asked me to call her "X," or "Madame X.") She resembled Ingrid Bergman, or a flushed Romanian empress with a forceps-wide ribcage. At the reunion she stood suntanned in a cubist-patterned caftan by the Conservatory's garden wall with her two grown sons and her loyal husband, broken capillaries on his martyr cheeks. She told me, excitedly, "I'm writing my autobiography. Early sins." As a decoy, to prevent her from probing into my European breakdown, I embarked on a long horticultural description (*lobelia, allium, iris*). My words grew labored and my hands trembled, as if I were having a seizure, a repetition of the Toulon staggering, the Montepulciano palsy. Listening, Xenia looked uncomfortable, like a nurse uncertain how to manage a difficult patient who was going to die soon anyway and didn't merit attention. Then she said, "Viterbo." She'd heard about my hospitalization. I turned quickly away from her. I didn't want to start telling stories, again, of our "therapy" sessions, the smooth slow intercourse, her shaved pubis. A teacher's vagina has no particular smell, only a reasonableness, ductility and articulateness, like forearms when playing rapid-fire octaves.

*

My father's people, originally dairy farmers, matured into dairy capitalists. My inheritance, based on butter manufacture, is small but secure. Duties come with the sinecure—correspondence, and lunches with estate lawyers in Manhattan, to convince them of my *bona fides,* and to conceal from them my personality's gradual disintegration, my incomprehension of what scrupulous Alma calls "reality." On the telephone to Buenos Aires, I ask Alma about her psychotropics, and she dissembles, as do I, whenever possible, to my reputation's detriment.

*

No one has called me Theodore since childhood. For a time, at the *conservatoire,* I went by "Thad," but "Thad" implies an unhappy paucity of erectile tissue. "Theo," Alma agrees, is a meditative, masculine nickname. I produce twenty erections per day (all under Alma's indirect supervision, and some in celebration of my sister Tanaquil) but I'm not a victim of that unfortunate medical condition known as priapism. Erections aren't painful. Out of the twenty, my wife Anita takes care of two. They prove me a semi-husband. The other eighteen erections are handled by Friedman, Marco, Stefan, Eduardo, Siddhartha, Franco, Isaac, Battista, Sing—friendly hustlers at the East Kill Sauna, Space Bar, Fortune 500, Statute of Limitations, Transit Factory, Contact, Liberty Alley, Stadium, Camera Baths, and other clubs in the water district.

My libido is out of control. Even ninety-year-old men, when I see them naked, excite me, though I won't interrupt my piano-practicing to service them.

*

Dr. Crick calls me "bisexual." I married my wife, Anita, during a month-long snowstorm that paralyzed East Kill's economy and clouded my consciousness. My mother never approved of the marriage: she called Anita "ordinary." Anita is a tall blonde with a weak chin and strong cheekbones; she walks with the grace of a Kabuki dancer, though she received no training in movement arts. To simulate her coloring, dilute strawberry ice cream with milk, to undo the pink's intensity, and then love the result. A sun lamp in her private bedroom burnishes her skin. She likes when I use the word "sign"; it makes me seem a sociologist, and she married me for my analytic abilities, not my musical skills. She'd like me to retire, so we could move to Portland, Maine, where the only well-to-do branch of her destitute family still owns a house that could become hers if she sues for it. In New Rochelle, late 1960s, she agitated for nuclear disarmament, and she has an East Kill University master's diploma in aesthetics. For a time she taught at the East Kill Community College: "Introduction to Aesthetics," a core course, boycotted. Aesthetics are passé. Students prefer engineering. Contrary to Alma's critical claim, my wife is not "ordinary." She is fussy about details and physical sensations. She appreciates my bottom, which she calls "your special provider." I like intercourse; I am not a fan of the vagina, *per se,* but I enjoy its tight yet permissive grip. A man's holes only roughly compare. I was not bad at math in school; Anita's initial assessment of me as a sociopath *in utero* does not miss the mark. My groin: an area she wants sole rights to. No one deserves a monopoly. Preoccupied with her collection of dollhouse furniture, she avoids the full-sized. Dr. Crick calls her "obsessive." From the hobby shop I bring home special-ordered miniature fauteuils and whatnots, to keep her amused. Her late father, Hal Ackroyd, a drunk, ran a tire shop in Manchester, thirty miles from East Kill, and slapped her around the kitchen. Her mother has remarried serially: her current name is Mrs. Wax, and she is indifferent to her daughter's existence. Anita has a sister, Astrud, whose wine-colored nevis, on her cheek, repulses me; she moved to Taipei to be a missionary. When my wife smiles, her face undergoes reversal, and approximates a frown, so I can't accurately judge her moods: dejection, joy? Does she hate being married to a two-timing failure? Does she think me a narcissist or does she have other words for what Dr. Crick calls my "malady," and what my sister Tanaquil calls my "squalor"?

*

Toward a new philosophy of music:

I dreamt that, along a factory assembly-line, a hand-made orange metronome moved—a propagandistic inducement to be kind, to care about other people's rhythms and prisons . . .

*

The first time I remember seeing Alma perform, I noted (*déjà vu*) her relative flatchestedness. (I regret the frequent linkage of "bosom" and "piano" in the musical journals I skim before bedtime.) Alma's breasts, as I recall them under her saffron gown, were flapjacks, round, palm-sized, not protruding, making no demand on eye or memory. The gown didn't hug the breasts: it gave them room to breathe, to enjoy their lack of distinction, in privacy. A breast, like a pianist, wants solitude, separation from judge and voyeur. Alma was playing the Schubert *Wanderer* Fantasy. As she reached the final, difficult, loud pages, endless ascensions toward a C-major climax already reached, her hands seemed fatigued. I connected exhaustion with unprotuberant breasts. Their flatness made me feel superior—undeservedly.

East Kill residents think it bizarre that I, at forty-three, live not only with my wife but with my mother and sister. Most of the year, Alma is in

Buenos Aires; Tanaquil, a recluse, rarely leaves the house. She stays in her locked bedroom, with its wallpaper of Big Ben and Buckingham Palace, and amuses herself with Tauchnitz classics, frozen waffles heated in a toaster oven, diet shakes from a private fridge. Demanding, paranoid, she never grew to full height. As a child, she had a nearly fatal fever (Alma called it "red brain": a combination of meningitis and scarlet fever). Tanaquil is two years my junior, but she skipped two grades, so we were in the same classes; she never went to college or seriously played an instrument, though for a year she tried sax. Quick academic advancement led, by slow degrees, to her perpetual arrest, upstairs, in her bedroom, away from the productive, rebuking world. Tanaquil fears that I will interrupt her progress toward the next drink, the next defecation. We meet in the hallway at midnight to complain about Alma. Tanaquil's dream: to be a madam in an important bordello. She fastidiously plucks her eyebrows, unto absence.

*

I have one pierced ear with a gold hoop, dark hair neatly plastered to my skull, a low brow, well-proportioned legs, clear fair skin, large blue eyes eager for companionship, wide hands, long tapered fingers. I wear "Montmorency" citrus eau de toilette and black cashmere sweaters, have stiff posture, am rarely depressed, often affect a British accent, speak kindly of "the people," hate bankers, sympathize with the working class, could easily become a Marxist if I were not a bourgeois Catholic, a conscientious objector, a pacifist, kind to family, especially to Alma; I regret cruelties—erect flashings—administered early in life to Tanaquil, and I am patient with Anita, though I can't fathom our bond. She married me for "butter" money: separate bedrooms, the lot. For world peace, I keep three cactus plants on my best Bösendorfer and wear black briefs: they give me a voice.

*

In an earlier notebook I described the time that Alma took me to the East Kill carnival, but I failed to do descriptive justice to it, and to the fine discriminations that Alma exercised, as we strolled past Ferris wheel, cakewalk, tattoo parlor, freakshow. Tanaquil didn't accompany us; she stayed home and sulked in her bedroom, reading (she later told me) a nonfiction book about traffic in Tahitian girls. Another year I will have the strength to describe that carnival—Tanaquil's willful absence, Alma's pride of place near the Ferris wheel, East Kill's populace genuflecting to her grandeur. Wise, she cautioned me against snacking on cotton candy, and yet she let me loose in the jackpot area, where I won a sloppily mocha-frosted sheet-cake; a decade ago, I stayed up all night describing, in a notebook, my victory, and the flashing lights, periwinkle and chartreuse, surrounding the merry-go-round. I should have read that description to Alma, but, shy, I hid it from her critique. I am keeping new notebooks to remedy my former, regrettable reticence, my failure, in the past, to describe the many carnivals that have confused East Kill. We are not a pleasure town, but incongruously, without warning, a carnival will lay its tents and freaks upon our public park.

*

When I was a teenager, Alma kicked Tanaquil's pet terrier and then locked it in a cage: more later on this episode. More, too, about Alma's household rules? The lock on the refrigerator, in the old days, when she was a nearly full-time East Kill resident? Discuss the time that, during an altercation, Tanaquil hit Alma's left breast, and Alma yelled, "You hit my breast!" Also I must discuss my drunkenness and my evaporated talent.

*

Unsurprisingly, I present HIV symptoms. Rashes and sweats. I won't give details. These are the Aigues-Mortes notebooks, not the sickness notebooks, and Dr. Crick has encouraged me not to dwell on decay. He says I should ignore it, until difficulties reach unbearable clarity. A dreary recital of physical symptoms is the last thing I'll welcome, when I read these notebooks, later, after my comeback.

Utopia: Dr. Crick tells me I may be permanently asymptomatic, that I need not fear degenerating organs and faculties. He loads me up with pills. I take them when it pleases me. When I'm not in the mood, I flush them down the toilet, and lie to him. He practices medicine in the water district, his office a freestanding white stucco cottage. Some of the sex clubs have an incongruous Positano appearance, clashing with the neighborhood's brick vernacular. Going to Dr. Crick's for a checkup is tantamount to a return to Atrani, on the Amalfi, where once I played Schumann's *Novelletten,* and suffered a fainting spell during an undemanding cantilena. Dr. Crick used to be a full-time abortionist, in the years when it was illegal. Right-to-Lifers picketed his office. Dr. Crick has a limited range of facial expressions, and no wrinkles, although he is nearly sixty. A fat face is incapable of crease. He drives a lizard-green Jaguar. I drive an ivory Volvo, badly. I nearly crash—from nerves and inattentiveness—every time I take it on the road.

*

Many pseudo-friends have died of AIDS: now I needn't fear their recriminations. Todd Brest, with fine white-blond hair, looked like Baby Cadum—the broad, doughy, dropsical face of Down Syndrome. He graduated from Oxford and wrote a study of Sanskrit spiritual texts (translated into ten languages). His grandmother, Velma Brest, a dowager, owns half the town, though no one wants to have anything to do with her. After one impeccable blow job, I shunned Todd—but first I memorized his buttocks' abstention from the sun. When I refused to hug him at Jeffrey's Diner, he called me a "shunner." Others have leveled the same accusation. After I'm finished with a "boyfriend," I consign him to the dustbin; an ex-trick dies, and I think, "Another person out of the way." Heartlessness is a symptom.

*

Thom Mangrove, my late father, crowded with visions, didn't like my glints of promise; he ignored my first fugues, bold, on the Guadalquivar Bösendorfer. Alma called him a liar, and yet she liked the financial package. My "butter" inheritance comes to me not directly through his estate but through a dead uncle's bequest, and no other family member can touch the funds. Alma makes her own money in Buenos Aires, every weekend playing at a different theater, church, museum, plaza, or tango palace.

I fritter away my income on water district sex. Thom liked to "brain" me: squeeze my forehead hard, affectionately, to obliterate my wrong, invasive, curious thoughts about Tanaquil's body, or about how Alma deserved death for not enjoying my youthful (at age seven!) performance of Cécile Chaminade's "Scarf Dance" at East Kill Public Library.

*

I am working up to my Aigues-Mortes comeback by playing petty concerts in East Kill. Each has a theme. Recently I played a *Totentanz* evening at the Lyceum. Katherine Hepburn, elderly, in the front row, beamed. Afterward, she came backstage. I studied closely the celebrated face and realized that she wasn't Hepburn, just some local woman with mange. Fullness enveloped her rear: diapers? She whispered, "Mom's cerebral today," which, someone explained, was a distortion: her "Mom" was long dead, but her daughter had a brain tumor. No one famous ever comes to East Kill. Alma Guadalquivar Mangrove is undisputed empress of the town, and I am crown prince. Half of East Kill hates our family.

*

Hermaphroditism of the appoggiatura:
    After breakfast I felt dizzy, and, napping, dreamt that Alma grew a beard. She still wore concert gowns and pretended to look the imposing matriarch. No one dared mention the amply downed chin.

*

Alma's opinion: I should stop practicing for a year and let the nerves heal. If I were to consider her point of view, the notebooks would suffer a breakdown. And yet why not respect her verdicts? Didn't she once meet Princess Radziwill, after a benefit concert in Monte Carlo? Fatal flaw: the notebooks have no desire to figure out whether she enjoyed meeting the Princess. Nor have the notebooks tried to imagine Alma's emotions while she lies on the couch and smokes Camels while listening to unreleased tapes of her concerts, turning off the machine so she can dip back into her Agatha Christie mystery and reapply lipstick and adjust her bathrobe and then put down the paperback and switch on the tape again, the piece containing too many dissonances this time, forcing her to turn it off and say, "This performance we shall leave unreleased, even though in principle I insist that each of my taped concerts is remastered on CD and offered to the public." Dissonances discomfit listeners, so she purged discord from her repertoire; she did not rewrite the music to make it more churchy, but chose pieces that kept at bay the maddening minor second. I cannot tolerate music that moves forward; my Aigues-Mortes recital must eddy and retreat.

*

Don't get your hopes up. The object in your hands is not a novel. Call it a still life: sentences without development, incident, or kindness. I wish I could speak with greater forbearance about the people I know, and about my own fate. Instead, I atomize noxious events and unwanted persons, turn them into particles.

*

Definition of the lyric:

Snow outside my window is lyric because I pay no attention to it.

Our dead-end block, Mechanical Street, mostly residential, has some specialty businesses: a nougat and spice dealer, a toy railroad repair shop, and a psychic, whose red neon sign has a missing *p*, so it flashes *sychic*. When I last visited the psychic, Mrs. Clemovitz, she said I had no future, only a past, and the past was not the province of clairvoyants.

Notebook Two

I have never been to Aigues-Mortes. I remember my late father drinking café con leche on a second-floor hotel balcony in Portbou, a tiny Spanish town bordering France; while Alma was away on tour, Father often took Tanaquil and me on vacation to Portbou, a few hours from Aigues-Mortes. We never bothered to drive to Aigues-Mortes, and he never described it as desirable. Portbou colleagues clamored for his ambiguous services, despite his bantam-weight smallness; about size, Alma said, he was always defensive. He had shell-shocked cousins in Portbou: I can't remember their names. One had a withered arm. Another had a large rear-end. After Thom's death we never tracked them down.

In Portbou, at the unprepossessing Hotel Flora, Father watched Tanaquil and me swimming, below the balcony, in the meager pool. He had no desire to join us; he preferred to watch. He called Portbou magnetic: it had some mysterious connection to the Guadalquivars. Though eager to escape Alma's tempestuousness, he was happy to research her origins. I, however, found nothing to recommend Portbou. There was no cinema, race track, or concert hall. Thom spent the nights gambling at cards in a local bar. Tanaquil and I wasted every afternoon by the dull pool, a few hundred yards from the Mediterranean. If the Hotel Flora has been torn down, I want to write its epitaph. My sister and I failed our father, slowly, and he let us know; we apologized every morning, on the Hotel Flora balcony, as we sat on folding chairs, looking out at the ocean. Are Guadalquivars buried in Portbou? Ask Alma.

*

Yesterday, my favorite escort, Friedman, at his water-district loft, its window overlooking the almost lake, burned incense cones and played Mozart's *Zaïde* while roughhousing me. Friedman, who looks like an extra in a Pasolini film, is educated: he hustles for information. He wants a wide experience of the world so he can write about it later. Other careers that Friedman has pursued (flute-playing, spying, gardening) no longer interest him; though he may return to law school, he has temporarily "retired" into hustling, as others retire by opening a rural bed-and-breakfast.

Friedman took a Polaroid of me, for his collection: he intends art, not blackmail. I spilled cum (three spurts) on his unshaved buttocks, worthy of ruining (by desiring them I desecrate them). He told me that his first reading experience was comic strips and that his world-view was based on square frames, articulation bubbles, outlined figures, punch lines, and superheroes, and that I seemed to him a "Sunday Funnies" character who appears only in a single episode and is never again heard from but is more intensely loved than the regulars. A *tone color* surrounds me, he said. He forgave me for romanticizing his temporary profession, hustling. He sometimes follows my wife to the grocery store and surreptitiously watches her wandering the aisles and pushing a cart.

After an intense orgasm, we produce voice from our head rather than our chest. I went to the window to see what passed as a body of water. To be surrounded, in the water district, by water, and yet to doubt its existence, is the East Kill dilemma.

*

Chicago's best hotel, the Palmer House, might have been where I caught HIV from Fabio Abruzzi, my current piano coach, a slim native Italian, my age, asymptomatic. We were playing a four-hand concert (including Poulenc) at the university; in our hotel suite he told me about his infection but I asked him to enter me without condom anyway. It may seem odd that a professional pianist has a coach, but everyone, no matter how advanced, needs instruction. A teacher can correct bad habits. Fabio, who looks like a shopworn Alain Delon, or a partially erased Picasso harlequin-urchin, studied with a pupil of the great Egon Petri, himself a Ferruccio Busoni protégé. I might have already been infected, before Fabio. Infection's origin doesn't concern me.

*

Possible repertoire for the Aigues-Mortes recital includes Rachmaninoff's *Moments Musicaux*, which lasts twenty-six minutes. Extra notes fool the listener into thinking the piano a monstrous new step in human evolution. There's too much ecstasy in Rachmaninoff—an atmosphere of Chanukah, of soiled time. I'm Catholic, but my references are Semitic. Tanaquil insists that we are indirectly Sephardic Jews, through the maternal line. Alma has a hush-hush relation to genealogy. About Mangroves she is silent, and about Guadalquivars she likes to be obfuscating and theatrical, claiming family origins in Pamplona, Buenos Aires, Lisbon, anywhere she has been applauded.

*

My Aigues-Mortes comeback will be recorded, so that, as CD, it might be sold by subscription to members of "Alma's List," a mail-order club of listeners loyal to her career. In Aigues-Mortes I should avoid programming any music that Alma has already monopolized. She's made over forty discs, everything from Haydn to the Spanish masters— Mompou, de Falla, Montsalvatge. Alma says I lack microphone experience—hence the importance of the Aigues-Mortes recital, which I have the power to cancel. My hands, from over-practicing, are rediscovering their primary ruin, the damage they sustained years ago, under Alma's tutelage, and then afterward, *au conservatoire*, near the East Kill Pantheon, ten hours a day until I could no longer concentrate, and then tea in a chipped bowl at Jeffrey's Diner, where I still repair for refreshment— Jeffrey's, with opaque windows, on the corner of Lucinda and Lavinia, the center of the water district; Jeffrey's, the only eatery obscure and dingy enough to mirror my insignificance and secretly reverse it (turn it into magnificence) via the deceitfulness of mirrors. A reflective surface lies: pretending to send back the same, it pollutes the original.

*

After playing Liszt's "Funérailles" for Fabio yesterday I stepped into the Roman Catholic church on the corner of Mechanical and Vine; I wanted to see God in the light or dark of Fabio's prescriptions. I told the Lord's likeness, "Give me a romantic sound, like Artur Rubinstein's. Give me the sound that Alma once envied."

I could play more than one comeback recital in Aigues-Mortes. The second program could consist of two mammoth works, Schumann's Fantasy in C, and Liszt's B Minor Sonata, plus an impromptu lecture explaining how words fail to describe water. I must find the score for Schoenberg's *Transfigured Night* in piano reduction, or if such a score doesn't exist, I must do the reduction myself. I want my listeners to be frightened, worried that I might go into platform convulsions. Breakdown bestows clout on a performer. Audiences are frightened that the crisis will repeat, and this fear rivets their attention. Alma became kinder to me after my Viterbo institutionalization. She no longer harped on the maleficent tendency of my left hand's second finger's first joint to collapse during passagework. Whenever she is in East Kill she watches me practice. I beg her to watch. She doesn't impose the surveillance. She may well be reading this notebook.

*

I have asked France to sponsor my Aigues-Mortes concert, but France is reluctant. I have asked New York to sponsor my Aigues-Mortes concert, but New York is reluctant. I alone hold the power to wrestle the recital—should there be two, or three?—into existence.

Failures are intricate, and not each earns fossilization; not each deserves its Vedantic diorama.

Six years ago in Toulon, I performed *Il Trovatore* in piano reduction. One critic called my performance "cancerous," and wrote, "Find a way to let him end his career with dignity."

I should arrange a piano reduction of the Verdi *Requiem* and play it in Aigues-Mortes to end my career with dignity.

*

Alma briefly intersected with the American avant-garde: she was pianist mascot for Abstract Expressionism and for Fluxus, though artists eventually found her too rigid and monarchical. My temperament's most revolutionary aspect is lack of follow-through. I abandon my statements, midstream. Would Alma consider Scriabin avant-garde? Until today's practice session, I never understood his silences—trills and triplets accelerating toward flame. Alma said, "We need more silence in our family." She praises reticence yet performs raucous *Iberia*.

My recitals reflect a subway aesthetic. Aigues-Mortes is a tiny town, mostly pedestrians and bicycles. Public transportation must push its way into Aigues-Mortes's heart.

*

My favorite hustler, Friedman, resembles a vintage porn star, Bruno, a 1960s legend in San Francisco and New York, an "all-over" porn star like the "all-over" Abstract Expressionist paintings that Alma loved (and, with her performances, brought to life). I keep Bruno's photos in the Guadalquivar armoire: unsafe hiding place. Bruno took a few customers. I came of age too late to hire him.

*

I will never live long enough to perform the complete works of Liszt. Influenza worsening, I'm woozy from three glasses of port tonight and sore from Friedman's back-door invasions. I feel the urge to end my life, but first I must describe it, so that readers who care to look for a pattern in the last days will have the resources to find it. If I could wear Liszt's ratty, repetitive, lovesick compositions like dahlias in my hair, then I'd have the confidence to present myself to Europe again: the problem with music is that I must *play* it, not *wear* it.

Chopin's music communicates *żal*, which Liszt defines as "inconsolable regret after an irrevocable loss . . . a ferment of resentment, premeditation of vengeance . . . sterile bitterness . . ."

Alma says I shouldn't burden the Aigues-Mortes notebooks with scholarly quotations.

*

Friedman visited Mechanical Street but instead of following me into my bedroom he went to Tanaquil's lair and disappeared for an hour. Ignored, I ran through my Liszt program—"Orage" from *Années des pèlerinage*, "Pensée des morts" from *Harmonies poétiques et religieuses*, and "Bagatelle sans tonalité." When Friedman reappeared to say goodbye to me and ask for payment ($100), his palms (I kissed them) were fragrant and sticky. I may never again hire him for an in-call. I don't want Tanaquil to become sexually three-dimensional on my dollar. I remember shouting "Tanaquil has tits!" an eternity ago, humiliating her, in a public place.

*

My European agent Alfonso Reyes called to ask whether he should bill me as a Liszt specialist, a Scriabin specialist, or a master of blurry twilight illusions—because of the "brush" or "melting" touch I learned *au conservatoire*, and because of my taste for slow, eviscerated tempi, wandering in the suburbs of continuity. I hate noise! Fragmentation has invaded my playing. I told Alfonso to advertise me as a French pianist with an Italian temperament, or as a social theorist disguised as a Liszt specialist. Performing his *Années*, I give a disquisition on chill. Voyage anaesthetizes: reapparreling sewage in filigree, Liszt's curlicue circumnavigations imitate Chopin copying Bellini.

*

The classical music industry, in which I play a minor part, is the last bastion of whoredom; after my European seizures, amnesias, and palpitations, and after my Viterbo hospitalization, I staged a monastic withdrawal from the concert-giving world. If I outlive Alma, I may sell our pianos and take a vow of silence. Meanwhile, I could learn a sweep of the Busoni oeuvre and wow Aigues-Mortes. Alma cautions against excess repertoire. Her magic number, she says, is four, not five. "Instead of five cities, Theo, play in four. Instead of five sonatas, play four." I ignore her advice: I pity the fifth city, the fifth sonata.

*

Was it twenty-five years ago I debuted at Alice Tully Hall? Had Alice Tully Hall been built? I don't keep careful records. Sam Wagstaff and Robert Mapplethorpe, Alma's friends, understood the necrophiliac properties of the Fauré nocturnes I played. *Con amore,* Liszt indicates, in *Vallée d'Obermann,* but I don't caress the keyboard's soprano register. I don't make friends with the C above middle C. Xenia Lamont, my first master, taught me how to curve the finger but not so rigidly that it becomes a claw; she taught me how to keep fingerpads alert to *Liebesträume's* lyric dangers. Xenia's breasts reminded me of flesh-toned water balloons. Powerful muscles held them up.

*

Revelation: I shall not perform solo in Aigues-Mortes! I shall do a song recital with loyal Derva Nile! Tonight we will sort through repertoire in my studio. Fauré, Debussy, Poulenc, Satie? We must include Reynaldo Hahn: his piano parts are negligible, but the tessitura suits Derva's troubled voice. Two years ago she broke down, singing Rachmaninoff in Tulsa, but she has a good muscle memory, and she consulted a laryngeal specialist, Madeline Tarnow, in New York. (I daren't hurt Derva by admitting I want to go solo in Aigues-Mortes.) We will repeat the program in Aix-en-Provence and Bergamo. I will call Alfonso, but first I must ask Alma in Buenos Aires whether she thinks it unwise to share the Aigues-Mortes concerts, on which my career depends, with Derva. Alma's rule: "Never waste time trying to please a fickle public." And yet audiences love a pretty soprano. Buxom, dark-haired Derva, posed next to the piano in the posture of Ingres's *La Source,* will doll up my autoerotic folderol, which fooled San Antonio, where the memory of Van Cliburn is vivid, but may fail in Aigues-Mortes, a town with a conquering spirit. I must go to church, on the corner of Mechanical and Vine, and pray for guidance.

*

Last night, after reading songs with Derva Nile, whose voice has improved so radically, I fear she'll overshadow me in Aigues-Mortes, I went to Friedman's loft, and he gave me a regular's discount. He said, "You have red bumps on your ass." Irritation, from sitting too long at the piano. My excitement level was abnormal, Aigues-Mortes-endangering. From Friedman I received an orgasm, the usual tugging sensation, like a major seventh held overlong by flute and oboe, flutist and oboist naked, oboist a sixteen-year-old boy with untidy pubes, and flutist a seventy-year-old woman, slender, silver-haired, happy to hold the major seventh for its full duration. When I come, I contain hemispheres. Wars are fought, countries demolished, during my least orgasm. I have nothing better to offer you, Alma. Didn't you want to murder me last Christmas, when I insisted on playing Scriabin preludes before breakfast, and then, after dinner, I screened the BBC documentary about preparations for my Barcelona consecration, the time I dedicated Bach's partitas and *Well-Tempered Clavier* to a new god, one I was inventing that afternoon, for the film's sake, script worked out in advance with the director, though we pretended the performance was unpremeditated? I wanted to sexualize Bach in honor of Barcelona. I'd received many propositions on the Ramblas; I'd squatted in the trenches with Bach long before Bolshevik strains in modern Baroque performance practice rendered me unfit to play partitas in public—exiling me to vulgar, amorphous nineteenth-century works, perverse dream-pieces in the spirit of Massenet's *Hérodiade*.

Time to re-enter my orgone box.

Notebook Three

I drank two bottles of Rioja last night while watching a 1962 videotape of Moira Orfei, queen of the Italian circus, dancing in sync with Mozart's "Là ci darem la mano." Moira's head wiggled: is she doublejointed? Proprietor and protector of her legend, I fear that I will drop it, that it will crack. "Moira Orfei is a beautiful woman and also a major circus artiste," Anita said, begrudgingly, as we watched the video. Anita in the boxy armchair was falling asleep. Poor Anita, enslaved by my circus connoisseurship. I woke her when Orfei tightrope-walked to a potpourri from Gounod's *Roméo et Juliette*. Later Orfei swallowed fire to "Mi chiamano Mimì." I was tempted to telephone Moira in Montecatini (if I only had the number!) and say that her circus artistry was still appreciated, that she would be named a national treasure of Japan or a Dame of the British Empire, that her beauty would be visited on unsuspecting third-world nations, and that I would write think-pieces on her behalf in the *East Kill Times* if the right-wing editor would step down: in these squibs, I would say that circus is currently in shambles, and that new, infuriating artistes try to claim techniques that Moira Orfei invented when she was a child star, never paid enough for her troubles, traveling from piazza to piazza in Italy.

Montecatini Terme, a spa town in Tuscany, between Pisa and Pistoia, was the place I first saw her perform, in the 1970s, when I was visiting the healing baths. Moira Orfei was considered, at the time, merely second-rate, and yet she had been a star for years. Watch the 1962 Mimì fire-eating act: she seems ready to eat spectators. Moira Orfei is my original Cimmerian shore, superior to any pretender to her circus throne. And yet in Catania she was reported to have *slept among the tigers*. She had nowhere else to rest. Circus conditions in those days were a scandal.

Anita won't tolerate another evening of Orfei reclamation—so tonight alone I will watch the forgotten Jean Renoir melodrama starring Moira Orfei. Moira sent me an armful of her obscure lost videos, and I am systematically watching them, trying to rise to her defense, once again, even if this effort compromises the health of my Aigues-Mortes comeback.

*

Last night I saw the rare Renoir opus, *Massage*, starring Moira Orfei. She plays a Basque masseuse, Tania, working in Morocco. Locals don't appreciate her feline beauty and therapeutic skills. She turns her lack of renown into a political cause. Sublimating her unhappiness, morphing it into idealistic fervor, she mobilizes indigenous peoples against French colonial oppression. Mostly the film is long shots of angry Orfei against sand dunes and ships. She relies on silent pantomime. Renoir didn't trust her with dialogue.

Her nipples, exposed in the film, upset me. They visually rhyme with her left shoulder's two beauty marks. Why did she feel compelled to do a nude scene? No matter the climate or scenario, in every film Moira performs an obligatory, knee-jerk, *nouvelle vague* striptease, usually as finale. In *Massage*, topless, she serves drinks on the joint's patio; male intellectuals, Che Guevara types, nudge her ribcage and make snide, weighty, historical-materialist comments on her breasts, as if her nipples were political ripostes. In my favorite scene, the screen Moira Orfei flips through movie magazines, looking at pictures of the real Moira Orfei.

*

This afternoon I must accompany Derva Nile, soprano, in Hugo Wolf songs at the East Kill Home for the Blind. I should save my hands for Aigues-Mortes instead of frittering them away on Derva Nile. An East Kill resident, she splits her time between teaching at the Rorschach Musical Institute in New London (she commutes biweekly), and giving free recitals for the elderly and handicapped. Her husband, the moody, barrel-chested Morris Nile, disapproves of my alliance with Derva, and finds me "uppity," but I almost blew him (steam-room backrubs crescendoing to a kiss) last year in the East Kill YMCA's locker room. Afterward we ate stale carrot cake at the café.

It would be a mistake to bring Derva to Aigues-Mortes. I got involved with her because we both have been visited by technical disaster, and because she resembles Moira Orfei—the same heavy-lidded eyes, square jaw, tiny nose, gazelle neck. I needn't describe Moira Orfei, because she is acknowledged queen of the Italian circus, and pictures abound. I have pasted her photograph on each Aigues-Mortes notebook's front cover. Let these pictures replace my paltry verbal evocations. Alma (in her Marxist phase) told me that pictures will bring on the revolution long before words.

*

A few years ago I met Moira Orfei in Rome, at the Hotel de Anza; and after leisurely tea (we talked of elephants, ponies, circus travails, tightrope-walking, flame-swallowing, man-eating beasts, wrist bangles, the difficulty of pleasing one's father), we went to Bulgari, where she tried on rings. I wanted to buy her a modest *tronchetto.* My "butter" money permits extravagance. The clerk bungled the sale; ignoring us, he played poker with the janitor in the shop's rear. I told the rude clerk, "The great Moira Orfei is here. I'm ready to purchase a ring. If you'd only treat us with respect!"

*

I must begin planning the Aigues-Mortes festival: the historic reunion of Moira Orfei and Theo Mangrove. I haven't yet told Derva Nile. I will share the intricate, foolproof plans with no one except Mangrove family members and my international agent Alfonso Reyes. Nor will I surrender to grandiosity. Arrangements will be practical, concrete. If Moira decides to tell the press, I can't stop her, but I'd like Aigues-Mortes to remain our secret. Our choreography must incorporate Aigues-Mortes's arcades, of which I have, alas, no knowledge.

*

Notes for further discussion:

    (a) Moira's nipples in the Renoir film;

    (b) the Aigues-Mortes arcades;

    (c) stiff wrists when I play Liszt;

    (d) my left pinkie's near-paralysis.

*

Moira Orfei has more talent than all the circus upstarts you could name. She is equal to anyone in the Carré family, and superior to Babette, the Talo Boys, and Miss Renee Jolliffe. Move over, Elsie Wallenda! Moira Orfei's ensemble outclasses the Poutier and Clasners touring companies. Moira feels circus in her veins; she swallows flame in dotted rhythm. Her can-cans have more charm than Rigolette's or Frichette's. Moira's eyes (in documentary footage) express unfeigned panic when she approaches the jaguar's cage. Her emotions are genuine, she told me, when we ate oysters in Marseilles; she feels what she pretends to feel.

When her ex-husband, a gay set-designer for the circus, first saw her perform, he called her (the description appeared in *Oggi*) a "gold mine," a rare combination of stunt-artist and sexpot, and he immediately put her on Italian TV, re-choreographed her act, and gave pointers on how to tightrope-walk with breasts pushed forward as if they hurt her feelings and she wanted to shed responsibility for their beauty.

Perhaps I will lower my immunity and bring on convulsions by involving Moira Orfei in Aigues-Mortes.

I must retreat from East Kill locals by intensifying my love for Moira Orfei. I repeat: no circus star of the current generation can match Moira's authentic artifice.

*

Only now, at this advanced age, am I executing the elementary lesson Alma taught me as a child: drop the hand's weight, without forcing. My left pinkie this month is virtually paralyzed. It forgets to seek in key-beds a velvety launchingpad for leaps.

I learned technique from Alma; I could use a brush-up, but she has departed for South America. My European breakdown satisfies her, because it bolsters the family legend: in musical-gazette interviews, she describes my memory lapses and fainting fits as if they redounded to her credit. Palpitations and seizures I experienced in Aix-en-Provence, Carpentras, Toulon, Montepulciano, Ferrara, and elsewhere, resemble Alma's 1964 São Paulo "nervous breakdown," onstage, in the midst of playing Liszt's "Chasse-neige" from the Transcendental Etudes—a collapse that did not end her career, but catapulted her to tabloid immortality.

"I am God," Scriabin once said, and I understand: while our lordly sight expands, it narrows to a claustrophobic, smelly extent.

*

If I could find a hustler this afternoon I'd be happy. Every escort in East Kill is booked—I've paged them all. I should have prepared for this eventuality. Horniness jeopardizes my Aigues-Mortes concerts as well as the interim's piddling engagements. If I were at Marseilles's Hotel de Anza with Moira Orfei, we'd drink a bottle of Petit Chablis and eat a platter of raw Marennes-Oléron oysters and criticize the circus performers she's surpassed—Mesquita, Mary Patricia, the Canadian Wonders. But I am home on Mechanical Street.

I telephoned Derva Nile and told her that she could not accompany me to Aigues-Mortes. She didn't mind. She respects Moira Orfei's priority.

*

Long ago, beside schoolhouse bushes, I found a dead Protestant boy, Tom Watley, his face bloody, gouged, disfigured. I didn't report the body. When I returned later, he was gone. I've often wondered whether I knew his murderer, unapprehended: perhaps the culprit was Miss Kash, freckled redhead teacher whose Sunday-school description of limbo made sick sense.

How vulnerable was young Chopin to sexual assaults? Did young Scriabin experience mild molestation at the home of his revered teacher Mr. Zverev, perhaps in the presence of Siloti, to whom Rachmaninoff dedicates his unpopular preludes? My interpretation of the sixth prelude, in E-flat major, fumigates lyricism by suggesting graves and cradles. In Aigues-Mortes, I will lecture on Mr. Zverev's sexual appetites.

*

Alma, on tour in Rio, telephoned from Hotel Valetti, while preparing for the evening performance of de Falla's *Nights in the Gardens of Spain*. She wants to forget gowns and friendliness, to skip hair-washing: "If you think you've wasted your life, honey, then I've wasted mine, too." She speaks with a smacking sound: dentures? I once saw them in a cup beside her bed. She threatens to cancel tour, return to East Kill, and supervise the household, which, in her absence, careens out of control. Tanaquil's room smells of rotten apples. I mentioned to Alma my epicurean afternoon at the East Kill Sauna; she approves. She frowns on Aigues-Mortes: "It's a career-wrecker." Why not, instead, the nearby Stes-Maries-de-la-Mer, where gypsies—apropos to Liszt!—gather every year on May 24 and 25 to celebrate the feast of Black Sarah? The gypsies could be chorus for Scriabin's *Poem of Fire*, featuring me as piano soloist. Alma bragged about her 1960s civil rights activism, her Lady Bird Johnson medal. She was photographed with Malcolm X outside the Hotel Bon Soir on the Lower East Side, near the pickle shop.

I like discussing, with Alma, my sex life, using an illogical code we have perfected over the years. I never say "fellatio": I say "Granados." If she were a doctor, she would prescribe the water district as anodyne: it corrects cramped phrasing. Let's hope I can unparalyze my left pinkie by the time I walk onto the Aigues-Mortes stage and face my executioners.

*

When my father lay down in bed with me, his chest was an electric fence whose electricity had been temporarily turned off for safe climbing. We rested together like two AA batteries snugly powering a transistor radio. Alma barged into the unlit bedroom and asked if we had sanitized our position, reduced its intimacy, after she'd entered. Alma wore glittering "Bridge of San Luis Rey" eyeglasses—a special pair for score-studying. Despite darkness, she could probably see Father's portly chest and the thrifty place, below, where my hands delved; and she could guess I enjoyed special treatment, a chance to "take cuts" in line, ahead of competitors.

My father, asleep beneath earth's ultimatum . . .

These and other nostalgias, useless . . .

Notebook Four

In a week, I fly to Boston to try a new hustler, Dustin, whose photo, on the web, resembles Friedman: Sephardic-Lebanese. I had three orgasms based on Dustin's photo. While in Boston I'll visit Alma's younger sister Matilda, sphinx of Back Bay, who lives in a Clarendon Street townhouse near Joan Kennedy's. The Guadalquivar sisters haven't spoken in ten years—not since Alma suffered food-poisoning after Matilda served suspicious oysters at brunch. My mother insists that Matilda is an adopted—not biological—Guadalquivar. My aunt is freckled, fat, her coiffure a cumulus cloud; my mother, like her mother Gertrude, is gaunt, pallid, unblemished, with a long rope of straight hair sometimes rolled into a ponderous bun and pinned up with a silver barrette.

Matilda, a decent pianist, still capable of reading through Mozart's "Duport" Variations if she hasn't started tippling, let her talent rot by never practicing. She reads tarot cards. Through psychic tricks, a Guadalquivar *Santería,* she hopes to decimate Alma from afar. A gossipy *Musical America* article once spotlit Matilda's grudge.

The state of music today is Alma's to adjudicate; Matilda's to envy; mine to destroy. (Here comes a forgetful fit.)

On my nuclear family's behalf, soon I will make the monthly, propitiatory journey to Clarendon Street. Matilda will ask about hustlers I've been hiring. Will she countenance my notebooks, or will she want me to siphon strength into preparing Aigues-Mortes?

I mustn't tell jealous Alma about the visit. She said, once, intercepting a gushing note my aunt had written me: "Don't trust Matilda. She fawns over you to irritate me."

Prodigal aunt, I picture you, lonely in brown leather armchair, your swollen feet propped beside unsent letters on an ottoman: *Sister, I will never forgive you for stealing the career that should have been mine . . .*

I miss Alma, off to South America. I wish she'd return. I'd help her unpack. Anita could fetch take-out from Juanita's Pizza, and we'd let Tanaquil lock herself upstairs. Tanaquil, a fainter, doesn't deserve the cruel treatment I dish out. Later I'll try to make amends for flashing her in the hallway long ago.

Alma rarely writes letters. Why not an occasional get-well card, to cheer me up, when she is abroad, on her perpetual, Mechanical-Street-denying tour? And yet, if she remained here, year-round, our house would no longer be the ideal place for planning triumphal Aigues-Mortes comebacks.

*

Tanaquil's door is locked—from the inside. I press my ear to it and hear a Sinatra record, and then, in the pauses between songs, her stertorous breathing. I could use a sister's counsel. Playing possum, she wants sympathy and a boyfriend.

Carcinogens in our house: I can smell them. Ash from the fireplace. Household cleansers and disinfectants. No way to rebegin with an ecologically safe environment—invasive agents have already corrupted my cells. I want to pen-knife my arm and gouge out the damaged molecules.

How can I become more likeable? By diligently describing Aigues-Mortes preparations in these notebooks. I wish I had Moira Orfei's telephone number. An immediate conversational fix would do me good. Thinking of her dimples cheers me up.

*

Try to work from what I already know of Scriabin, rather than start from scratch, like a schizophrenic. Don't behave like a leper if you don't want to be treated like one. Imitate Alma. Copy anyone but yourself. Be disciplined, and notice how a good composer develops material and avoids tubercular fantasia. Don't behave like a toccata. Prance like the sonata-allegro form. Ask basic questions about your musical conduct: *Is it real? Does it help society? Can it be repeated? What would Busoni have said about your behavior?* Don't make grandiose plans. Treat morning work-hours as they were treated by wise Christians in the nineteenth century, when Wagner wrote *Parsifal*, and Liszt wrote "The Lugubrious Gondola."

*

I paid Friedman for an all-night "party." We discussed Moira Orfei's greatness while he twisted my cock. I showed him the 1962 videotape. He said, "Moira's amazing," a punishably meager tribute.

To quote Alma, I'm wasting my life and I don't know how to stop wasting it. Only Moira Orfei can help, but she has forgotten my existence. For a few years I had her phone number, and then she went into hiding. I know her sister Chloe's number, but Chloe won't help.

*

On a parchment scroll I want to diagram every musical affect: one hundred types of emotion and gesture, as rendered in Western tonal composition. With this master plan, I could ride triumphant to Aigues-Mortes. First I will show the chart to Matilda, who will function as *cambio*, changing the dogged list into a tithe, payable toward my crimes against Tanaquil.

I don't know how to tell Matilda the tragic fact that I'm not an ideal interpreter of Liszt. His "Forest Murmurs" woke me to puberty and the legs of Frank Stark, the first legs I had an orgasm in front of, but I could never do justice to the etude's left-hand ostinato, despite my local success with technically taxing *Iberia*, Alma's property.

Matilda hates her mother, the grumpy, imperious Gertrude, still alive, over one hundred. Tended by expensive nurses, she dwells in Springs, Long Island (not far from the grave of her former friend, Jackson Pollock); Alma never visits. Alone, Gertrude broods on disloyal daughters, maniacal grandchildren (me, Tanaquil), and her conceptual art collection, including Duchamp readymades. My grandfather, the composer Ricardo Guadalquivar, died a long time ago: cherry chewing tobacco, long yellow fingernails. I play his virtuoso nothings as encores.

*

The last time I saw Moira Orfei she was sitting, tawny-faced, in an out-door Montecatini café, recovering from Sicilian tour, reading yellowed scrapbooks that documented her early servitude to her circus-manager father, who led Moira from town to town, forcing her to perform, locking her every night in the hotel room so her miraculousness could recharge, apart from the soft drinks and nickelodeons of the seaside towns through which their sordid act passed. I stopped by Moira's table and praised her scrapbooks, but she looked glazed, indifferent, as if I were a billboard on a highway her chauffeured limo sped down. Abruptly, she leaned toward my face and held out a black-and-gold cigarette; she didn't intend to burn me, though the glowing ash approached my eyes, which I quickly shielded, pretending noncha-lance. (I didn't want to insult her.) I haven't visited Montecatini in years, and I lack the rigor, after tonight's bottle of Rioja, to describe the café where Moira sat, leafing through a scrapbook's doomed early pages, her father dead now.

Attempting to explain Moira Orfei's power, I once wrote, in the score of Liszt's B Minor Sonata (above the irregular theme's first state-ment): *Consciousness as predicament.*

*

Matilda is a problem. Anticipating my visit, she pesters me with middle-of-the-night phone calls. And yet have I made a decent nephew's attempt to understand her sexual rages, or the garret she once slept in, receiving customers, believing true gratification took place only in department stores from which her whore self would be barred? Do I remember the women's shoes sold in the Matilda-refusing department stores? And do I love these emporia because they once barred her entrance, when she was a teenager? Why is Matilda stained? Do I repeat myself? She may sicken before I arrive. Bedside, I will meekly sit, and she will compliment my comprehension of what she calls "the femi-nine"—her round red Mary Magdalene face a rebuke. Matilda's dead husband (she never took his name) bequeathed her—in addition to the Clarendon Street townhouse—a Miami apartment and a Cape Cod bun-galow. In Wellfleet, usually she is too tired for a walk on the beach. On good days, when hallucinations retreat, she hunts morels.

Matilda made me spend years (ages twenty to thirty) catering to her sickbed needs, just because she'd drunkenly promised me concert bookings superior to Alma's. As if Matilda in Back Bay were the new Sol Hurok! Delusional Matilda, whose agoraphobia I love: gin drives the Clarendon Street version of *The Scarlet Letter*, a Signet edition in her pocketbook, along with black-market Percocet. She got addicted to Percocet during an episode of lower back pain. The drug mellows Guadalquivar unpleasantness.

*

Matilda has a small dark friend named Lu, a skinny French-Algerian girl who wants to study piano with me. She needs the sensual freedom that only a train ride to East Kill can provide. Lu played me a Mendelssohn song without words. My evaluation: "You must break the back of the four-bar phrase." She may turn out to be a great wallpaper designer. Lu showed me a sample—Jack-and-the-beanstalk motifs—of a design she intends for Matilda's library. I managed to unclothe myself inconspicuously by the end of Lu's lesson: I hid the nudity behind a huge armchair. She asked for my nudity, and Matilda OK-ed it, in advance. My action wasn't statutory rape: Lu, twenty, looks thirteen. Her father's opinion of the exchange, I don't know. Matilda prefers girls with dead fathers: they're easier to train.

I'll bring my Super 8 movie projector to Matilda's and show her the three-minute film I made of nude Lu playing Mendelssohn. Only Tanaquil and I have seen my home-made Super 8 erotica, which we call "Mechanical Street Cinema." Perhaps I will incorporate the movies into my Aigues-Mortes piano performance, with Moira Orfei's permission.

*

I visited Matilda in Boston. Before going to her townhouse, I stepped into the Copley Plaza public library tearoom and jerked off at the urinals next to a young redhead with acne, whose suddenly revealed, educable penis made me want to send condolence cards to tricks whose identities I've forgotten.

I stared at her townhouse's Gothic front as if its brick intricacies held keys to my formerly criminal mind. I dreaded buzzing: perhaps Matilda wasn't worth the bother. Perhaps she'd break down in tears the second she saw me, or start shuddering in sexual ecstasy.

As I sat in her armchair, listening to her criticize Alma, I knew I had experienced this humiliation (on Alma's behalf) before, near a swingset, or near a row of pastel classrooms, a fatigued school, a conservatory in the mountains near Biarritz. I listened to Matilda's abuse: *déjà vu*. I would continue to fail Matilda. She would not bring me new concert bookings. Clump clump on the stairs leading to the Clarendon Street bedroom: Matilda ascended, and I, for Alma's sake, paschally followed.

In bed, Matilda confirmed my "power," she called it; after showing me her Buddhist prayer rugs and her miniature Noah's Ark, she said that I was the unimpeachable foundation of Alma's reputation, that my recent nervous collapse was an irregularity, not a norm. She took off her glasses before we embraced. Her hair coloring was incoherent: should I call it sandy blonde, or silver, and shouldn't she ask her colorist to choose one shade or the other? Matilda told me that composers are superior to performers, and she asked, in a brutish, slurred, drunk undertone, why I wasn't more famous than Alma, why I insisted on the familial frame of reference, and why I had amnesia about my men. (This forgetfulness was especially intense at those moments when my glance, sated by lovemaking, fell on the Buddhist manuals piled on her armoire, the twin of my Guadalquivar armoire.) Boldly, though with elided vowels and consonants, she murmured that my Granados *Goyescas* was more daredevil than Alma's, and I envisioned a time when Matilda might defend my reputation against philistines like Hector Arens, who, in the *East Kill Times,* called my playing "leprous." As sunlight lineated the Clarendon Street bed, I regretted my months of inexcusable absence. She called me "show-off." At first I thought she was insulting me; then I remembered that she loved preeners. She quoted a line that she said was Edwin Arlington Robinson though it sounded like Ogden Nash, and she called me "supernal." Perhaps her standards are low.

During sex, Matilda's cough got on my nerves. Why couldn't she restrain herself, take Vicks? Her dryness forbade, at first, easy entrance, until she reached for the bedside tube of K-Y. She is a scholar with a great career ahead, if only a career of explicating *The Scarlet Letter*, and narrating, in videotaped essays, her private history of hospitalizations and libations.

Exhaustion forced me to cancel Dustin, my potential Dorchester escort. I spent the night at Matilda's townhouse, armory of anti-Alma balm.

*

Today, in the *East Kill Times,* I read about a cannibal who cooked little boys after molesting them. He prepared "little boy pot pies" and "little boy stews" for his neighbors, who complained about the strange taste.

Alma called from Buenos Aires, after her concert at Fundación Proa. She said the only reason I didn't commit suicide was my replenishable optimism, the utopian streak I inherited from her: "You got the bad genes and the good genes. My nerves, yes. But also my gifts." She mentioned "your birthright reservoir of lifted mood."

After a few Xanax I am tempted to write Matilda and ask for help making Aigues-Mortes arrangements. But I must check the impulse. She has enough problems (hallucinations, slurred speech) without being forced to face Moira Orfei's supremacy. Matilda's pathological jealousy of other famous women caused her long-ago break with Alma: poisoned oysters were the alibi.

*

I spent the night strategizing my next overture to Moira Orfei, the only living epitome of drunken romanticism, a cult I want to lead, if she would agree to share her dimity throne. The climaxes we'd be capable of reaching together! The weird disjunctions between feeling and rationality! Her circus tricks might mingle with my impromptu lectures on hallucinogens—diatribes delivered from the piano during Debussy etudes. Orfei/Mangrove possibilities flood me as I work on the impressionist's tricky, unostentatious show-pieces, perfect foil for Moira's leaps and near-disasters. Hemiola—beguiling distraction from regular beat-division—will fill the audience with panic. How about "The Moira Orfei and Theo Mangrove Show," a TV variety hour, on cable?

Fear that we might never meet in Aigues-Mortes, that Moira might misunderstand my instructions, breaks my heart, in advance; I imagine waiting—in boulevard Gambetta's moldering arcades, after a lunch of monkfish with saffron—for a never-materializing Moira. How much longer can I bear to wait for word? Her pale skin and black hair and large fake eyelashes—where would I be without their corrupt consolation, their telegram of fatigue and repetition, like the same mortadella sandwich I ordered every day in Lucca from the butcher near the Giardino Botanico, even when his sultry daughter watched me order it, and I thought, ashamed, "She knows I'm addicted to mortadella, she knows my weakness, and that's close to damnation, being known by the butcher's dark-haired daughter"—assuming she was not his wife or concubine, hanging out near the beaded curtain, observing customers, in an unfrequented part of Lucca, close to the ramparts and the filthy public swimming hole. On the via del Giardino Botanico, outside the butcher shop, I'd found pieces of smut, porn pictures cut into scraps, confetti. Had I torn a magazine, and then forgotten my rage?

Let me fall more frequently into trance, even at the risk of what Dr. Crick cheerfully calls "psychosis." France is the answer: Aigues-Mortes, a reunion with Moira Orfei. I will restore her reputation to its lost zenith.

Notebook Five

The house smells of asparagus piss. Thoughts of Mechanical Street's disarray prematurely age me: see my worry lines, crow's feet, tummy spread. Friedman notices it all. Messy Anita claims to be a "neatnik" but leaves carpets unvacuumed so she can concentrate on her insignificance, which she finds comforting, as do all small people.

As a teen, I gave recitals at an East Kill rug shop, in the antique district, one block long, not major enough to attract tourists. Temporarily docile Tanaquil handed out programs, took tickets, and poured water into Dixie cups during intermission. Those were my Couperin days: avoiding romantic repertoire, I feared plush sounds, early death.

Incoherently I lectured Tanaquil last night on tonality. Dissonance isn't unpleasantness; it's simply a sign that movement is about to take place. Alma tolerated dissonance because of her Greenwich Village friendships and her schoolgirl participation in Communist cells.

Before Tanaquil shut her door for the night, she said, "It's difficult, being the only straight shooter in a household of Malibrans."

*

When I was a cocky teenager, my boxer shorts sometimes served as outerwear. Tanaquil and I rode swanboats at East Kill Public Park. My boxer flap opened as I rowed. She laughed at the display and handed me the joint she was smoking; I wanted to give up my musicianship, at that moment, or take on a major disease, like epilepsy. Also, I wanted my feigned epilepsy to be a guestpass to her forgiveness. No longer to dwell in a false system of downbeats! Regardless how frequently the key signature changes, it always reverts to the home.

*

The rooms in which my sexual escapades take place are small, white, rented; given the dimness, I can't know how many infected people are present. Despite my terminal condition, I am asymptomatic, to an historically unprecedented degree, and resistant to the newer viral varieties, protected though I remain in sexual encounters, within an envelope of "safety" as fictitious or provisional as the belief that forgiving bodies of water surround East Kill. I am the town metaphysician. Every streetcorner is ineffable, dying to be explained. I travel from bedroom to bedroom, hotel to hotel, keeping praise to a minimum.

*

Anita doesn't want our sexual relations to continue. She finds my coital style vulgar, my mouth and fingers never coordinated. Why not consider Moira Orfei a safety valve, leaving Anita free to pursue local romances with valet-parking attendants? Moira Orfei wears paste tiaras and bangles that look authentic and expensive (some actually are!), while Anita wears basic pearl studs and a fourteen-karat chain that I bought her in Lourdes when I played my Abbé Liszt program, and steak tartare on the Place des Pyrénées poisoned me.

*

If I look back at my life, I'm afraid I will see a design. Matilda is empress of patterns. She drafts astrological charts. In her bedroom she spread out my map and said, "Ignore the present moment's claim to be the only truth. Look at the messy web I've drawn." She pointed to arrows leading off the page. "Your life is smaller than you recognize. Dark forces crimp your borders and cut you down in your prime. I see factions." She drew the stolen white terry Solhotel (Banyuls-sur-Mer) bathrobe around her shoulders and swallowed another Percocet and said, "Yes, you've experienced this rushing sense of power and endangerment before." In a sleepy fist, she held my cock, and it rose, happy to be recognized as a family member, an international talent.

*

My hopes for Moira Orfei are so large and unformed that I fear they will be disappointed. Dr. Crick can't cure soul-sickness. Later, I must describe Moira's knees and inky hair, beyond words, but still worth the futile effort.

*

Alma is home from tour—cheeks drawn, shoulders slumped. Was she jilted by a Buenos Aires consort? We discussed Aigues-Mortes over cod-fish lunch, served by silent Tanaquil. (Anita was absent—taking care of a girlfriend hit by a speeding ambulance.) Alma called Aigues-Mortes a mistake: it might pander to voyeurs charting our family's ups and downs. Aigues-Mortes has a subtlety beyond Alma's ken. Not for her the trivial festival, the remote gig.

"Moira Orfei is the enemy of serious music," Alma said, disapproving of circus/piano hybrids. Hector Arens once called Alma "the Deborah Kerr of the piano." I'd like to outlaw such analogies.

I mentioned my plan to compile a glossary of the emotions that classical music catalyzes, and Alma expressed delight: "Then I wouldn't be responsible for your melancholy!" She compiles lists during consultations with Helen Jole, her Argentinian psychoanalyst. Listmaking cures.

"Your Milhaud disc," Alma said, "didn't sell." (She was referring to my CD of his small works, including the *Rag-Caprices*.) "One hundred total. Why not record my father's nothings?" I love Ricardo Guadalquivar's piano *morceaux* (despite their smallness and mediocrity) for their embrace of boredom, waiting, and misapprehension. Why didn't Alma spend her entire career reclaiming them?

Alma enumerated problems while chewing cod: "My son's extravagance, my daughter's reclusiveness; my son's reclusiveness, my daughter's extravagance; my cluster headaches, my son's cluster headaches." I found myself falling asleep. It was my turn to ask if she was dating anyone in the southern hemisphere, or to compare numerologically symbolic passages in our repertoires.

She startled me awake by recapturing, in words, London during the Blitz, the times she helped Myra Hess soothe terrified, bomb-wary listeners. About Myra's principle of weight transfer, Alma said: "I apply it to late Schumann, withhold it from Fauré. Schumann demands turgidity. Fauré wants sweetness. I prefer Fauré, though the public wants Schumann. Buenos Aires, however, wants what I give her."

I should describe Alma's face, body, and wardrobe, but my readers, if they exist, already know, from record jackets, videos, and live performances, what she looks like.

*

Quickly I need to take a trip to one of East Kill's hustler bars in the water district and remedy the career situation. Find a recommended escort and slowly undress him and bury the indiscretion later in sherry with Alma after dinner and after playing our two-piano repertoire— Robert Casadesus's *Danses Méditerranéennes,* Arthur Benjamin's "Jamaican Rumba from San Domingo," Ernst Bacon's "Kankakee River Burr Frolic," Manuel Infante's *Trois Danses Andalouses,* Paul A. Pisk's "My Pretty Little Pink"—as if no recriminations had earlier been exchanged.

How can I tell when I am entering the hustler neighborhood? My water district, its borders uncertain: Ocean Drive, River Street, Lake Street, Marina Way. . . . Despite these names, and a purported stream dividing our town, we have no verifiable—no consoling—connection to multiple bodies of water.

*

I met Friedman for a session: beyond oral, beyond anal: a practice we call "detente," or "fracture." Diplomatic, visceral, frightened of the law and yet expert at evading it, he specializes, as hustler, in unknown, painful positions (ads call him "The Wrecker"), positions he renames after legal cases, physical ailments, political maneuvers. Sex's purpose is nomenclature. Friedman is more interested in words than in sensations.

*

Dear Moira Orfei,
Though I tried your patience on earlier tours, let's work up a minimal program. Move our repertoire toward silence—toward the infantile and the stopped-short. Must loudness be our specialty? Must every piece

climax? In the past I never respected the difference between mezzo forte and forte. I'd love to see you inflict expressionism on Aigues-Mortes. If I could lure you there!

Remember: waltzes sell.

Picture May in the Camargue, our circus tent surrounded by wild horses, flamingos.

Love,

Theo Mangrove

*

Alma departs tonight for Buenos Aires. I'll visit the water district after her limo leaves Mechanical Street. Dr. Crick says, "As long as you're safe, have as much sex as you want." But he never defines safety.

East Kill inspires its residents with ambitions they can never fulfill. No person is at home in a home town, but this is especially the case in East Kill, where glumness has settled over the rooftops and the cars and the poetic aspirations of the girls and boys at East Kill Prep, and the slow students at the conservatory, learning voice-leading though they will never use it.

Didn't Moira Orfei warn me, at Trapani's Hotel de Anza, against career suicide? Didn't she urge me to perform Liszt? I may never be as popular as Alma. My staccato octaves resemble hers, though I lack the pioneer grit that sent her career from Peru to Colombia to Venezuela to Argentina to Guam, the Balearics, too, and Sardinia, and the former Yugoslavia. Praising Alma is a ploy. In Aigues-Mortes I may figure out why I flashed Tanaquil and arrested her life.

Why hadn't I studied the violin instead, as Alma once advised, trying to steer me away from imitating her career? She would have liked a string player in the house, to relieve the horrors of equal temperament; she would have enjoyed a son's vibrato. She worried about my infant earaches; she told an interviewer, "I kept watch over that child every moment during his first four years."

I haven't shaved in two weeks, not since my night with Friedman at the Empire Motel, outside East Kill, on Highway 15, leading nowhere. I don't know what's wrong with me this year—something Friedman said, at the motel, the lobby desk manned by an emaciated, gap-toothed cowboy with a lopsided beard, who seemed not intelligent enough for the job, and apologized to us for the malfunctioning thermostat. Atavistic Friedman had depressive circles under his eyes. He didn't want me to suck his cock, only to stroke the area behind it, a transition—Dr. Crick calls it the "perineum"—that makes masculinity a hallway rather than a throne-room.

*

I spent a lovely evening alone at home on Mechanical Street, eating complimentary chocolates. That's the only pleasant recent event—the arrival of one pound of free chocolates in the mail from Siddhartha, who'd offended me at our last tryst by refusing to kiss though we'd worked out the scene in advance.

*

My slow student Reuben, a redhead struggling to learn the complete Chopin etudes, has a blurry, damp, erased complexion. I fear for his safety. He motorcycles, without helmet, on Lucinda Way, in the water district; he wants to impress functionaries at the plant where his father manufactures pain management kits. The mayor and Reuben's father are having an affair. Mayor Dreyfus would stop at nothing to keep Reuben's father happy, to keep the pain-management business in East Kill, rather than see it relocate to West Kill, a more logical home.

*

Tanaquil ventures downstairs: upset, glowering, re-reading *Ivanhoe* but not concentrating, she sits on the pink damask sofa. I should permanently retire from performing. After my nervous collapse, which she called an "auto-da-fé," she said I should limit myself to *Totentanz* recitals in East Kill, and teaching private students, like slow Reuben and nude Lu.

I used up too much sperm last night at Friedman's. There's none left for escorts who might call back—Max, Stefan, Siddhartha, Brett, Isaac, Aaron, Tucker, Ransom. Wouldn't Alma, if she were home, permit my trip tonight through snow to the only neighborhood I like, the water district? I want soft-shell crabs at Jeffrey's, the diner where I am known to staff—forgiven, my mediocre aspirations.

*

The first time I saw Moira Orfei at home in Montecatini, she was sitting around with nothing to do. Touring season hadn't started. Her shiny circus slacks were fathomless turquoise, like the bottom of a shallow East Kill stream where I used to wade, afraid of rocks yet drawn to them, curious about drowning. Her open-toed sandals proved a few points, or would, later, when I remembered them. On her right index finger, a ring sparkled. (Gem specifics elude me.) She wore a striped turtleneck: brown and blue, a non-intuitive combination, ensured circus success. Her lip gloss, white-pink, suggested flamenco capabilities; her black sunglasses, large and interfering, carried, on their temples, the Orfei family crest. Her jet hair, teased into a triumphal puff, avoided movement, and she lay on a chaise longue near cacti and palm trees; she was waiting for meaning to arrive, or else a phone call, a visitor from the past, anything to wake her from stupor, anything to suggest bazaars, glasswort, caprioles. She wasn't fussy.

*

Years ago, before my career was ruined by scandal (escorts, drunkenness, hand paralysis), I met Moira frequently for high tea at the Hotel de Anza, when we were touring together and found ourselves in any European or American town that featured one of this famous chain of luxury hotels, noted for its *Jugendstil* lobby furniture and its exotic finger sandwiches. In any Hotel de Anza we would meet, snack, waltz (if a *ländler* were playing), plan films (sci-fi or romance), discuss Orfei scandals (always in danger of re-surfacing) and acts we might try out together. False gaiety punctured our afternoons, damaged my equilibrium, thrust me farther into the past than I wished to go, back to the bandstand where I first saw Moira dance, a park in Montecatini, remote and unpopular, where a clarinetist and guitarist were playing, and Moira was two-stepping, lost, separated from her father and her early training: she was a replica of Lola Montès, seasoned spectators said, unafraid to go out on a limb. After her debut in the bandstand, Moira became a subject of manifestos, aesthetic dicta circling around the miracle of the Montecatini bandstand and around my involuntary spectatorship, which tastes, when I remember it, of baked meringue. Simple conversation with Moira was a strain; my comments were hesitant, for her reputation dwarfed mine. My hands shook when I stood in the bandstand and saw Moira twirl and shimmy in a modern, unprecedented pavane. (I'd traveled to Montecatini, without Alma's knowledge or consent, to take healing baths.) I wanted to introduce myself to Moira but didn't know how. Eventually the crowd dwindled to four elderly men watching her slow rotation, and I summoned the courage to approach her and describe my musical aspirations and how she might become part of them. She was indifferent to my schemes, narrated with old-world stiffness. Her modernity shamed my East Kill persiflage. Later, when we toured together, she forgave me for disappearing to find an escort; such diversions neutralized the minimal sexual charge between us. In all our years of tour, I never made a pass at her: commendable restraint.

Touring with Moira Orfei, I could use my imagination, enjoy pastiche, and taste brittle candy—slim pink boxes of white-chocolate-coated almonds, sold in Hotel de Anza lobbies. If a Hotel de Anza opened in Montecatini, I'd book a room and wait for Moira's reappearance. But the Hotel de Anza may never start a franchise there—just as it may never spread its regality to East Kill. And so I must live perpetually distant from the Hotel de Anza, and the moods its lobby allows: Saturn and Mars, frescoed on blue ceilings.

Moira's hairstyle, at every stage of her career, has always been the same, which affords her management the ease of not needing new posters to advertise her circus spectaculars. She performs conventional stunts (mastering dangerous animals), but also tableaux that border on the musical, requiring drums, triangles, whistles, castanets, and repetition, always the same sound-effect repeated frequently enough to prod listeners into lachrymose imaginings of earlier times they heard those sounds, produced not by Moira but by women who looked like Moira, whose earrings always seem to be the agent—the activator—of the music-box effect. Tone seems to emerge not out of her percussive bijoux but out of her flesh, her musculature the resonating instrument for sounds paradoxically mechanical, silvery, originating in metallic and man-made substances, like maple armoires, or amber jewelboxes fashioned to resemble human skulls and coconut gourds.

I was unshaven when I first met Moira in Montecatini, but my three-day's growth of beard and my sloppy attire didn't stop her from being polite. She acknowledged that I, male but unexemplary, stood in her vicinity; she performed no obeisance and advanced no hostility. She rotated in a bizarre galliard on the bandstand, and palm trees swayed like warnings; her cloudy skirt seemed grass or beads. Posters around Montecatini advertised a rags-to-riches aspect of her stage persona. I gleaned, from the chatter of four elderly men, watching, that she came from affluent Montecatini's poor periphery, and that the town fathers, noticing Moira and her talented sisters, assisted Signor Orfei in organizing his daughters into a group act, dramatizing their successful battle against poverty; but I distrust any account of Moira Orfei that does not originate in her own words. Without her language, I am forced to speculate, and I dislike hypotheses. In the Hotel de Anza, whichever Hotel de Anza we chanced to find, during our slow peregrination of a Europe that had limited patience for our effects, she would tell me parts of her story, but they never added up, and, intoxicated, I probed no further. I was grateful that Moira Orfei was endless, and that she never told me the true story of her difficult life.

Notebook Six

Tanaquil, hunting for boyfriends in the water district, caused a minor car accident this morning, but she escaped unharmed. She left our totalled Volvo on River Street, to be towed. The smashed car's connection to water never quite present in the presumptively-named water district reminded me of the time that Alma and Tanaquil and I drove to a Finger Lake, parked at the shore, and waded into sludge, whose instability disturbed my sister—she lost balance and fell down. Thirsty now, as I sit in my studio, looking out to ceaseless downpour on Mechanical Street, I recall my many bodies of water, and the harm I have done Tanaquil, and how, in Aigues-Mortes, I might make amends by entrusting Moira Orfei with the secret, and assisting (through dextrous piano playing) her trapeze dramatizations of Tanaquil's trauma, repealed. How can I convince Moira Orfei to wend her way through Tanaquil's intricacies, not as "psychotic" (says Alma) as mine, but still deserving respect, contrition, and triage?

*

Today, anticipating Aigues-Mortes, I practiced Debussy preludes. To be a worthy customer of local hustlers, I must develop chest and shoulders. Also I must memorize the second volume of Liszt's *Années*, because he exploits the keyboard's mephitic lower register. Aigues-Mortes needs to hear about the bottom. My right hand's second finger has cracked open at the tip, thanks to Liszt; hustler jism could enter the cut and compromise my immunity. I should program preludes by Debussy, Bach, Chopin, Scriabin, Rachmaninoff, Griffes, and Gershwin. How will Moira Orfei demonstrate prelude? While wire-walking, she could discuss her friendship with Catherine Deneuve when Catherine was still a Dorléac, not yet famous, her sister Françoise not yet dead. Moira is best at fugue.

*

Last night Friedman, in his water-district loft, deprived me of orgasm, though I paid full price. He thinks it therapeutic if I don't conclude. He claims to be part Algerian. After sex, we walked along what passes for a river, and, while we looked into black water, or pseudo-water, he described his literary ambitions. He calls himself "the new Mary McCarthy." With kohl-circled eyes he resembles a weary Cocteau. His surly speaking voice, low as the left-hand murmurings in Liszt's *Années*, attracts customers. Chainsmoking, he bragged that his roman à clef will blow the lid off East Kill's secrets. Balderdash. I doubt that Friedman has the discipline to be a writer.

I complained to Friedman about blue balls. Near water, or pseudo-water, Friedman finished me off: he clutched my head, squeezed it, as if wanting to strangle me, but also as if to forgive whatever I did, earlier, to earn his wrath.

We ended the night foodshopping at Lucky. We talked to the good butcher, Vincent Crick. Physically and temperamentally he resembles his brother, Dr. Felix Crick, my internist, with stucco freestanding office on Lucinda Way.

*

I visited Eduardo, former escort, at the public hospital, where he was dying, helped into afterlife by his long-suffering mother. (He retired, at thirty, from hustling, and became—under the name "Eduardo Ochs"—a well-known local painter of still lives; then he got sick and lost sight.) His mother, in the hospital room, said, "Breathe, Becky." Incomprehensibly, she called her son "Becky." "Becky, do you want more drip?" she asked. To ease the way to death, Eduardo sang, wordlessly, with shamanic virtuosity. His unscripted moaning sounded like Rachmaninoff's "Vocalise." He was heading to heaven. I had no part in sending him there.

He was trying to die in a sideways posture, as Dr. Crick had recommended. The mother soothed his bedsores; he was small and shriveled, like a rag doll on Tanaquil's bureau once. Dim, the room in which Eduardo met death: I couldn't see accurately.

I held Eduardo's hand, rubbed his shoulders: he shuddered at my insensitive touch. One of his paintings hung on the wall: *nature morte* of apple, knife, book. While I massaged Eduardo, his mother complained, "Damn it, Dr. Crick, Becky needs a painkiller." The doctor was absent, so she took out a hypodermic and gave Eduardo a shot. "It's the strongest morphine in the western hemisphere," she said. Dr. Crick tolerated sexually profligate patients, but he was chintzy with morphine. Sometimes the family had to supply it.

*

When I see Moira Orfei in Aigues-Mortes, we will play cards. I will bring my Tiffany deck. My fellow *conservatoire* students were card sharps: any cheap amusement to distract them from mastering impossible instruments.

Moira Orfei's knees, when she wears a skirt, are attractive and legendary enough to justify any hyperbole, and they explain her ungraspable, tumultuous career. The knee is not a vivid, memorable, or sexually charged portion of anatomy, and yet Moira's knees establish a compromise-formation between plumpness and boniness—a middle ground that makes me jealous: envious not of her skirts, their cut and comeliness, but of the knee's immodesty beneath the hemline. The knee, when I look at it, or at a picture of it, proves that Moira Orfei has the right to ignore me—and that she is younger and more beautiful than most circus followers realize. Why didn't her friend Eric Rohmer call his film *Moira Orfei's Knee*?

When Moira is seated, she presses knees together: she respects Montecatini's conservatism. Before Aigues-Mortes I could use a trip to Montecatini, to stoke up on Orfei moral fibre.

Moira's knees are almost as big as her head. Have other suppliants noticed this fact?

Debase myself before Moira's knees. Be nervous, so my behavior will be impressively deferential. She could tell me, when we meet, that I lack discipline, but I will distract her by flashing my playing cards and my willingness to deal.

Every performance must do its humble best to remedy some historical catastrophe. I must figure out whether Jews or other ethnic groups were persecuted in Aigues-Mortes, and then dedicate my performances to them. Perhaps Messiaen wrote a solo piano piece that would be appropriate elegy for Aigues-Mortes's war dead. Moira wants our act to honor the memory of her mad father in Lucca, locked in the asylum where the Giardino Botanico meets the ramparts; his hallucinations paled, she said, beside her circus eminence's tragic magnitude.

*

Mechanical Street holds a block party every July fourth. One year, a neighbor boy—Arnie, one of the slummy Sante family—lost a fingertip. The amputation made him more attractive, more sought after, by his entrepreneurial father, for illicit photo shoots: Arnie starred in pictures accompanying his father's porno novelettes. This year I will stay in Aigues-Mortes until August, despite humidity and mosquitoes; Tanaquil could be the block party's star, without my overshadowing presence. She has not attended a block party in years, ever since the July fourth she tripped on a curb and split open her lip.

*

Alma wastes time on the phone with me; last night she called, fresh from a walk along Buenos Aires's seedy Calle Necochea. After praising Cantina Rimini's orchids, she tried to manage, from afar, my technical crisis. A piano note cannot be altered once it has sounded, but Alma has achieved the illusion of vibrato through pedalling, not pressure. I, too, could simulate vibrato, if I followed Alma's late-night advice from Latin America.

Alma said, "Have you finished memorizing the Liszt Sonata?" No, I told her; I have also forgotten *Au bord d'une source* and *Gaspard de la nuit*, my repertoire's discomfited core. She mentioned the water district. I said, "My good friend Friedman is twenty-eight." Well past the age of discretion. Tomorrow night, Alma will play at Planetario Galileo Galilei.

*

In early life, I wanted the easy outlet of elegy and murder—first, murder, so, afterward, I could indulge in elegy, my favorite posture.

I considered murdering Tanaquil because her protuberant genitals, casually revealed in restaurants, cut into my tranquillity. I remember the crack, and her habit, when bored or nervous, of handling it. If she were wearing a skirt, her hand would reach toward the hidden place. These genital explorations reinforced Alma's prominence; Tanaquil, pressing a palm against her crotch, was playing a duet with Alma's fame. I considered murdering my sister—ridding us of the embarrassment. I never mentioned my plan or pushed it to fruition. Simple eye contact between Thom and me (Father I never called him) sufficed to communicate my plots.

*

As a child, I held Thom up as my model prisoner and model jailor. In conversation he threw around the words "Nobel Prize" and "suicide," as if the concepts were twins; no one we knew had committed suicide or won a Nobel Prize. His vocations were vague, plural, promiscuous: he had been the president of a chain of music conservatories; a rare book dealer; a forger of paintings and documents (portraits, passports, treaties, star autographs); a financial consultant to lesser-known French vineyards. His death was mysterious. We experimented with at least five versions. None pleased Alma, who wanted to homogenize them into a single, graspable truth. He drowned off La Spezia; he committed suicide in Rome; he died of exposure, homeless in Bryn Mawr; he died of autoerotic asphyxiation in our house on Mechanical Street; he died as a mercenary, fighting in Egypt. No tale of his death had the monopoly on veracity. Pleased by his posthumousness, we watched rumors multiply. I don't want a conventional death; I'd like to split my demise into a dozen explanations. Unsteady, Alma drifted toward South America because she never knew exactly how Thom died; if she could fix the facts of his termination, she might have been content to remain on Mechanical Street. She dislikes East Kill because Thom's ancestors, dairy farmers, founded it.

Thom never met Moira Orfei; he died before she entered my life. He might not have appreciated her—or he might have claimed her as his investment, his discovery. I have failed to avoid mentioning my father. Thoughts of long-ago events in Montecatini—revolutions that provoked Moira's repeated descents into circus danger—are my only protection against Thom's return into this still life's expanding frame.

Notebook Seven

I visited Matilda in Boston yesterday, and when I entered her body, she complained of pain. Though the dryness wasn't my fault, I saw its piano aspects. Alma, if she were here in the Clarendon Street bedroom, would understand. Events derive meaning from adjacencies. No vaginal dryness or penile soreness is disconnected from a fate's other compartments. The Mangroves do not suffer "dissociation of sensibility." For us, a spiral staircase links every incident to forgotten dungeons.

I slept upstairs in Matilda's house, the bedroom next to hers, my door unlocked. She couldn't explain why my pillow was blood-soaked this morning. Nor could Dr. Crick. I telephoned him from Matilda's townhouse, and he hesitated to diagnose. I described her nonviolent core: its pinkness, its immunity. Dr. Crick told me to stop worrying—his usual response, whenever I mention bleeding. Avoiding direct words on my condition, he told me to study Exodus for news about human need and wilderness. His touchstones, like mine, are Semitic.

*

When I returned to East Kill, I gave blood and enjoyed a battery of medical tests, including my year's second colonoscopy. Dr. Crick saw nothing immediately wrong, though he had a troubled look on his face after delving. Maybe I was so "down under" from Valium that I am an inaccurate judge. He described my throat's laceration and swelling. An infected cut—red, throbbing, on my right hand's index finger—bears on Aigues-Mortes.

Today, weak from colonoscopy, I can't begin to narrate Alma Guadalquivar's Teatro Colón debut or to describe the fourth-grade cloak-

room where my teacher Mrs. Retalbo kept her fur coat, a wrap like the one
Moira Orfei wore when she brought her Bengal tiger act to Göteborg.

*

Moira Orfei is not my muse. We can't pinpoint what she is. Nor need we
limit her claim. She lives far from East Kill and yet governs my water-
district afternoons. Of my escorts she never gets wind; her image sends
me to their embraces. Under her spell, I grow afraid of "all," of totali-
ty: I dread summarizing my erotic life and thus ending it.

Moira Orfei could leave me adrift and what comfort would remain?
No engagements in my calendar, except a few Derva Nile benefits.
Should I commit suicide before May and leave dramatic word for
Moira? Stop exaggerating!

Perhaps an Orfei sister's illness explains Moira's silence—not Chloe,
but one of the many other sisters, all jealous of Moira, their persevera-
tions never attaining circus pinnacle. Perhaps Moira is weighing a marriage proposal, or enjoying a religious retreat in Castelfranco. Does my
name mean nothing to Tuscan audiences? Her fan clubs have not elected me president. I don't want her to think me demanding or over-
attentive.

*

I remember waiting, outside Hotel de Anza in Barcelona, for Moira
Orfei to appear; waiting, outside Hotel de Anza in San Sebastian, and
outside Hotel de Anza in Collioure . . .

*

In Aigues-Mortes I shall play Ravel's complete works for solo piano,
with Moira's trapeze dance as accompaniment—or Liszt's *Années* vol. 2
(*Italie*) with Moira's *penseroso* act, involving flame, swords, lions, hoops,
jewels, stillness, chains, obedience, memories of Signor Orfei's incarceration. Her act is elegiac and *doloroso*, like Hadrian's Villa becomes,
even without visitors, after she has performed in its vicinity, or like Villa
d'Este becomes when she repeats her performance there, despite tour

buses, despite Orfei intermarriage with descendants of Liszt's adulterous mistress, Marie d'Agoult. My busy practice schedule leaves no time to explain the Orfei/d'Agoult calamity. Moira alone has the right to mourn Alphonsine Duplessis, the original consumptive Lady of the Camellias. Moira has the monopoly on remembering Alphonsine, because of their physical resemblance, and because Great-Great-Grandmother Orfei attended the Duplessis salon, or so Moira told me, in Atrani, at the Hotel de Anza, after she led cream ponies on Grand Parade through Positano.

I'm drinking schnapps at Jeffrey's Diner. Friedman enters, wearing sweats, tank top, and sneakers, despite snow: heavy late-autumn sludge, paralyzing the roads. Interrupting my meditations, he sits in my booth; soon I must put down my pen. How can I concentrate on Moira's resemblance to Alphonsine, and on my pipeline to Alphonsine's grave in Montmartre Cemetery, via my upcoming performances with Moira, when rude, swarthy Friedman has ruptured my hemisphere? He is multi-ethnic, an untraceable hybrid—Palestinian, Algerian, Lebanese? His forehead has permanent welts, as if someone dropped weights on his skull when he was a baby. The men I love are dented.

*

Pleasant paid sex with Friedman, regular's rate. After hamburgers at Jeffrey's, we went to his loft. I insisted he shower. He is a criminal with a rancid canola oil smell on his person; his attractiveness dismantles my homely attainments. Like many hirsute Levantines, he naturally produces a nutty odor (chickpeas?). As he entered me, I admitted my desire to make a Super 8 film of him, in jockstrap, on the Cross: I have embarked on a series of films, Mechanical Street Cinema, using the Bolex that Thom bought for Alma, on Swiss tour, when she felt a sudden hunger to record the mountains surrounding her greatness. The film I made of nude Lu playing piano is my best so far. In it, she looks punishably diligent, small. Tiny people, like Lu, incite my pity, my wish to bar them from concert stages, and my wish to film them. Discussion of Mechanical Street Cinema has no place in the Aigues-Mortes notebooks. Watch me fail at nudity and music, my twin vocations.

*

Another date with Friedman, at his raw loft: regular's rate, three hours. The more I think about Aigues-Mortes, the more I want to hire Friedman. His treatment bruises my rear, a jiffy pak. He kisses with sloppy gaping mouth and doesn't compliment my body. Perhaps he hates it, considers it just a john's. I do Alma an injustice to fetishize Friedman's secondary sexual characteristics. She will be pleased that I am mastering Ives's *Concord* Sonata for Aigues-Mortes. As a teen, Friedman gave tours of Walden Pond and Amherst. This afternoon, caressing his calves, I decided that I have evaded my true work, which is to lie in bed with an escort while contemplating earlier naked bodies I've known, and explaining past nude nuances to the present hour's companion.

After sex, we walked through the water district and failed to ascertain its borders. Its rowhouses are too near pseudo-water; walking on the gutter, between sidewalk and river, or what passes for a river, I lost gravity (did Friedman push me?) and almost fell in.

Although elevated trains have been dismantled, our colonial house still remembers their vibrations; rafters squeak and shake. Now I hear a passing train, perhaps carrying Alma home. It brakes at a near station. But this vehicle no longer exists.

It may be too late to read Nietzsche, as I had meant to, in my youth, when Alma told me that the greater part of a pianist's education took place away from the keyboard, among books and "the people," her euphemism for escorts and my other colleagues in the water district, competitive as *conservatoire*. I could live nowhere but here, in East Kill, the epicenter of the musical uncanny. Friedman is the first hustler whose body I have managed to memorize—as opposed to Marco, Ransom, Siddhartha, Carlos, Stefan, and Friedman's other cronies, whose names and muscles I forget, despite this documentation.

An early Mangrove, first settler of East Kill, and his euphony-seeking successors, lived in our Mechanical Street house. Progenitor portraits line our upstairs halls. My studio walls are covered with posters of Moira Orfei's Italian, French, and Spanish appearances, her hairstyle and maquillage the same in every picture, her circus inventiveness an antidote to Mangrove pomposity, ancestral infatuations dooming me to stay in a town that tolerated my *Totentanz* concert but otherwise ignores me.

*

Listeners may not understand why I resort to a teacher when I am a respected pedagogue and pianist, best known for spectacular failure in Europe, fits of mental absence during performances.

Advanced, I turn to Fabio Abruzzi to heal my crippled pianism, formerly aristocratic. He helps me forget our infection, the virus given me, or so I reconstruct, at Palmer House, a hotel about which I have no strong feelings. I would not wish to have been infected at a Hotel de Anza.

Fabio's penis, its mushroom head, frightened me today, after I played the Liszt B Minor Sonata, unmemorized. I have, at times, enjoyed Fabio's size; this afternoon I almost choked. He tries to purge my musical faults, though it is improbable that I, Alma Mangrove's son, a recording artist in my own right, can find a master capable of curing my pathology. For indeed I suffer a malady, an infection of pianistic equipment; spasms and staggerings intrude on my Alma-acquired (genetic?) keyboard athleticism, my way of negotiating leaps, and my ability to curve fingers for incisive sound. If the trance that holds my frail career in place should falter, I will resort to theft, assault—any felony to regain propulsive phrasing, sharp rhythm, *messa di voce*.

My oldest student, Rabbi Gershon, eighty years old, will want embraces after tomorrow's lesson; the bearded sot leaves his fly unzipped.

When Anita and I were first married, I kept a series of notebooks about our sex life. She read and then destroyed them: left them out on the curb for the garbageman. I was relieved to see the notebooks exterminated.

*

I hired a nineteen-year-old boy named Enrico, together with Friedman: work partners. An extra $150 for the younger. I said to the kid, "I wish it were twenty years ago," and he, misinterpreting, pushed harder, as if he were angling inwardly for some favor—some description—I had no power to reward. I wish I had a photo of Enrico to paste in this notebook. What good would the photo do? Prove Enrico. Help me remember Enrico. Every escort lasts in my memory for one day only. I dread the waylessness between escort appointments. "Waylessness" is Alma's word. If I think about Buenos Aires, the notebooks will shut down.

*

On my behalf, Anita made telephone inquiries about flights to France. I will fly into Nice, then hire a chauffeur for the drive to Aigues-Mortes. I fear my wife's intentions. She must harbor malign reasons for remaining my buffer. Perhaps she plans eventually to deplete me, turning me into a grisaille automaton, empty as Alma becomes in conversation when home from tour.

All I care about, tonight, is Géricault's *Raft of the "Medusa,"* for Janson's *History of Art* is Alma's toilet reading. In her absence, I take the liberty of using her bathroom, to be near her pipes and porcelain. I am not otherwise permitted in that sanctum. I prefer it to my own, and have admired it since adolescence, when I discovered that her superiority extended from piano to hygiene. She has more fears than I do. Mine are local; hers are international. Her nervousness has spread a mesh—a net veil—over proximate emblems: dying elms, uneven bricks, fog, TV antenna on the grim Sante family's roof, and the curve in the crook of Mechanical Street, where our block intersects itself, greets its own aborted destination.

Notebook Eight

Anita's stepfather died. No melodrama. Mr. Wax, a postal employee with high cholesterol and prostate cancer, was due for death—no point in keening a foreknown demise. Anita took the news in stride. She'd not spent enough time with Sam Wax to develop a more than perfunctory affection. Stoic Mrs. Wax said her day would go on just the same, despite Sam's passing. She repeated, "I remember, Anita, when you were little, you'd play on the front lawn and watch the traffic. I wasn't afraid you'd run into the street. You were happy to wave at the cars and eat your applesauce and fritters." I caught the mourning undertone. Mrs. Wax has a God-fearing desire to revise Anita's memories, to erase Anita's early love of accidents and self-wounding.

Mr. Wax will be buried tomorrow in Albany. Grief is not my forte. After the funeral, I may look up DeSantos, an Iranian-Cuban escort I've been e-mailing. His hips, on the webpage, look wide enough to bear a child; his naïve, cheese-like face appeals.

Why doesn't Anita divorce me? She needs my "butter" holdings, my ancestral dairy sinecure. Maybe she loves my unnaturally large skull, like Swinburne's, nearly an anatomical monstrosity.

Why do I stay married to Anita? My degraded loyalty to what I already know; my addiction to the habitual, the disappointing.

Montecatini's old-world lady-of-the-evening glamour outshines Anita's round-faced, smirking modernity.

*

At the funeral, no Wax wept. Anita's sister, Astrud, stayed away in Taipei. We haven't seen her since our wedding. Her photo remains on our dining-room hutch. When, beneath the Guadalquivar chandelier, I sit, pan-

icked that suppertime has arrived but I've not yet visited the water district
to see the sun set over tawdry cat-houses and fish-houses, this photo of
Astrud and her burgundy facial birthmark, shaped like Newfoundland,
prognosticates my errors. Her nevis, a stormcloud, blocks the sun and
casts aspersions on my idiotic heliotropism.

*

Hot hour, after the Albany funeral, with DeSantos. He has hairy thighs,
and Jung's *Man and His Symbols* on his coffeetable. As we split an orange
together in bed, I remembered the fresh, illegal oranges that Alma
smuggled back from Andalusian tour, when I was a child. My father
praised their acidity. I hope DeSantos won't jinx my potential Liszt
grandeur in Aigues-Mortes, where I'd hoped to reverse the hold of the
fetish, the bought ass.

*

Yesterday while checking out Luigi Nono scores at the East Kill
Conservatory library I saw my friend Matteo. Formerly a hustler, currently a music librarian, he uses a cane. He shelves, alphabetizes: light
tasks. His ailments include shingles, spinal deformation, and hallucinations—due to pills his mother took while pregnant. Because of his dis-
eased, aristocratic mien, my imagination, in his presence, disembarks;
I want suddenly to press his sick face against the Xerox machine's plate
glass and press the copy button. He reminds me of Guadalquivar cousins
I knew as a child, frail refugees from Catalan purges. Seeking jobs and
renown, my cousins bootlessly congregated around Alma in East Kill.

Matteo told me that in a few days his girlfriend Solly will become his
boyfriend: she is a pre-op transsexual. Matteo considers the operation
an "upgrade." He described how a doctor creates a penis from scratch.
He showed me a photo of Solly. She looked as if she'd been hit by a
truck, her face then reassembled.

As a hustler, Matteo was a nitpicker, doing demolition work on my
body; during sex, he ignored context and periphery, harped on a detail
(abdomen, buttock, nipple), and said nasty things about it.

*

I met a percussionist today in a Camera Baths cubicle. He had a large, curved erection, but his chest hair did not conform to my prefered Louisiana pattern: it resembled Rhode Island.

"I miss melody," he said. Drums precluded lyricism. He knew I was a bathhouse regular, but he had never succeeded in tricking with me. I apologized for avoiding him. My sexual appetites are irregular, and not within my control. He told me that other percussionists agreed with my self-diagnosis; my hasty arousal, its tendency to happen in any milieu, however inappropriate, led locals to dismiss me as a snobbish Casanova. After 69, I told him my theory of spasmodic erotics, and mentioned (imprudently) my plans for Aigues-Mortes, including a possible recital focused on the spasm. In my studio archive I already have a sizeable "spasm" dossier. The percussionist came, four spurts. The moment a trick comes, I detest him, though I pretend to feel inexpressible love.

*

"Parallel fifths are out of the question in proper voice leading," I told Anita, over swordfish and potato salad. I love inculcation—receiving knowledge, passing it on. After dinner I made an index of Lisztian aspects I must convey—verbally or musically—in Aigues-Mortes, and recited it to Alma, on the phone from Buenos Aires, before bedtime. She described her concert at El Viejo Almacén, her favorite *tanguería,* and said, "Your eloquence is a fetishist's game of pick-up-sticks."

I should program Mompou's *Suburbis,* including Moira Orfei's favorite piece about the little blind girl. If I cannot mention masturbation in my pre-concert lecture, then I will cancel Aigues-Mortes. Moira won't mind my adolescent explicitness. Think of the rushed sex she's witnessed in Montecatini alleys. She stands a head taller than I, and has a football player's collarbone. She favors off-the-shoulder gowns. Real or fake jewels spangled across the chest define her as Italy's first treasure, the only hope of contemporary circus art. She hopes not to bungle her responsibilities. Next spring in Italy, her new TV show will air; this low-budget revue hour will be directed by a former husband, who tends to film her in unflattering poses. Her Medean intensity compensates for his sloppy eye. On her show, she may interview me—to cement my shaky hold on Italian audiences. I will wear my celery velvet suit and will summarize my method in five minutes, without digressions.

*

I rediscovered my Moira Orfei scrapbook, in the upstairs closet, under a pink wool blanket (Alma's gift from Costa Rica). I hid the scrapbook a year ago, so its messages wouldn't distract me—photos of tall Moira and her shorter sisters, lined up outside their hut in Montecatini's ghetto, Moira's dimples evident. My passion for Moira is the latest and most lasting in a series of what Alma calls "drunken episodes without the drink."

I am no longer a child—my primary regret. And yet I don't envy Moira's early years in Montecatini, competing for food and attention with her sisters. Eventually she triumphed over them: at town fiestas, her equestrian stunt, harness strung with fairy lights, thrilled vigilantes, who later committed her father to the asylum.

*

On the books for Aigues-Mortes is an elegy program featuring Ravel's *Tombeau* for soldiers slain in World War I. God knows if amid Moira's farrago of fakeries, she can find a funeral posture. She is more celebrated for giddiness than for grief, her dead mother notwithstanding. But every artist is an elegist, and Moira will concoct jujitsu pliés to suit artificial Ravel's rigaudon and forlane. Perhaps she will at last articulate what she felt when her mother died.

Everyone knew about Mrs. Orfei's weak heart, and prevented her from circusgoing, its excitement producing palpitations. But, *un bel dì*, she attended and—watching Moira pirouette with a tiger and a flaming hoop—suffered a coronary. At least Moira believed the autopsy's hypothesis of cause-and-effect. She told me this tale in the Hotel de Anza lobby, Marseilles, as we sat recovering from a less-than-stellar co-performance. (I had suffered a memory lapse during *Miroirs.*) "Mother loved circus," Moira said. "No one in Italy felt it more deeply." If Mrs.

Orfei had died watching her daughter perform, how could Moira renounce the ring?

*

Define the Guadalquivar attitude toward escort escalation, moving from the $120 category to the $300. Define the Guadalquivar attitude toward the ecstasy obtainable only from paid partners. Define the Guadaquivar attitude toward DeSantos's cock filling my mouth, the very orifice that must explain the history of Liszt's *Années de pèlerinage* to Aigues-Mortes audiences, but first to Anita, and then to Moira Orfei, so she can develop suitable circus moves. Define the covert lure of Aigues-Mortes, the logic of its seedy, rarefied arcades, and the aroma of dead water, salty and murmurous, that infiltrates the cafés.

Notebook Nine

"Buenos Aires, as a musical locale, is superior to Aigues-Mortes," Alma told me at dinner. Angry, she is back from tour: no escorts allowed in the house. Argentina reacted badly to news of her imminent retirement. She presumed that they would sympathize with her career's natural termination, and yet they griped, like the Peruvians the year before: in Lima, she'd proclaimed the limits of nineteenth-century music ("I've exhausted the romantics, I can play no more"). Scoffers left the concert hall before she'd finished the Schumann Fantasy.

After dinner she practiced Ravel in her upstairs coign. Concerto in G is *my* piece. I need to steal it back. I don't wish her to flop, but I can't be known solely as "the guy who writes Alma Mangrove's liner notes."

*

I visited Friedman, who tied me up and experimented with my perineum, which, as Dr. Crick attests, is to the buttocks what a Bach prelude is to the fugue. I hope this analogy won't offend Alma, should she choose, later, unbeknownst to me, to read this notebook, or the others stacked on my bedroom's Guadalquivar armoire. I don't care if Anita reads the notebooks. Tanaquil may read them if she wishes. She would understand their contents; and she keeps rival notebooks, which intend to assassinate Alma's career. If I am not more precise about Tanaquil's role in recent events, I will not have fulfilled my long-ago promise to repair her wounds by careful description.

I told Friedman that he could come over to tea, that I would endeavor to introduce him to Alma. He has no wish to finagle a backdoor entrance to the Mangrove clan. As an adolescent he spent time in the Marseilles skin-trade. Moira Orfei is no stranger to Marseilles—it was a live-action site for her TV pilot ("The Moira Orfei Show"). Her father, leading the Montecatini *partigiani,* knew members of the French Resistance hiding (in full view) on the Quai de la Fraternité. Our Aigues-Mortes program will celebrate Orfei anti-fascism.

*

I persuaded Friedman to visit Mechanical Street and hear me play Liszt's B Minor Sonata. He showered in the private bathroom adjoining my studio. I diligently soaped his crack and asked him to remain unclothed while he listened to Liszt: nudity constituted his "punishment," though I was the humiliated party.

After I finished, Friedman said, sitting judgmental and naked on the Queen Anne daybed, that he admired my flow. I asked him why he used abstractions to evade simple praise. All music flows, so to make a sonata flow is no virtue. He said that Liszt performances often stagnate: I'd impregnated the dead silence between recitative's spasms. Alma knocked. I told her (through the closed door) that now was not a good time. Friedman, screwing me, said, "You're moving in circles." I threw the accusation back at him, told him he was penetrating in circles, like a convict tunneling an escape by means of ratiocination. I heard scuffling at the door: Alma had returned. Friedman and I got dressed. I opened the door and introduced him to Alma. Wearing the cheap blue glass necklace I'd given her, she pretended interest, and asked about Friedman's background. Later he told me that she was much more attractive in person than in photos. He said "whore" was just a word, like "cocotte" or "lioness."

*

Alma at dinner discussed her happy early years with Thom.

"Our relationship boiled down to buttons," she said. "Opalescent. When we made love, they broke off my blouse as he undid them."

I told her, "I want to understand Scriabin's cloudy essays on *falling*— as Emma Bovary or Mary Magdalene fell, but also as a suicide falls from the top of the Empire State Building."

"Yes," she said, with customary, comprehensible weariness. Everyone is tired of my theories.

Scriabin incarnates his *falling* essays as preludes, etudes, and "poèmes" for solo piano, the mystic chords descending in arpeggios from sky to ground, like a nose-dive into identification with someone's father's autoerotic asphyxiation, a death I once read about in a memoir.

*

No one on the local front is prepared for the splash I will make in Aigues-Mortes, bringing the bounty of a new interpretive style, *schmaltz* refigured as analysis. Unsympathetic East Kill deprives me of venue, and limits the time I can spend in water-district acts of drunken fornication.

Alfonso Reyes says that the Aigues-Mortes entertainment office expects to unleash a blitz of publicity on the south of France—signage, skywriting.

I don't think our concerts are as important as the Aigues-Mortes folks make them out to be; I'd prefer the performances to remain low-profile.

My inability—in Tanaquil's sloe-eyed opinion—to have a "normal" human relationship, without the infection of power, detaches me from regular concert-hall gigs, so I have sought alternative sites: at first, rug stores in East Kill; and now, the obscure arcades of Aigues-Mortes, rivaling Paris. Over coddled eggs this morning Alma said that I exaggerate the prominence of the Aigues-Mortes arcades. I showed her a map. Aigues-Mortes is the original experimental community, like Fourier's—a socialist dream.

*

Derva Nile came over for rehearsal. We worked on Liszt's "Oh! quand je dors" and "Comment, disaient-ils," her Fracas perfume an abundance I could lose my mind contemplating. She said I was playing too loudly. Her nervous addiction to the limelight prevents her from accurately judging volume.

Her breasts, if I were predisposed toward them, would entice me. Theoretically desireable, they remind me of pleasures I had with Anita in Beaugency, on the Loire, near the Tour du Diable, where we had our only entirely satisfying intercourse—it lasted three hours, an ideal, even by Alma's standards.

Anita left for a musical-comedy coaching session with Ross Sachs. Slowly, she is developing her own act, which will recycle material she aborted earlier in life.

Derva and I have nothing to show for our labors, though we still hope to do a program of Fauré mélodies that will draw critics who have long avoided our concerts. I wonder why I am taking Derva's talent seriously and placing it above my own. Her tempi are slow and mannered, however much I try to prod her to the next beat. My metaphysical urgency—God-fearing haste—led Moira Orfei to notice me in the first place, among all the pianists who sent study tapes so she could prepare circus accompaniments to Elliott Carter and Milton Babbitt songs and choose a pianist who would reveal the underground link between circus and *lied*.

Alma suggested I commission a piano sonata inspired by Catullus epigrams. Good idea. Brad Olney, a local composer who physically resembles me, deserves my commission. Because Brad can't make a living as a composer, he runs a boutique for men and women, Olney Clothes, and designs the garments himself. He's better known for his shirts than for his sonatas, though both show the same concern for laborious pattern. We had sex a few times in the changing rooms. He clips his silver chest hair, as if he were auditioning for a role in one of Moira Orfei's gladiator pictures. He wants to join the Israeli army, though he's not Jewish. He believes in aggression, lost causes, and apartness. He told me that he composes music because he wants to separate himself from the world. Moira Orfei is the major contemporary exponent of *l'art pour l'art*.

*

Tanaquil should get a job. She has worked at makeup counters; she has worked washing floors at ballet studios; she has worked as a security guard at a women's psychiatric residence. Tanaquil's range of career accomplishment is staggering, if we believe the jobs she *says* she's held. No one tries to check up on her stories, and why should we? Isn't it your privilege, as adult, to lie about your vocation if you're ashamed of the truth and want to invent something more glamorous or else (in her case) something lowlier and more linked to masturbation, the family trademark?

*

Silence from Moira Orfei. Has she reconsidered Aigues-Mortes? Is she undergoing emergency surgery, as her sister Chloe intimated when we last spoke? Chloe never had a significant career on the Continent—sure, the odd appearance in India, on a talk show, confessing travails of living with a famous sister, but no genuine circus appearances, no effort to give posthumous satisfaction to their mother, who died of circus delights.

Chloe, in a convent school when Mrs. Orfei died, rushed to the funeral in Montecatini, but never figured out how to pay tribute to her mother's memory; every deviation from circus insulted the maternal ghost, and yet Chloe lacked trapeze talent. Her main interest was leukemia, and the Italian battle against it.

My distance from Moira Orfei turns East Kill's boulevards, as I drive down them, into rows of soldiers felled in forgotten battles: why bother being a pianist if I can't imagine that there are Camargue flamingos nearby?

Some talents ask to be squandered—and if Moira is the means I employ to waste what Alma has given me, then I am fulfilling her gift's secret purpose, self-extinction.

*

"You were nearly a caesarean," Alma said last night at dinner, veal stew with frozen peas. "I was in terrible pain. But nothing as intense as the earlier miscarriage, the first. Your father thought I was going to die. He hated bloodshed and screaming, so he stayed away from the hospital."

After the Industrial Revolution, Branch Way was rechristened Mechanical Street, because of East Kill's burdened consciousness of factories, not enough degradation, a hunger for more assembly-lines, so that the working classes could be ground even farther into the dirt.

The sun is setting over the water district, which I can see from the window, here on Mechanical Street, in the private garret where I write my Aigues-Mortes notebooks, and where no one ever disturbs me, not even to say an exciting new or old movie is playing at the Empire and do I wish to interrupt my meditations to catch the late show? I don't live in the water district, but its sunsets are my property; from my window I can see the rosy-fingered vulgarity and know that my house and the hustler neighborhood occupy one city, one time, and in God's eye are the same—a single experiment in dying near what passes for a body of water, or what is believed, by most of us, to be a body of water, with pleasure- and fish-houses along its shores, despite inclement weather, the Provençal mistral shaking the weak buildings and giving pneumonia to the prurient patrons. My ecstasies are false, despite Alma's claims, whispered to me since adolescence. "You're no Rachmaninoff," she said recently, "but nor am I. We're imitation Rachmaninoffs, which is nobler than being a real Stokowski or a real Leinsdorf—or a real Clara Haskil. I was fond of Clara, but I can't claim that her Mozart was my Mozart." I took this advice as encouragement: I needn't be Rachmaninoff, I need only impose his personality on my entire repertoire. Thus I habitually transported the water district's coloration into my playing: I smuggled chance encounters, fatal windstorms, and declining property values into musical phrases composed long before rigid modern zoning divided our city into sectarian parts.

I have empathy with underdogs, although I've been accused, in print, and on radio, and by Alma's fans, of cultural imperialism, a charge she skirts because of her loyal Latin American following. Ignorant of Buenos Aires folkways, Alma stuffs Western art music down proletarian throats.

*

Tonight Anita and I celebrated our anniversary. She cooked us a two-pound lobster. Alma, steering clear of the celebration, took a limo to New York and met with her agent to discuss the next farewell tour. I have become a dirty and unpleasant middle-aged man of no interest to Alma, and yet perhaps I can save face in town, make her proud when she gets wind of my accomplishment—not directly from me, I'm not a braggart, but from others in the area, family, the *East Kill Times;* or perhaps she'll intuit kudos from the silence surrounding me locally, no one wishing to speak to me in public. I need a chihuahua to walk every morning after I play Poulenc's *Mouvements perpétuels*, the only divertissements that can get me out of bed. Suicide would be one easy and dramatic solution to the Aigues-Mortes quandary, though I doubt it would please Alma or the peoples of East Kill or any other American and European cities in which I have performed or resided during my long career, now petering out.

*

Before nightfall, I must memorize Scriabin's *Vers la flamme*, on the program tomorrow at the East Kill Home for the Blind (duo recital, benefit, with Derva Nile); but first I must write to Moira Orfei. If I publish an open letter in the *Corriere della Sera*, then Italy will notice my endangerment and Moira's callow abandonment of our cause. Possibly she will telephone tonight and prevent me from publicly denouncing her perfidy. I don't want to badmouth Moira, I merely want to send the love note she has been waiting a decade to receive. She is jittery from réclame. Each new ad is a slap in the face, a reiteration that she is *known*. And to be known is to be underestimated.

If the keys obeyed me when I played the Fauré Ballade, then I wouldn't need to grovel before Moira Orfei. Even now, I am failing her, and I haven't begun writing the letter denouncing her for having failed me— and yet I meant to reverse that hypothetical letter's burden, and compose a statement so brief and loving she'd want to thumbtack it to her closet door, as, once, Alma taped to her studio mirror a note I wrote her from Portbou, the last time I visited it, a message I presumptuously called "My Life and Work," as if private correspondence needed a title.

I may begin the letter to Moira Orfei in a fortnight, if she hasn't faxed a firm pledge to appear with me in Aigues-Mortes, to achieve our public reunion, a rendezvous in a seaside bandstand so much like Montecatini's, one might be forgiven for thinking Aigues-Mortes an Italian protectorate.

*

Fabio lay nude on his living room rug while I struggled to play the Scriabin *Black Mass* Sonata. Scriabin requires a teacher's nudity for reasons I can't explain: Ajaccio violets, tropical stars. Fabio doubts I have the sonata's mechanics down pat enough to perform it in Aigues-Mortes. He called my playing "fatally hesitant." He thinks I should play Bartók's "Diary of a Fly" instead. Anything can qualify as a god, if I am in the mood for worship.

Toxins from the pesticide plant have left chalky deposits on our windows and on Mechanical Street's elm tree leaves. My molecules are fake, infected, and porous, unlike those nights of endlessly postponed sunset, of waiting for Moira Orfei outside Trapani's Hotel de Anza, beneath its orange awning.

*

Now Alma is back in Buenos Aires, spreading good news to the masses. I miss our hectoring dinners, arguments over Aigues-Mortes, a comeback she wants me to abort.

She told me last night, on the phone, about her childhood deprivations, sensual pleasures that her father Ricardo, piously disliking popular songs, forbade. Economies to extinguish the flesh: she wanted a white silk communion dress like her best friend Rosa's, but she got a drab cotton hand-me-down from the church organist's daughter. Alma's flesh rose in rebellion. For revolt, she chose *conservatoire*. Now, I'm discarding gifts she planted—Guadalquivar seeds. She said, "I must run through de Falla before orchestra rehearsal tonight. I always look at the score to refresh the memory. I fear technical mishap, ghosts of my forefathers. The bottled water tastes bad." Her melancholy is East Kill's climate: I can't interpret snow or rain apart from Alma's early losses. If I could turn back the clock and give Alma the dress she'd wanted as a girl, the dress her father refused to give her, then I wouldn't need to be a pianist; music's purpose is Alma-reparation, and if I could directly make amends, I wouldn't rely on the keyboard.

*

If I don't buckle down and memorize Scriabin's *Black Mass* Sonata I will humiliate myself in front of the discerning Aigues-Morges populace and Moira, who may then decide never to work with me again. Moira Orfei is my ideal woman if I imagine someone else watching us cross a street in Les Baux-de-Provence together: we clutch each other when the wind nearly knocks us down, and laugh, *pace* the mistral, as we contemplate our upcoming string of recitals and shock appearances—a Mangrove/Orfei blitzkrieg in the Languedoc. Moira Orfei is my ideal woman if I imagine myself ten years ago watching someone in Les Baux watching us walk hand-in-hand to a bistro with a corner banquette which we regularly claim; seated there, under this person's jealous surveillance, we order our usual negronis. (Alma once told me that negronis were the cocktail-of-choice for the Abstract Expressionists. Moira Orfei's beauty embodies the Abstract Expressionist mandate to combat entropy.) While someone watches Moira and I drink our negronis, we discuss Baltic political disintegration, the religious observances of subaltern tribes. Moira has pan-European sympathies. Watchdog agencies urge her to mourn deaths in Jerusalem and Beirut. Moira Orfei is my ideal woman if I imagine someone watching me help her pick a belt and apply jasmine eau de toilette behind the neck at a department store counter in Paris. I needn't merely imagine this scene: it happened, the last time Moira and I were in Printemps together. We chose a jangly belt to uphold her harem pants; a man with black briefcase and aviator sunglasses watched us at the belt department and followed us to the perfume counter. I put down my credit card and asked if my presence fatigued her. With a *Die Fledermaus* laugh, inoffensive and flirtatious, she deflected the question. I have not succeeded in justifying myself to Moira: Chloe, in her Luccan palazzo, refuses to give me Moira's phone number. Is Moira staying with Chloe, or living alone in Montecatini? I misspoke when I said that Moira is my ideal woman *if I imagine:* wrong. She is real, and I should stop pestering her with letters. If Moira hadn't once nearly overdosed on sleeping pills, I wouldn't worry about her current disappearance. Someone should telephone the Montecatini chamber of commerce.

*

Describe the water district. The notebooks must prove its value. But I cannot anatomize a place whose beauty lies in resistance to description. (That is an excuse.) Could I sketch the harbors, the intimations of a port, the inlets and false streams, the real streams confusing the eye?

Could I reproduce the canals, the repetitions of Venice, the almost lake, the pond and bridge, the falls, the waterfalls, the trysts beside the almost lake, the paradise of ferns in summer below the falls, the small bridge over the canal, near the highway, forbidding pedestrians? East Kill will not accommodate a *flâneur* unless I describe him.

And where does Mechanical Street fit in? Can I describe its distance, mercurial and shifting, from the water district? Carnival nights, the water district forbids foot traffic. How many times have I stood on the bandstand stage, looking out to the falls, when carnival has been cancelled but I am hoping it will be reinstated simply because I am waiting there, a fool, below a Fourth of July banner not present in November?

Once, years ago, when I walked with Alma along the water district's dangerously uneven brick pavements, toward a carnival that vanished as our longing for its presence intensified, she tripped, and nearly broke her ankle.

On the water district's border, the cemetery contains our nest of Mangrove family graves, untended stones defaced by the musically disenfranchised.

Notebook Ten

Letter from Moira Orfei (translated from the Italian)

Dear Signor Mangrove,

Until now I have been too fatigued to answer your letters. Ordinary American lingo can't measure my exhaustion. Chloe still can't comprehend it. My needs and destiny exceed yours. I command more land, more syntax. Methodical, I practice stricter forms. You failed to synchronize your music with my equestrian acts, and yet nostalgically I recall our bizarre wanderings through Les Baux, when circus art—historically speaking—was just getting off the ground. I won't forget Viterbo, where you coughed, sneezed, swelled, pustulated . . . Chloe called it puerperal fever.

Bernard Herrmann ("Vertigo" and other treasures) composed for me his finest secret scores; I danced to his "Fantasia in Lilac" (for toy piano and orchestra), and managed animals and flames while Gaby Casadesus played, my movements influenced by Satie and Cage, family sycophants, whose philosophies gave Orfei routines a lazy, arctic purity. Remember Mont Blanc's theater-in-the-round? That night, you played toy piano, and I forgave you for exaggerating your importance—overstating your imbrication in my sphere, which is "vast as opera," as your beloved muse once said, in her cups.

I am tired of ecstasies I produce in others and ecstasies I must manufacture in the Villa d'Este manner as if I were to Villa d'Este born rather than to the hut (reproduced the world over) on Montecatini's outskirts, far from the ducal palace where I now apparently belong.

The moat between East Kill and Montecatini protects me from your infection, your nasal disorder, your gastric distress (is it not prevalent among pianists?), your nightly manias, your miscomprehension of what you call "passing tones," pedantically needing to find le mot juste for every damn shade of your feelings, especially your devotion to me, moving between minor and major key sans detente, like two rivers, the Jura and the Rhine, meeting, when they have no right. Your head-on collisions have led to trouble before, as my splendor endangers me each spring at Auberge La Fontaine, Venasque, where annually I give an all-night demon-

stration and broadcast it internationally, though in Russia my goose is cooked because I obstruct Galina Vishnevskaya's arrangement with the Bolshoi to avoid all Orfei-isms.

I am usually silent, but tonight I feel histrionic, in memory of Father and Mother, their size, how they got me started in things circus. You plan to send us on tour despite my fear of trains and buses, of terminals and loitering sleaze, and despite my wish to stay home, family goats and rabbits wandering our palace as it were a dirty hut. In Montecatini's piazza I do a mini-circus, gratis, without clearance from town fathers.

"Rachmaninoff is not music," you told me Alma Guadalquivar Mangrove insisted when you presented "Moments Musicaux" at your first recital, but together in Aix we proved his saturnine worth. How large and tulip-like you have convinced me to be in Napoli, Orta, Ischia, where Auden watched me and said not a word: I had silenced him as only Martha Graham had done before, observers claimed. Not that Alma Guadalquivar, as Auden referred to her, refusing the last name, would have noticed my performance's distinction or thought it deserved your accompaniment. Perhaps my medical crises (dare I specify?) make me a fit companion for you, whose physical condition is subject to alterations, like a gown changed at the last minute for the Black and White Ball. Italy's recent elections push us close to fascism; Chloe seeks to keep Orfei blood unpolluted by your sexual indulgence's "passing tones." I too suffer "sins of the fathers," but I've stayed uninfected, medically normal. Spleen, liver, kidney, uterus, lungs, heart, intestines, et al., are there, and shall always, pray God, remain, but I won't mention them, not in a letter I instruct you to burn after reading, lest you transcribe it in a notebook meant to keep my nonchalance at bay.

These Italian subtleties, old as Petrarch, grow labored in translation: that is the problem when an artist enlarges her sphere and communicates to the masses. Speaking of you, Arturo Benedetti Michelangeli once told me, "Leave well enough alone"—let your aesthetic mistakes remain unpersecuted; they will turn into my circus terms soon enough. That has always been the Orfei salvation: I can convert any painful subject into circus. Our vocation allows us to travel across Europe in caravans and disguises and confuse everyone we behold by charging a small admission fee and making noise and sending sparklers into the air over the centro storico where medieval streets have seen the persecution of Jews and other outcasts, pogroms and exclusions now reversed through circus generosities. Critics call me, after Scriabin, a "poem of ecstasy," because I let you illustrate my circus arguments by playing, in piano reduction, that opulent manifesto. Without your musical garnish I deserve ecstatic title, for I am always out-of-place, even when I simulate situation.

Fan letters reach my Montecatini winter palace, hothouse through which I wander at will, despite heavy circus responsibilities; brooding, I evade tasks and verify what Father told me when he died, a fable that translated thermodynamics into synesthetic atmospheres that Walter

Pater praised. Every cream pony I climb upon to dance exacts revenge against Fascists who top-pled Father's sanity.

Aspirin, taken all day, has not lowered my temperature, 103 degrees. Chloe will lay cold compresses on my face and monitor my pulse so that Aigues-Mortes might come to pass; though I have avoided you for weeks—months—the original dream of a reunion remains a succulence to contemplate. I could concentrate and plan Aigues-Mortes if your letters were not driving me mad; even my visit to Chamonix gave me the shakes. If you lead our Aigues-Mortes demonstration toward Liszt's Swiss "Années de pelèrinage" I may lose Languedoc credibility; and yet, seeing gentians bloom outside my villa in pointless profusion, I understand the repertoire manias that drove you, five years ago, to a Viterbo asylum where electroshock achieved what my mere words could not.

You have told me, with unwanted explicitness, about the "water district." How it must drain your manhood! Montecatini has no equivalent ghetto. Nervous about civil war, Chloe stimulates my flesh with stiff brushes.

I'm no Marie d'Agoult. Perhaps Liszt won't ruin me in Aigues-Mortes eyes. Exhausted from tour, I visited cemeteries in nearby Collodi—Pinocchio's town—and Pescia, where I prayed to the della Robbia Madonna. Respect my fatigue, if you wish to attain circus. Chloe offers whisky to calm my fevered brain and cold rosemary compresses to clear my passages. Listen to me inhale effluvia. Are you, in East Kill, inhaling fumes self-formed? If you think I don't exist, think twice.

Factually,
Moira Orfei

Notebook Eleven

It's time to list what I must accomplish:

    play Messiaen's "Les sons impalpables du rêve . . ." in Aigues-Mortes;

    research my ancestry, to clear up mysteries (am I a Sephardic Jew, not a Roman Catholic?);

    visit the graves of Moira Orfei's parents;

    get a colonic;

    discuss drug side-effects with Dr. Crick;

    begin planning the Moira Orfei Living Museum;

    buy a building in the water district and convert it into the Moira Orfei Living Museum;

    clarify Moira's exact relation to Alphonsine Duplessis and Marie d'Agoult;

    mark up my scores more legibly and donate them to the Moira Orfei Living Museum;

    ask Moira Orfei if she will mind being a museum and if she will contribute memorabilia;

    get a lawyer to draft a contract with Moira Orfei so she will not sue the museum for breach of copyright;

    ask Richard Avedon if we can use his photos of Moira Orfei as permanent installations;

    ask Alma to be honorary president of the Moira Orfei Living Museum board of directors;

    make sure that Alma's duties are merely symbolic, so that she won't interfere with day-to-day museum operations;

    choose one composer (Ravel? Poulenc? Scriabin? Liszt?) to preside over the Aigues-Mortes recitals, and quickly communicate the decision to Moira so she can begin coordinating her

act (not that she needs much advance warning, so spontaneous are her stunts);

figure out the Orfei family reaction to my Aigues-Mortes plans
(does the Orfei clan object to me?);

stop communicating with Chloe Orfei;

clarify my link to circus arts;

answer Moira Orfei's letter.

*

Anita, vacuuming, found, bedside, a pile of my shaved body hair. I had
forgotten to transport the fuzz to the kitchen wastebasket. Now she realizes my recidivism: I've fallen into the emasculation habit again. The
hair pile upset Tanaquil, too, when Anita told her. Smooth, I lose
household authority, and Tanaquil asserts her hairlessness as an
antiphonal superiority, according veto power. Body hair is sadism's origin: we shave it off only to see it regrow in cursed, Esau profusion.

Does Tanaquil hold my childhood nudity against me? She wanted it,
a warlock diversion from Alma's reign. At the time, Tanaquil seemed
indifferent to my penis, and yet I let her witness its frothy glee. Not content with hallway gymnastics, I admitted her to my coded bedroom;
wanting to be an ideal brother, a musician, I swallowed every rule and
made myself giggly on her behalf.

*

Visit to Matilda a failure. It took me one minute to come. She said, however, that she liked my new shaved status—legs smooth as Alma's. In youth,
the Guadalquivar sisters traveled the southern hemisphere together, led by
Ricardo and Gertrude—inattentive, cultured vagabonds, locking the girls
in the hotel room at night. Ask Alma: did Ricardo Guadalquivar's phallus
resemble ginger root?

*

Alma, home from tour, yelled at Tanaquil, who spends every night reading on her rocking chair. Now she is tackling *Return of the Native.* Last year

was *Tess of the D'Urbervilles.* One book a year, like a Los Angeleno. She intravenously absorbs the text, a substitute for dance hall and gin bottle. Contentious, rheumy-eyed, we Mangroves amend the Bill of Rights to add new luxuries. Tanaquil has a chronically bloody nose. In her bathroom, I see piles of incarnadine washcloths, sinkside. The last housekeeper, Mrs. Freundlich, nearly deaf, left Lemon Pledge stains on the grand pianos, though I told her not to shine them. My unlikeable, snobbish intolerance for disorder: where went Marxism?

*

After my all-Poulenc concert in Trinity Church, the only house of worship in the water district, Dr. Crick introduced me to his new patient, Frieda, with fuchsia lips, mahagony triangular eyeglasses, and a kinked nimbus of white hair. She kissed me ("congratulations!") on the lips, and now I am sick. Dr. Crick calls her "Patient Zero." She is singlehandedly responsible for carrying new contagion from East Hampton to East Kill. A virus on top of another virus is exponentially more lethal. I will lock myself in the house rather than risk running into Frieda on the street.

*

I sucked off Friedman in the Fortune 500 sauna and then visited Alma's birthplace, a white Georgian mansion on East Kill's outskirts, near torn-down-railroad-station traces. Will Richard Avedon take my picture for Aigues-Mortes? Figure out repertoire. A night of minor American modern composers? Aigues-Mortes, a puny town, has a "major" complex—it despises its own smallness and longs for the big time. When Moira Orfei visited me at the Viterbo asylum, we talked career disparity—wounding, to compare one's own small accomplishments to someone else's monuments. Viterbo asylum physicians taperecorded the conversation for future diagnostic study. Moira Orfei asked if I had an odor problem.

*

Mid-colonic this morning at Dr. Crick's stucco office I smoked pot and came up with multiple recital (rectal?) programs. Afterward, I read in the *East Kill Times* about an Albany maniac who'd murdered five underage male hustlers. Pictures ran: I recognized none of the victims. I never dip below the age of consent. I should transcribe in the Aigues-Mortes notebooks my letters to Moira Orfei, for the sake of scholarly thoroughness.

*

I want to screen Moira Orfei's films in a specially constructed pavilion in Aigues-Mortes. Later tonight if I have the energy I'll list all her movies, including the ones she made with Chloe, before the boating accident, on Lago d'Orta, that forced Chloe's premature retirement from the screen. I am tired of Moira Orfei's filmwork not getting the international attention it deserves, and I am also afraid (to quote Alma) that I am "using up my talent."

I will reserve a room at the Hotel de Anza in St. Malo, for Moira and myself, in April, so we might repair our fractured relationship before Aigues-Mortes tests it. The friendship fell apart after the Viterbo institutionalization; returning to East Kill, I stopped communicating with Moira Orfei, on Dr. Crick's orders. Her presence produced altered "ideation." That I prefered the new ideation did not dissuade him from banning further contact with my glossolalia's catalyst.

In Aigues-Mortes, I plan to revere the passing tone at the expense of the central pitch; to break every chord; to speed up and slow down unpredictably; to emphasize each phrase's unhappy isolation from its neighbor.

Alma asked, "What will Moira Orfei perform, and what repertoire will you bring to bear on the salty Bouches-du-Rhône?" My answer was evasive. Every local wants too much of my body. Patient Zero telephoned. She nattered on about Poulenc. Why did Dr. Crick give her my number? I want to hide from the world, but also I want to rule it.

*

When sleepy Friedman came in my mouth I felt his testicles rise, reneging their long-ago descent. I thought of the deep, unexplored gorges surrounding East Kill, and I remembered my father's memorial service, cold cuts and rolls served afterward in the church basement, momentary sympathy from Miss Kash, Sunday School instructress who preached hospitality: she said that on Easter and other festival days we must open our homes to indigent and ill strangers. The Santes offered no sympathy after my father died. He'd accused them of anti-Semitism, because they tried to prevent a Jew—the psychic, Mrs. Clemovitz—from moving onto Mechanical Street, and opening a business that, Mr. Sante claimed, fed the Zionist mafia. I doubt that fortunetelling and Zionism interleave. Mrs. Clemovitz does no harm. She predicted Aigues-Mortes. In her Jewish crystal ball she saw my fate.

I enjoy a near-constant erection, even when I play piano, in private or in public. Cock has no destination, nowhere to land, and so I resort to silence, imitating my father the night before his death, when (according to Alma) he withdrew money from his savings account and deposited it God knows where, in what secret illegal Continental bank—Marseilles, Toulon, Portbou, Girona, Collioure, Bandol, Banyuls-sur-Mer, Viterbo?

We survivors went out for a pizza the night after his memorial. (The next morning Alma departed on tour to Guam, Tokyo, and Okinawa.) I probably had an erection (why not?), and I may have discussed it with Alma, who liked information about bodily eruption; in our pizzeria booth, Tanaquil and I giggled about the unsightly waitress, who had a third-eye pimple on her forehead. The waitress's head wiggled separately from the body, as she walked: "head walk." (Ladies whose heads have independent ambulatory motion are head walkers. Mrs. Sante, across the street, has head walk. Moira Orfei has head walk, a superior variety. It is easiest to head walk if you are wearing high heels.) We'd ordered pepperoni. No lights in the pizzeria. I shouldn't seek order and counterpoint in every historical event. Why explain pizza after memorial?

Alma wants me to seek a new physician; she calls Dr. Crick a quack, and threatens to sue for malpractice. Dr. Crick, fawning, heals. He avoids my rectum. I have a disease he calls incurable, though infinitely manageable. He choreographs it so deftly, I hardly need describe its symptoms in the notebooks, which would fall apart if I placed too heavy a medical emphasis.

It is possible, Alma has often said, for a person of musical gift to *run out* of ability—to see it vanish. My talent fled when I met Moira Orfei; it soon returned, but it disappears frequently, and I have no control over its exit. It dispersed when I met Moira because I realized her magnificence was larger than I could accompany or narrate with my music, though the contract required me to tranquilize her circus virtuosity's violence.

*

Impregnate Anita? No. She considers herself too old.

Adopt? No. I am too selfish to be a father. Parenthood will interrupt my career.

Have a baby with Moira Orfei? Include the baby in future Aigues-Mortes acts? Would Moira permit fertilization? *Moira Orfei, please bear my child!* Dictatorial tendencies exacerbate my viral load. Alma, are you reading this notebook? Put it down.

Notebook Twelve

Dear Theo,

In Montecatini I think of you with love. For a time, I needed distance, silence; too much chatter in my life, too many mod orange dolmens. I wanted sexual abstinence, too. Explicitness is unbecoming. Intercourse is not a detail for circus-loving ears.

Your breakdown shouldn't worry you. Forget perfectionism. Enjoy retirement, nights of shame! In Viterbo I held your hand while doctors watched, taking notes. Do you have copies of their reports? Did doctors dissuade you from seeing me? They applauded, when I entered the electroshock room. Never before had a circus artiste visited the asylum; never before had a guest been admitted to the psychosurgery chamber. No one considered me a voyeur. Having seen the juggling video, or the live act, they understood my motives, my defiance of gravity. Before elec- troshock, I fear, they were distracted by my presence and paid me too much heed, attentions preventing them from precisely administering voltage. You seemed to enjoy the procedure. Later, when we spoke, you mentioned a new ebullience. Suddenly you could discuss the past. What you'd forgotten arose into recollection with colorful, falsely vivacious vividness.

You may marvel, Theo, that I can put together words. Circus is an abstract art and I have never stinted in public exhibitions. Now Chloe is preparing pasta con le sarde; she waits on me during tour hiatuses. She leaves her Lucca palace in trustworthy hands—our other sisters, not worth mentioning. I may never send this letter. I write consolations but rarely mail them. My soul's largeness, today, is like the St. Eustache church after you took me through Passage de la Reine de Hongrie, Passage de Bourg l'Abbé, Galerie Vivienne, and Galerie Véro-Dodat; you tried to explain the passages, but I couldn't pay attention. Your hands trembled. That sum- mer, your decline began. I've had what critics call "the big career." Need I prove your exis- tence? Doesn't circus sentimentality provide you—my failed friend—with an interior? The Aigues-Mortes tableaux require flames. My medium will never be water, though you suggest- ed I attempt marine effects. Do you want to drown? I daren't imitate a lake. Nor do I wish to burn you with my nearness, as you claim I did, that first day, with a cigarette, in a

Montecatini café, when you disturbed my repose, as I browsed through my early career's for-
gotten scrapbook—snapshots of incarceration and forced performance. If I seemed to singe
you, that is because you approached me the moment I moved my cigarette in a direction I did-
n't calibrate as yours until the second you appeared, uninvited, in its lit radius.

Chloe, lisping, calls; delay offends her. Trust the unseen.
Moira Orfei

*

Time to distract myself from sorrow by calling Lost European Cinema,
and mail-ordering bootleg copies of the complete films of Moira Orfei
(she has hesitated to send me the gladiator flicks), or else by conceptu-
alizing Moira's possible contribution to Aigues-Mortes. Repertoire:
Chausson, Messiaen, Honegger, Roussel, Auric, Satie. For starters. The
second night's concert will describe my love for Rachmaninoff's passing
tones: clusters of abbreviated, decorative notes wander out of bounds
and disobey key norms we once genuflected toward. Moira will tame
horses and tigers while I demonstrate passing tones. I wish I were living
in the Hotel de Anza on the shores of Lago d'Orta, with Moira, in the
adjacent suite, preparing her giddy-goat number.

*

Friedman, like me, has shaved off his body hair. I can't get aroused without an underling's fur to ground my dreaming. His prick seems longer
and darker than the last time I blew it. It informs most pricks I've seen,
held, tasted, etcetera, in my life, though his is a relative latecomer to my
gallery. Retroactively his prick grandfathers every earlier prick I've
known; today, its darkness—the stained ridge—authors all previous big
organs I've encountered. N.B.: dank smelly glans.

*

Life was supposed to be simple in East Kill, near bodies of water we
could never verify (rivers I can't prove are rivers, lakes I wish were
oceans and fear may merely be streams), and surrounded in our house
by the sounds of Alma playing Déodat de Sévérac's *Baigneuses au soleil*, the

occasional zarzuela, the saints of a musical past never dominating us because we had a liberated relation to harmony, a glass of water, like melancholy, always nearby, optimism, too, if we felt like it, and depression if we wanted it, no social obligations interfering. Gone are exuberant days on the town green, when I put up a banner advertising Moira Orfei's return, a performance that never occurred: she cut East Kill from her tour.

*

I bought an hour with rosy-cheeked Franco Idol: Roman emperor bangs. Easy, to tell him about my bleeding, labored swallowing, numb limbs, vertigo. I explained major ninths, and my conviction that I had caused Tanaquil's "red brain." I told Franco about outdoor sex with Siddhartha and Sing near attractive family mausoleums. Alma is away on tour, so I can bring escorts home. In Aigues-Mortes I will do a Granados night, trumping Alma. She gets silent on the phone whenever I float the possiblity that I might bring *Goyescas* to Aigues-Mortes. Perhaps I should concoct a program honoring the cocktail piano tradition—Fanny Mendelssohn, Gabriel Fauré, Michel Legrand? I'll show slides of Alma's bedroom and explain my grandmother Gertrude Guadalquivar's incontinence. Of course I haven't told senile Gertrude about Aigues-Mortes. The last time I spoke to her, in Springs, Long Island, she was in pain. I asked if the pains were specific. She said, "I spoiled you. The pains are everywhere."

*

Impatience will ruin Aigues-Mortes, as cold hands destroyed my Toronto recital. A critic wrote, "He brings the flaws of East Kill to a North that has no need of remembering."

I forget my entrance in *Nights in the Gardens of Spain*. Should I wake Tanaquil and mention the lapse? Dr. Crick says my disease, including neurological complaints, need not be terminal, if I minimize distracting ventures into the outside world. Keep clear of "female" baffles: he believes that the world is "female," an alembic of forfeited promise. Second themes of sonatas communicate "woman" in available codes. Is it possible to be more emotional, or have I forfeited that right? Must "feeling" be music's center?

*

Nora Sten, bad omen in fringed purple scarf, cowboy hat, and vintage Balmain dress, attended my Scriabin concert in Trinity Church. We conversed afterward at the pulpit. Her hands thrashed nervously at her face, as if to pick off scabs, as if her features were an enemy I'd forced upon her.

I first met Nora Sten years ago *au conservatoire.* In the days before the tendency to slobber overtook her enunciation and rendered her beauty farcical, a schoolgirl chum took her on a tram to visit Walter Benjamin's mistress, Vera Marcus, a German-speaking recluse living in East Kill, subsisting on coffee cake and moldering stories of Kabbalist experiments. The Orfei family were friendly with Walter Benjamin, Moira told me. In Siracusa's Hotel de Anza, drinking her negroni, she described socialism's place in circus stunts. She mentioned the Messiah: Moira, suspended upon the trapeze, helped him arrive through the strait gate of circus.

*

Someone has been rifling through my notebooks. One possible culprit is Tanaquil; another is Nora Sten, whom I have hired to do occasional, lackadaisical tasks. While she mops, dusts, and launders, she tells stories about Walter Benjamin's mistress and her lunatic numerological theories.

Nora Sten, music critic, experiments with social boundaries by housecleaning for pianists as a revolutionary praxis, a form of spying and fieldwork. That Nora's theories often take the servile form of scrubbing is a paradox questioned by skeptics on the *East Kill Times* arts page. By pretending to be a domestic, she hopes to undermine Alma's principles, like a mole, from within, burrowing into Alma's ideological fortress via Ajax and Bon Ami.

I must define Nora's "slobber" more precisely. (Walter Benjamin's mistress once told Nora Sten, "Only the dead are capable of precise description.") Spittle collects below the lip and minds its own business

and is neither beautiful nor ugly. By offering a Kleenex to wipe the wet-
ness, I offend her, and condescend to her cultural practices. Enthusiasm
produces slobber; maybe I, too, drool when I play. (I don't practice in
front of a mirror, and I've never seen a video of myself.) Inspiration is
disfiguring: the more transported the artist, the more freakish.

*

In the kitchen, when Nora thought I wasn't paying attention, she put on
mime makeup and read aloud passages from my Aigues-Mortes notebooks—paragraphs describing bodily functions. (I try to keep physical
matters in the sickness notebooks, but sometimes segregation fails.)
Nora brought her daughter, Tammy, to the house. Tammy wants piano
lessons. She's only mildly retarded. Start her with Hanon, Anna
Magdalena Bach. Time is already ruined, squandered; since I have
already wasted my life, there is no point in engineering last-ditch efforts
to redeem it.

*

Success last night, playing Scriabin in Elmira, New York. My performance of his blankness—the places in his etudes and preludes when he
communicates nothing—met enthusiastic response. The dozen people
in the audience appreciated my newfound love of nullity and faux pas.
My higher purpose is not to perform the music, but to circumvent it, to
describe as wide a circle around it as is possible, within the limits of the
plebeian ear's endurance. Friedman came to the concert, and we spent
the night in Elmira. He came inside me as antidote to the quintessen-
tial Scriabin prelude never arriving at a still point—so short, so nothing,
these preludes, composed in Moscow, St. Petersburg, Paris, Heidelberg,
Dresden; not one of them important, permanent, describable; not one
of them a material object to which words can be attached, despite the
occasional urgent affective marking (*affetuoso, appassionato, maestoso, contem-
platif, belliqueux, douloureux, déchirant*). *Déchirant* means "agonizing," and
indeed my audience was agonized by my performance of opus 74;
belliqueux means "bellicose," and indeed I roused the twelve people in my
audience to war-like intensity. An audience never gives me solid proof

that they have absorbed my medicine. If, once, an audience reciprocat-
ed, I could permanently retire, satisfied. Instead, I must play concert
after concert, each time attempting what the last episode failed to
accomplish: if *rubato* is stolen time, time robbed from one beat to give to
another, then my business is *rubato,* redividing time's wealth, redistrib-
uting the durations. I engage, as well, in familial and erotic *rubato.* I steal
love from one body and bestow it on another. Not for expressivity's sake.
Not because I am a noble Robin Hood. Thom taught me reapportion-
ment: when he moved his money from East Kill, before his death, to
bank accounts in Europe, private locations we've still not tracked down,
he gave me a posthumous indication that I should never keep an erotic
resource in one place, but, under cover of night, I should move it elsewhere, always guarding against capture, terrorism, monopoly.

*

The Middle Eastern man at Fortune 500 is back. He has a hairy chest (the
Alaska pattern) and likes my ass but refuses to tell me his name: he is a
political honcho, a Tammany Hall type, linked to East Kill Council graft,
and he doesn't want to depress his constituency by "outing" himself. His
mid-coital aside: "I remember seeing guys, at the Calistoga baths, with
missing hands." I am attracted to his expertise, the way he precisely com-
pliments my "glutes" and describes remembered amputations. Fisting
injuries? I should underline with pink felt-tip pen the notebook entries
containing unpleasant sexual resonances, so Alma can skip them.

*

Friedman's loft burned to a crisp. His pet rabbit died in the blaze.
Friedman and I met this morning at Jeffrey's Diner for French toast. He
listed his losses. Fat deposits have developed on his neck; his eyelids
droop. He is more seriously ill than I had reckoned. In early life I committed small-scale arson—burning Tanaquil's copy of *Little Men*, and her
"Madame Alexander" Emma Bovary doll. Since then I have apologized
for these violations. She is too "scarred" (Alma's term for Tanaquil's
mental damage, the aftermath of "red brain") to absorb my contrition.
I gave Friedman $1,000, to tide him over. He's secretly wealthy; he's

mentioned his mother, Samantha, and her house on Corfu. Why he stays here is a mystery. East Kill, however, is a good town in which to be chronically, monotonously ill.

*

Strange: as Aigues-Mortes preparations intensify, I think nonstop about my grandmother's incontinence. On Gertrude Guadalquivar's birthday, I took a town car to Springs, Long Island, and we went out to dinner. She lost control en route to the restaurant. I can't bear to describe the humiliating scene in the car: Gertrude sprawled out in the back seat, liquid dripping down her seamed stockings. Tanaquil refused to accompany us; she stayed in East Kill. Alma, neglectful of her mother, was in Buenos Aires. Gertrude said that Alma didn't even call to wish her a happy birthday. I'm not a dutiful grandson, but at least I traveled to Springs. I exaggerate incontinence's horror. Gertrude's accident was my fault: stimulating chatter about crib-death in German art songs overtired her.

Notebook Thirteen

Letter from Moira Orfei (translated from the Italian)

Dear Theo,

The mails are slow. Word from you is occasional; your letters arrive in floods, and then, without prediction, they dry up. I swallow flame while playing Granados tapes in preparation for Aigues-Mortes. Chloe disapproves of the delight I take in calisthenics. Jealous, she can't sustain her own circus act anywhere on the Continent, so I am alone with my complexities, no mother, no father, only Italy to protect and comfort me, and my endless paying audiences, never faction-torn, always loyal. Hence I hew close to "publicity" as my primary art form, at the risk of seeming fascist. Italian history contains many circus performers but only one Moira Orfei, who can dance to Mompou, or battle a tiger while making the struggle seem part of the flame. The circus circuit has confined me, sweaty and overburdened, for many years, but until you I never had an appropriate melodic context, an imp to call my own.

I trust you're diligently preparing Ravel: you realize my stature in Italian society. Much rests on our level of polish in Aigues-Mortes: we need an ineffable rightness, melismatic, a flourish as of castanets, and an artificiality, so no one believes we are real and rhythmic, though the ill spectator longs for our milieu. Fearful solitude will be my fate if you do not prepare, if you stay out late in your zone of promiscuity, your water district: my health will suffer if you continue to indulge. Heed my warnings. Broadcast this loud truth on your NBC, your ABC: I am your destiny, and only if you are technically competent can you simulate my circus omnipotence, circular as the Colosseum in Father's tiny desktop model when he was alive and had a desk at which to plan my punishing tours.

Best circus ideas germinate away from home; here, winter palace, Montecatini, I reproduce gyrations dreamt in the Hotel de Anza overlooking the Necropolis of Tarquinia. Were you staying there, too? Did we walk together along the Via Ripagretta, and, later, on the Lido di Tarquinia, discover salt flats that augured Aigues-Mortes? Do you know how simply I said my prayers, trusting you were their foundation? I fear to end this letter. Birds rise from the salt flats.

Viterbo's doctors warned you what distance from me would bring. You and I visited the Tomba del Fiore di Loto, and a cloaked apparition rose from the lotus-flower's heart, though you, trying to describe it, almost fainted in my circus-weary arms.

Moira Orfei

*

Alma is hospitalized in Lima, Peru: doctors will remove a blood clot from her leg. Although I hope she speedily recovers, I cherish this motherless interlude on Mechanical Street—time to puzzle out the fifth Scriabin sonata's *accarezzevole* passage. One day, my recording of Scriabin preludes and etudes may stand next to hers and not be humiliated by the juxtaposition. Is the Bergamo choir director I fucked fourteen years ago dead? I lied to him and told him my name was Ugo Mangrove. He asked if I was related to Alma Mangrove. I said no, but I was related to Theo Mangrove. That name meant nothing to the choir director. I never claimed to have a gift for friendship.

*

During rehearsal, Derva Nile, wearing a bronze turban, her face rouge-darkened, complained of crime in East Kill. She brandished tabloid photos of mangled bodies on bungalow porches. Derva has her own clipping service for violence. Fatigue has become my keynote, fatigue in Fauré's *Valse-Caprices,* as if I were racing toward my death—my father's, reprised. Friedman is missing from town; he left before vetting legal inquiries into his apartment fire. He may have gone underground to avoid prosecution; perhaps he set the fire himself, to collect insurance money, although, as mere renter, he won't see significant profit. I'll find him at Space Bar; he sometimes occupies a furnished room on the second floor. Space Bar never charges Friedman for his spontaneous tenancy; he hides to disappear from his own futile longings. Maybe he escaped to Corfu, to spend time with his mother, Samantha. Friedman claims to be going deaf but refuses to wear a hearing aid.

*

At Camera Baths, Larry the Egyptian pharmacist removed the towel wrapped modestly around his middle and proved that he is a freak. He has two penises—a major, normal one, with a healthy scrotum, and then, below the balls, a smaller penis, tiny, vestigial, functionless. He is proud of the second penis, which doesn't get hard. Showing off the twin organs, he stood up from the wooden berth, gyrated his hips, belly-danced, said, "I'm an intellectual." I used to give Larry piano lessons: he advanced to the level of Aram Khatchaturian's *Adventures of Ivan*. Home: our dining room carpet is wet—leakage from Tanaquil's bath-room. I mopped up the flooded areas. I've cleaned up my sister's floods for decades. She always overstuffs the toilet, as if trying out a new econ-omy. Time passes. Nothing happens: eternal return. Tanaquil flushes the toilet; it overflows; I clean up the mess; repertoire piles up.

*

Alma has returned from Peru to recover from her blood clot. She shouldn't be playing—she should be sleeping—but she is practicing Falla in her studio. Work ethic can't remedy mental deficiencies. Did she really go blind for a few days in 1938 or did she invent that childhood incident to dress up her Teatro Colón program notes? Dr. Crick says I have incipient cataracts. Without disease I would have little to say to Alma. I sat on the foot of her bed last night; we discussed her former blood clot. I expected her to make light of it. Instead, she described it as a catastrophe, worse than the two miscarriages that framed my birth. At least she is not incontinent. That would stop her career.

*

Tanaquil and I argued in the hallway connecting our bedrooms. We talked about my daily nausea. She said I should go to Paris for treatment. I defended Dr. Crick's adequacy. She claimed that Aigues-Mortes lagoons were bad for my respiration. I asked her if she enjoyed keeping silent. She insisted that Anita looked like a drugstore Indian. I was dis-tressed that Tanaquil didn't automatically understand by osmosis every-thing I said: after forty years together in the same house, shouldn't our thoughts be synchronized? We mentioned degenerative diseases that run in our family: hemochromatosis, psychosis. She asked whether the medications Dr. Crick prescribes impair my sexual function. I asked Tanaquil if she had the power to enter a trance state. She expressed her dislike of my "sleazy" friends, and confessed, "I don't like to perform, and I don't like to watch. I struggle hard enough just to experience time's ebb." She reacts weirdly to Alma. Years ago, Tanaquil tore to pieces Alma's signed score of *Goyescas*. My reactions to Alma are not normal, but they sustain my career. I want to finish the Aigues-Mortes notebooks but I will be dead when they are completed. Their aim is perpetual, futile composition. I don't have any photos of Tanaquil or I'd include them in the notebooks. She bears an uncanny physical resemblance to her ballerina namesake, Mme. LeClercq, a friend of Alma's from Abstract Expressionist days, when Alma's performances changed the future of painting. Everything I say is in the past tense. Am I incapable of describing present action? History goes backward before it goes forward. The prospect of Aigues-Mortes arrests progress. There is no such thing as decline, and there is no such thing as advancement. I am the metaphysician of Mechanical Street. Tanaquil flushed the toilet.

*

In a poor housing project I visited an incompetent hustler—Guillermo, a cheap dyed blond, who moonlights as an operatic baritone; he recently appeared in the East Kill Lyric Opera production of *Manon*. His flabby ass flexed at will, a dull and winking mouth. I found value in his worthless hole: I relished thinking, "Your hole is worthless," while preparing to enter it. His buttock skin felt like breakfast cereal that clings to the bowl when I have not done the dishes until the afternoon and I can't help but rub my index finger along the rim of the bowl to feel the dried bits. His body hair was shaved: shoulder stubble remained. He opened the bedroom window to the winter air though I asked that he close it. His strong right thumb, without love, dug into my crevices. Superficially kind, he had anchovy breath, long nipples, and a drooping cock—not as dark as Friedman's, though thicker than Franco's. Fatigue stops me from describing the disappointing session. He gave me rough cheap torn towels to mop up leftover cum. I have many escorts at my disposal—why bother with Guillermo? Perhaps he is a carrier. Can I tolerate a disease on top of a disease? Why include Guillermo in the Aigues-Mortes notebooks? I should tell Alma about Guillermo. Alma and I watched *Jules et Jim* together on her bedroom's TV when she was recovering from an infection of the urethra. The set was so small, it cut off the subtitles. Alma's French was excellent, so she offered a nearly simultaneous translation.

*

Tanaquil and I had a second argument. She wants me to see outside events as real. I told her that the outside is not musical, and that in Aigues-Mortes I will experiment with silence. Tanaquil said, "Experiment first in East Kill before you show off in Aigues-Mortes." I told her that in this dark hallway she resembled Moira Orfei. Tanaquil said that everyone resembles everyone. I reminded Tanaquil that I'd already apologized, a long time ago. She said, "Yes, you've apologized, but you haven't described the violation."

*

I visited Matilda on Clarendon Street. At the bathroom mirror she filled with concealing-stick the crease between her plucked eyebrows and said, "I can't badmouth Alma's banality, though I wander through her contradictions in a fog." After sex she put on brown hose, and tucked her feet under her rear-end as she sat in a Biedermeier armchair (stolen from Gertrude Guadalquivar) and scolded me for exaggerating the seriousness of Alma's blood clot. Matilda said that there are always sick relatives to nurse, just as there are always TV programs to watch. She lectured me on my broken nature: a repeated diatribe. She said: "You have the Guadalquivar nose, the concentrated brow, and a cow-like tendency I remember in my mother, hesitating on the border of the dining room as if afraid of the nutrition she was about to give and receive." More opus 5 of Webern is what Matilda needs, to cut through the fatty and undigested parts of her thinking.

*

Matilda came to East Kill for a repeat performance. She stayed at the Hotel Westphalia, near the water district. She wore a pink plaid Burberry-esque dress and I made the mistake of calling her "Pinkie," which she said was racist. Her bubble-gum face sweated; cat spectacles blurred and magnified her bloodshot eyes. Fashion hound, she took a sleeping potion with aphrodisiac properties. Our embraces intensified; I told her that I'm certain her breasts have more sensitivity than Alma's. I will never outgrow my love of a simple unhurried ejaculation in Matilda's presence—a climax that begins in one country (hilly) and ends in another (rivery). I plan to end my love affair with tonality but I may not be ready for withdrawal rigors, the post-tonal DTs. Is it possible to concentrate so deeply on a piece of music that the world around the listener dissolves? Dr. Crick once suggested that I was autistic. Crick rarely sticks with a diagnosis; medical nomenclature for him is like flower arranging, a temporary art.

*

The second night with Matilda, I withheld my orgasm. Be brief, Matilda said, as she sunk into chemically-assisted slumber. (Her sleeping potion—she let me sip it—tasted like ginseng.) Possibly she woke hungover, but I had left the Hotel Westphalia, afraid she would berate me at breakfast for my missing orgasm. Last night I didn't want her to see my face contort with conventional pleasure. I look ugly when I come.

*

Long ago my schoolchum Freddy Ippoliti disappeared; the "kidnapping" made the papers, his body never found. He was also Tanaquil's friend, though I tried to interrupt: *carpe diem*, an arrow through a snake. Furtively reading my notebooks will not ease your path toward health, Alma. Keep notebooks of your own if you want entertainment or catharsis.

*

I played Scriabin's *Vers la flamme* competently for Alma after roast chicken and plum crumble. She said listening would speed up her blood clot's healing. No Orpheus, no *fée*, I didn't demand perfection. I offered notes in reasonable order, a bare-minimum communicative intensity. Scriabin didn't settle Alma's stomach. She dislikes pedantic lectures, but I tried to explain my new discovery: "A *walk-around* harmony seeks no obvious resolution but exhibits a paltry stasis, so we, listeners, *walk around* the chord rather than insist it move forward. A *walk-around* chord lets us circle it—did Keats call it a 'brede'?"

*

Underrated Frank Bridge: I may program his character pieces in Aigues-Mortes. "I see no virtue in Bridge," said Alma, as I brought lapsang tea and cream biscuits to her room, where she is convalescing. Alma had a psychic visitation from my father last night after she went to bed. Helen Jole, Alma's Buenos Aires psychoanalyst, says that ESP is an epilepsy symptom. Dr. Jole may have a beautiful office off Plaza Güemes north of Villa Freud in the Palermo Viejo, but she lacks a spiritual temperament. She is no artist. Alma said, "I'm sick of the pedestrian. I've been surrounded by it my whole life." I haven't broached the Frank Bridge question with Moira Orfei. Perhaps she should add Art Nouveau aspects to her kangaroo monstrances. The Orfei connection to Art Nouveau passes through the indirect filter of Mallarmé, whose open forms appealed to Moira's grandfather, Umberto Orfei, when he read "Un Coup de Dés" in Italian translation and intuited that Mallarmé was predicting the future of circus. I never told Moira Orfei much about my father, though I mentioned to her the early trips to Portbou, the experience of swimming, watched by my father, in the meager pool; his gambling; his secret deposits; my occasional evenings with Thom in darkness, our mutual delving; being "brained" by Thom, an experience leading to higher musicianship; his boxer shorts and then my briefs, their overlap and mutual prediction. Did his boxers predict my briefs, or did my briefs, as a future idea, exist before the supposed "past" of his boxers?

*

Last night, Alma-style, I had a psychic visitation from my greatest piano teacher, Xenia Lamont. (Pedagogic aetiology: Fabio Abruzzi infected me, but Xenia gave me pianistic foundation. She taught me how to approach big chords: from above. She taught me how to create a singing tone: through fakery. She taught me how to falsify a composer's intentions and how to make an "inner crescendo," a manipulative tactic to frighten the gullible listener. She taught me how to memorize a piece—in sections.) When she visited last night, she had nothing to say. She was simply a body, a bovine effigy in a Lanz nightgown, floating horizontally above my bed. I tried to recover from the apparition by staring in the bathroom mirror. The antidote failed. I drank a special solution picked up in a Portbou pharmacy: codeine-laced cough syrup. I remembered what Xenia once told me: "You'll never play Liszt properly unless you overcome your love for my body." Then she helped herself to my cock, which I was willing to offer. It exorcised her power. The more she wanted my cock, the less powerful she became. Erections grow on trees. She knew how to master Liszt's Transcendental Etudes but I had a useful cock, more alert than her soporific husband's. My cock cut through music's obfuscation; my cock had the momentary power to neutralize radioactivity.

*

I overheard a conversation between Anita and Tanaquil: rare colloquy between enemies. They stood by the microwave; unseen, I hovered at the threshold.

Anita said, "Whenever truth is told, Theo shuts the door."

Tanaquil replied, "The door's open now."

"What were you doing?"

"Escaping claims."

I retreated to my studio, practiced *Carnaval*, made mincemeat of the passage in which Schumann imitates Chopin, Alma's favorite: it portrays Schumann as unmanly. Listening is not the same as love. I'm not drunk enough. I should open a second bottle of Syrah and begin reading a biography of Schumann so I can figure out how he ruined his hand, lost his mind, and died of tertiary syphilis. Did Schumann have BO, like Nadia Boulanger pupils I slept with in the 1970s? I should send

Moira Orfei a detailed chart of my sexual past, so she can decide whether she still wants to work with me.

Notebook Fourteen

Letter from Moira Orfei (translated from the Italian)

> *Dear Theo—*
>
> *Just a quick note from Montecatini to East Kill, an undated goodnight, undisciplined and rash, without particulars to relate, only a sense of perpetual festival and religious admiration, size and wonder beneath the carnival tent I travel with, city to city, searching for the perfection my late father claimed was the lost essence of circus art, which I am lucky enough to practice with the largest possible sphere of influence and more spectators than ever before in the Italian republic's history.*
>
> *I spent three days in Atrani. Its sunsets convinced me I could reclaim my past by reconnoitering with Ernesto, old friend I met by chance, beside the gold-domed basilica where the Mediterranean meets the manmade ramparts upholding the town. Reunited, Ernesto and I imagined a permanent alliance, as if I were not married, widowed, married again, and now refusing conventional arrangements, like the courtesan Father feared I would become. Ernesto proposed, but I woke from infatuation: I need new men in my life, not revived romances with boys from my childhood who now are repentant adults wanting to hook up with me because of my circus eminence.*
>
> *Given the late hour, I have no time to record the ways your secret influence has elevated my art to the level of esteem it now enjoys in Italy. I must retire, though I regret the necessity—shades drawn in my front parlor, as when Father died.*
>
> *Moira Orfei*

*

Time to buy outfits for Aigues-Mortes. At Olney Clothes I chose two tight shirts: a black and a white. A black for my death. A white for my life. A black for Aigues-Mortes, if it fails. A white for Aigues-Mortes, if it fails. In the changing room I sucked Brad Olney's cock—prophylaxis against Aigues-Mortes failing. I asked him to write a piano sonata based on Catullus epigrams. He said that he had retired from composing: he was sick of critics castigating him. I said, why not compose "nothings," like my grandfather Ricardo Guadalquivar? If you compose a "nothing," no one can insult it.

*

Theo Mangrove and Moira Orfei at Aigues-Mortes: The Boxed Set. I'm salivating. I need to eat a hard-boiled egg, quick, for protein. Perhaps bourbon is indicated. Malnourishment destroys my Aigues-Mortes notebooks. Tanaquil had an anorexic year: her eighteenth. Then I took her to Jeffrey's for "Mental Health Day" and she binged on glazed crullers. She spent all year reading *The Bell Jar.* She complained nonstop about her aborted musical-comedy career—Alma's fault. Tanaquil never made it past the semi-finals in the East Kill Lyric Opera auditions for *Li'l Abner.* I play Liszt like a sister-ruiner. Moira never mentions Chloe Orfei's needs. Moira's infatuation with Ernesto foretells a season of new amours.

*

Friedman reappeared. He quoted today's *East Kill Times*—an article I'd overlooked, Hector Arens criticizing "the Mangrove monopoly on the modern." Friedman, formerly a Montessori student, told me how orgasms reverse his self-image, unpocking it. Ever since the apartment fire, my esteem for him has fallen. He suffered no skin burns. Moira Orfei's cigarette, held out to taunt or entice, did not singe me. I misinterpreted the gesture.

*

Derva Nile arrived from New London. Plastic surgery: widened cheekbones improve her tone production, though the doctor should have adjusted her chin to match the cheeks. I coached her on Fauré's "Les roses d'Ispahan." She wants to program "Give Me My Robe" from Barber's *Antony and Cleopatra.* We consummated our relationship. Her vagina's angle was satisfactory, its texture moist. She provided the slot I require. Mid-intercourse she mentioned her abusive father, who used to smack her face and call her "oceanic." She said, "I didn't want you as coach, but Madeline Tarnow told me about your charms . . ." Edgard Varèse is the only solution to the ruckus on Mechanical Street. I will immerse myself in making a piano transcription of his *Ionisation* and *Octandre*. How will I convert the flute in *Density 21.5* to piano form? I can't ask Derva. Derva and Varèse—ne'er the twain shall meet. Derva's final smile implied that more intercourse is expected, though not essential. We work well together because we don't insist on the sexual; if it comes, it comes. Morris Nile is out of the picture. Men can have dowager humps, too. I like to blow men I pity. I pity Dr. Crick's brother, Vincent, the butcher.

*

Alma has recovered, thanks to my bedside manner and Dr. Crick's. She agreed to consult him, despite her conviction that he's a quack. First she called Helen Jole, in Buenos Aires, who said mysterious things about the essential mind. Dr. Jole had separation anxiety, countertransferential. Tomorrow morning Alma returns to South America. Tonight she hangs between life and death: at supper, her face ashen, she removed her dentures and held a handkerchief to her mouth. During the soup course (cream of cucumber), Alma said that my playing, at its best, resembled shock treatment. She knows about Viterbo. I responded well to the treatment: historic paragon of receptivity to electroconvulsive therapy. Moira Orfei visited Viterbo, her all-white outfit Carmelite; convent-like, too, her perfume—nasturtiums, verbena, myrrh, rose, orchid, orange peel, grapefruit. Once Alma departs, I can have sex with escorts in the house. She might suffer a stroke in her glassy Buenos Aires penthouse. Dr. Helen Jole calls Alma "stroke-prone." Alma's stomach aches are as severe as mine. I treat her unkindly in the notebooks. My chest is in knots. I should be saving these details for the sickness notebooks. The Aigues-Mortes notebooks, not sacred, keep me alive.

*

Matilda drove me, in her Dodge, from Clarendon Street to her Zen master's country house in Beverly. She stopped several times to vomit on the side of the highway. We sat in the Zen master's living room, choosing CDs from his operetta collection. He was busy in the winter garden; a sudden warm spell had provoked the crocuses. We listened to excerpts from Suppé's *Boccaccio*. Matilda walked me to the gazebo and sat on the swingset. No underwear: her vagina's coral sufficiency regaled me. I looked at my watch and said, "Matilda, we should be getting back to Boston. Your psychoanalysis-and-Buddhism reading group meets tonight at seven." She kept swinging. "Tonight we're reading Bachofen on matriarchy," she said. She hasn't spoken to her mother in twenty years. Matilda is smarter than Alma, though Matilda doesn't know how to use facts. Watching Matilda swing, I tried to describe my devotion to Moira Orfei, and failed: I suffer spasms of inattention and can't complete a sentence . . . If only Moira Orfei could initiate me into her Wiccan mysteries!

*

After sex, I played Friedman my home-made cassette of the Fauré Ballade, and he inspected my body for infractions, bugbites, pimples, ingrown hairs. He gives my bleeding rectum appropriate treatment. I like the feeling of a tended prostate; sensation wanders through my body, like Debussy's description of Faure's undulating, feminine Ballade, a description Alma recited. If Alma were to suffer a heart attack by reading these notebooks, I would destroy them. Each year I tear my Schnabel edition of Beethoven sonatas into pieces, and then buy a new one. I don't ask to be powerful. I only ask to be clear.

*

I am Alma's emissary on the world's stages. No: only in cities, like Aigues-Mortes, in which she refuses to perform because she is too choleric and they are too insignificant. She will appear in Marseilles but not in Aigues-Mortes; in Cannes she adores a light she calls "reverberant"— Mediterranean sun frescoing the overpraised Hôtel Martinez. Château d'If's darkness stimulates her. She lacks visual acuity. My father was attuned to retinal stimulation. He described Alma playing Schumann's "Abegg" Variations in São Paolo—her voile gown's nectarine folds, her hands indicating dictatorial semi-circles over the keys. Thom's death is not yet, to me, a fixed event: it shimmers in February. Three months have elapsed since I began these notebooks. Three more months to go, before Aigues-Mortes. I should look for Thom's death certificate, among Alma's papers.

*

Alma called from South America: she asked me to ghostwrite *Alma Guadalquivar Mangrove's Easy Cookbook*. I said I was too busy preparing Aigues-Mortes. She asked if the Aigues-Mortes recitals were family events. I said their content was appropriate for all ages. She asked if they were scatological. I said they included romantic repertoire. She asked if I've begun learning the Diabelli Variations. I said that I had given up all hope of ever playing Beethoven again, after what happened to my *Hammerklavier* in San Martino di Castrozza.

*

Tanaquil and I argued in the upstairs hallway between our bedrooms. She said, "How can I get a job when I need fourteen hours of sleep a night?" I suggested she do telephone solicitations. I reminded her that I hit puberty early. She said that Alma loved a precocious maturation. I said that my puberty had a tornado's charm. Under the green blanket, hand on cock, I cut an adventurer's path through the world by dispensing with it, undoing it with each stroke; jerking off, I canceled reality, bore holes in it, drove it into hiding. Tanaquil once inscribed a litany of complaints in acrylics on her bedroom walls. Alma instructed me to paint the walls blue, covering up what Tanaquil had written. These simple anecdotes wish you to behave.

*

To repeat the Palmer House infection moment, I offered my body to Fabio yesterday. I played the five Fauré impromptus and then lay naked under Fabio's covers, below his photo of the great Egon Petri's hands. Fabio sat on the quilt. Once he saved a minor composer's diary from the conservatory library fire. My thumbs—the hand's thick, stupid fulcrums—have grown lazy. Fabio took off his running togs and boxers and lay beside me. His nudity never fatigues me. His lean body means education to me when it does not mean infection. My finger in his ass was a sign of uneducated, froward haste. My penis felt detached from proceedings it had instigated. When his fingers tugged listlessly at the root, I thought, "Is Teacher faking it?" He pushed the balls upward, to clear room around the rear; this renegotiation of testicular position upset my stomach. I had a noncommittal climax, anyway, as did he, and then I looked out his window at the facing apartment: three blonde women and one tall dark man, in bed, beneath a chandelier. My performance falls short of a combinatory Casanova's. Sex is a terrible, unforgiving master. I may re-try the *Hammerklavier*.

*

Last night, walking down Stream Drive with Friedman, I noticed an aristocratic memorial doorway. Above the heavy ornamental tarnished brass knocker, a small peephole gave onto a further room, like Marcel Duchamp's "Étant Donnés," an artwork which had scandalized my grandmother, Gertrude Guadalquivar, on first viewing, although later she grew friendly with Duchamp and bought a third-generation replica of his "Fountain." I looked into the peephole but saw nothing: dust, stones, cobwebs, dimness, branches, leaves, pottery shards, newspaper scraps, tin cans, bottles, broken appliances. An advertisement for nothing, the memorial was in disrepair, on the verge of being torn down to make room for a new ambiguous doorway with a new uncertain peephole. I wondered why the memorial didn't say what duchess or socialite it was commemorating. In the enigmatic doorway there hung a pair of headphones, so passersby could listen to taped messages about—a sticker proclaimed—"the healing properties of impeccable taste." Friedman and I put on the headphones and heard nothing. Once, Alma described her brief stay in a White Plains asylum: to recover from shock treatment, as per the doctor's instruction, she listened, on headphones, to tapes of her own performances, and, if she found fault with them, she had the

option of erasing the tapes. We must destroy music—tear it to pieces—
while we interpret it.

*

After Fabio and I lay together again in bed, he thought my performance
of the Aaron Copland Variations much improved. Alma studied with
Copland: he made her over as a modern, without tears. The surgery
wasn't painful. She'd overvalued lucidity. I envy her friendship with
homosexual modernists. Alma is mentioned in their memoirs. She falls
apart when she remembers her importance: and yet, when the sun sets
in Buenos Aires, she must remember her father's nothings, which
earned little fame. I wish Alma would call me at those moments when she
discovers that she is nothing. Once she fed me a soft apple that I refused
to eat. I watched Tanaquil being fed the same apple and eating it.

*

I took the train to Boston to see Matilda. She received me in a bathrobe,
loosely shut. I played the clotted Rachmaninoff Prelude in B-flat to
warm up, while she mopped the townhouse and repaired the ravages of
an equinoctial party she'd thrown the night before. I demonstrated a
decent inattention to downbeat. "Well-trained," she said, tightening
her terry robe. "We can thank Xenia Lamont, not Alma." Matilda asked
me to play the first movement of Schubert's penultimate sonata (A
major), its first theme a reversed, autocratic bugle-call. She led me to
her daybed and we kissed. I narrowed my mouth's opening, but her
tongue insinuated a path inward, past my teeth. (I hadn't played her the
Copland Variations, the purpose of my pilgrimage.) Matilda's tongue
haunts me as I re-memorize Fauré's underrated preludes. I will play
them in Aigues-Mortes. In Fauré and Liszt, the "sigh" predominates. I
am beholden to its void.

*

I sat in Friedman's interim apartment with his fellow escort Marco,
three of us naked on the futon. I was paying. Friedman likes to work with

a second hustler. Both Marco and Friedman are hirsute, but Marco has a more attractive hair pattern (the Louisiana arrangement). I tried to point my erection at him, so he would forgive my diffidence, but there were limits to how articulate I could make my cock. I haven't described Marco's or Friedman's bodies adequately in this notebook, and so I won't be able to remember them in later years, when I have moved on to other men, if I ever progress; and yet my concern is not exact description, but evasion of exactitude, for the pleasure of escaping it. I smeared Marco's ethnically imprecise ejaculate over his back, shoulders, stomach, thighs: fastidious reclamation of the dispersed. The sixth floor restroom at the East Kill University library is a reliable place to find young men to blow. I am forever tinkering with the unformed. After Derva and I play Fauré, I will visit that restroom and will satisfy nineteen-year-olds, who, later, I hope, will write about the experience in their own notebooks. I've fired our unpaid housekeeper Nora Sten; she spilled coffee in my good Bösendorfer and was rude to Derva Nile. Derva will now help me housekeep; after our inconclusive rehearsals, my mind bears a perilous shine, like a skating rink. Before departing, Nora Sten told me another story about Walter Benjamin's mistress, Vera Marcus. Vera waited for him, like a mystic, to return from the formless. In 1950, she realized that he would never come back, and that she was wasting her life. She sold his letters to a Frankfurt library. She bought a new dress, new scent, got her hair done. At night the memory of the sold letters returned.

*

I lead my days in A-B-A form. Section A states the problem; section B presents its antithesis; and then section A returns, in a different key. The valuable material occurs in section B. Fabio said that when I repeat A, I need to add new flavorings—brighter attack, accelerando, bombast. Music in A-B-A form sounds simple, but its performance is difficult. One must rearrange and re-outfit the already heard, disguise it as new material, convince the listener that the music moves forward. No listener will tolerate retreat, backtracking, regression. I, too, detest drone.

*

I woke from a long afternoon nap. Have I already described my theory of A-B-A form? A is the past. B is the present. When A returns, it thrusts listeners, again, into the unpleasant anterior. Another interpretation: A is now. B is then. A, when it repeats, is the returned "now." Another explanation: A is waking life. B is dream. A, when it returns, is reawakening. I could discuss A-B-A form in Chopin nocturnes. Another day, I will describe again my breakdown in Europe, my spasms, seizures, absences, staggerings, fits; another day, I will describe again the healing properties of electroconvulsive therapy in Viterbo, and Moira Orfei's fragrant, ministering visit. Those experiences are shut away from memory, and so I can't narrate them. I can only mention them, repeatedly, as in a flag-waving ceremony, attesting a patriotism one doesn't feel. I could analyze A-B-A form's relation to a church's apse and nave. If Alma were here, she might wax ecclesiastical. May I speak candidly? My first and greatest teacher, Xenia Lamont, died four months ago, October 14, though I didn't hear the news until today. She died seventeen days before I began keeping Aigues-Mortes notebooks. I haven't frequently mentioned her, and so the reader, should there be a reader, other than Alma (who already understands everything), won't know why Xenia's death distracts me from Moira Orfei. When Xenia Lamont lifted up her nightgown and showed me the hysterectomy scar, I was past the age of consent. I was twenty-two. She was fifty. She said, "Come here." I approached the hospital bed, put my hand on her vagina, as instructed. I enjoyed the act, a cross between conquest and capitulation. I didn't mind stopping my life: my hand, Xenia's crotch, a teaching hospital. Fourth floor. Room with a view of the stream. My hand hoped, like a savior, like a cooperative student, to move her genitals somewhere else (toward a fresh angle, a new phrase, a finer argument), to make the ailing, itchy, uncomfortable groin more pleased with its locale, more saturated with its moist stasis. I'm writing these words in the past—alone on Mechanical Street. I tend to get abstract at a notebook's end. The narrator is not me.

PART TWO
Dispersion

Notebook Fifteen

Dear Moira Orfei,

Xenia Lamont, the first piano teacher I ever had sex with, died. She resembled Ingrid Bergman in *Anastasia*.

Xenia's passing will not obstruct Aigues-Mortes.

Love,

Theo Mangrove

*

The Aigues-Mortes notebooks, blank, lined, come in many colors. This notebook has a red cover. Others are green, yellow, silver, white. I buy them at the *conservatoire* supply shop. Purchasing a notebook and planning to write in it can be more rewarding than the words one finally chooses.

I wish the notebooks could include candids of wide-faced drunk Xenia Lamont, but I threw out my Polaroids. "Oh, just call me X," she'd snarl. To show respect before sex I sometimes called her "Madame X" so she would believe I was an obedient, trustworthy receptacle. She said a "susurration" surrounded her playing. She had a lateral lisp. Struggling to say "susurration" highlighted the deformity. When she kissed me, her upper lip sweaty, my body dissolved into nonresisting molecules. Touching her breasts, I felt them melt, like a wax candle: hallucinations saved me from the coarse, the actual. To the right of her naked body, I saw blur. I stared more at the blur than at her. Just as my penis entered her, a burning sensation assaulted its tip; I asked to drown in Xenia, to dowse the flame in an unknowing that only she could provide. I lack patience to trace connections between each knot of incomprehension. Right before I entered Xenia, a cold sensation, like dry ice, enveloped me. When not melting, her breasts seemed tires—durable, full, unyielding. Unpleasant, to dwell on memories, and yet the only way I can appear on the Aigues-Mortes stage without humiliating myself is by first undergoing petty catharsis. My notebook behavior must be strict, cold: rigidity is prelude to circus fortitude. Tonight: re-see Moira Orfei's great 1964 film, *Terror of the Steppes*.

*

I did not know Xenia was dead, until yesterday, months too late, I discovered her obituary in our alumni journal (she'd studied and taught at East Kill Conservatory). I checked my notebooks and discovered that the night she died, October 14, I was out-of-town, performing, at the Key West public library, the Beethoven *Pastoral* Sonata, the Ned Rorem Barcarolles, and Schumann's *Papillons*, and that afterward I rented an escort (Alex Uptown), his blond body hair obeying the Nevada pattern: equidistance, blandness, divorce, medication, askesis, dehydration. I memorize hair arrangements.

Blur neighbored Xenia's nakedness. When I discovered that she was dead I did research on the Internet and learned that most of my teachers are gone. *Poor stinking corpses*, someone said: maybe Heinrich Heine.

*

Xenia suggested, years ago, that I be her psychiatric patient, though she was not trained or licensed. She wanted to experiment, to become a lay analyst; she hoped I'd volunteer as her first client. I refused treatment. She took me out to fancy Saturday-night dinners at Chez Madeleine— butter-garlic escargots, coquilles St. Jacques, sautéed morels, Grand Marnier soufflés, Châteauneuf-du-Pape. She said that although I was under six feet, I held myself like someone with Marfan's syndrome (Franz Liszt). She regretted her husband's impotence, a decade of no penetration; she missed the sight of a penis stiffening in her honor. She said, "It breaks my heart to see you get hard." I wanted to reply, "But the hard-on isn't 'about' you! It's non-specific!" She did a competent job sucking: if, before I was born, Xenia sodomized pianistic idols like Solomon and Edwin Fischer, then I belong to a lordly daisy chain. Getting blown by Madame X saved me from a nothingness that now, in notebooks, I seek. Cunnilingus with a teacher turned me into an unfeeling cartoon. After I went down on her, she said, "How strict Alma must have been!" It was my birthday; Xenia bought me the *Don Giovanni* score. Vaginal dryness plagued her. She enjoyed my aggressive "Toccata" from Ravel's *Tombeau de Couperin*. She bought sugar-and-jam cookies at the East Kill Bakery while I waited in her doubleparked Saab, and we ate them by the almost lake. Cookies proved she had a thoughtful, nurturing streak. I'm too cerebral about my former fucks.

It is always easier *not* to feel, *not* to remember. Memories of Xenia, like matinees at East Kill's Paris Theater, formerly a vaudeville house, stretch out the afternoons before Aigues-Mortes. The Paris Theater, a year ago, burnt down—arson. No one was apprehended: I pasted the crime-report clipping in an early notebook. Vaudeville is dead, circus is dying, and the Paris Theater will never be replaced.

Split pea soup tonight, Anita says, and asks if I am wasting money on escorts. I'll let her think I'm impotent; truth is, I'm avoiding her, diverting spunk to the water district.

Alma once said my playing must convey objects, not ideas: "Pretend the audience isn't listening. Conquer their indifference by raising your voice, speaking clearly." Alma taught me concision, though I rarely credit her. She showed me how to dominate experience. Describing an undertaking—drawing a circle of imprecise words around it—I slay it. Tonight: re-see Moira Orfei's 1964 gladiator film, *Triumph of Hercules,* and send her a fan letter, rehashing pivotal scenes.

*

Last night, long-distance, Alma reminded me that at birth I had an oversized brain and perfect pitch. We talked about career silences: Argentines resent her imminent retirement. Despite the Buenos Aires climate, she wears her mother's green fur coat: "I make an impression. Mother wants me to be a regular woman, though I don't like *woman*, the strictures it implies. Mother can't accept that I'm an artist." I may not call Alma "Mother." Rules divide Guadalquivars. I should ask Dr. Crick for stronger psychotropics, like Alma's. At least syntax no longer exhausts me. Tonight: beets and lentils.

*

Xenia's Boston Brahmin accent—gone. Xenia's taste for escargots—gone. Xenia's fugal voicing—gone. Xenia's presence at dying Dinu Lipatti's last recital—gone. Xenia's descriptions of anti-Semitic Cracow—gone. Xenia's 1977 candelit Trinity Church performance of Brahms intermezzi—gone. Xenia's refusal to call me "visionary"—gone. Xenia's urging me to walk through parks alone after midnight so I could experience the darkness and hopelessness of the poor—gone. Xenia's kindness after I tripped down her spiral staircase and got a concussion—gone. Xenia's fantasy (murmured post-coitally) that a world-without-tonality is quiet, large, manageable, empty—gone.

*

Alma, you may not believe it anatomically feasible for a woman to rape a man, but it happens: I am always erect, so erection does not signify (Emily Dickinson would say "signalize") consent. Xenia Lamont claimed there was more pianistic wisdom in Dickinson than in all the misguided teachings of Theodor Leschetizky.

Madame X derided my melancholy disposition: "Destroy it," she'd say. She hated sad pianists, platform mannerisms. When speaking to her, I became retarded; my mouth grew detestable, uneducated—thick stumbling tongue. She disliked my self-chastisement: she'd say, "The degradation Alma drives you to!" Once I lightly slapped Xenia's face and she applauded; she said, "Now you're acting like a man." I never again slapped her. She held the sore, struck side of her face. She disliked when my playing became "inner"; I took too literally Schumann's *innig* indication in *Fantasiestücke* ("Evening"). My hand still smells of Friedman's cum, despite pine soap.

Xenia chainsmoked Marlboros. In the hospital she lifted her Lanz nightgown and showed the hysterectomy scar. Repeatedly, I deposited semen in her vagina, without condom. She didn't suggest protection. I hated being taken over, but I also felt honored: how many student penises did she solicit? Did attentions paid to penis mean my piano playing would cease being arduous and unrewarded? During sex, her Yorkshire terrier barked at the foot of the bed. Alma knew Xenia, and

thought highly of Xenia's treatise on how to play *Jeux d'eau*, Xenia's
Bloody Marys, Xenia's handknit cardigans, Xenia's criticism of my self-
indulgent rubato, Xenia's distaste for my phrasing's fragmented
arrhythmia. The last time I saw her was summer, the East Kill
Conservatory garden party: she looked suntanned, unlined, healthy, a
silver headband pulling dyed black hair away from her wide, upper-crust
face. Once, after sex, when I told her that I'd recovered from gonor-
rhea, given me by a guy, Xenia said, "Don't bring your filth into my
clean marriage." I wonder if she ever told her faithful, impotent husband about our affair.

When my heart palpitations subside, I will visit the East Kill cemetery and look for her monument. Gone, she distracts me from Aigues-
Mortes preparations, Moira Orfei reparations.

*

Twenty years ago at a funeral parlor, Xenia said, watching me write in a
notebook, "You're an observer." I remember the inadequate air-condi-
tioning. I was overcoming the Guadalquivar curse by recording mortuary
details in a notebook under Xenia's approving eye. My flaws were numer-
ous and would not be easily corrected, though a line of hair (Cape Cod)
connected my navel and groin: hirsuteness proved immunity to trespass-
es I perversely enjoyed. At the wake, I wrote down Xenia's worst features
in a notebook. I merely imagined her culpability. I'm not an apologizer,
though dispensing a few—to Alma, Tanaquil, Friedman, Moira Orfei—
wouldn't hurt. I haven't had an orgasm in twenty-four hours.

*

When Xenia heard me play the Schumann Fantasy, at her house, she
noticed faulty voicing (too much soprano, not enough alto) and rhyth-
mically unstable left hand. She declared Schumann my "lonely vocation."
She was drinking her third Bloody Mary of the afternoon. Expertly she
choreographed our sex—slowness, rapidity. She wanted to make our
intercourse New England. The more geographically located the coitus,
the more therapeutic. She repeated, "You don't know what it's like living
with an impotent husband." She pointed out his cot in the study, and his

model sailboat, paternal heirloom. Xenia profited from accurate sexual placement, pubic hairs aligned, meshing, as in her cerebral Schoenberg performances, rests durable as notes. I can't define her mound of Venus, plumped-up, like a pillow; high and orthodox; a Roman Forum, visited.

*

Once, when I was hiding from Xenia, not returning her calls, wanting to break off our relation, she telephoned Matilda: "Hi, I'm Theo's therapist. Where is he?" Matilda refused to reveal my whereabouts. She considered Xenia "psychotic," catalyst of my nervous collapse during Anton Rubinstein's First Concerto with the East Kill Conservatory Orchestra. My aunt sometimes uses "psychotic" as a term of praise. She gives glowing reports of my "psychosis" to her psychoanalysis-and-Buddhism reading group. Alma on the phone from Buenos Aires told me that she was performing tomorrow with Lolita Torres at the Teatro Avenida, a program titled "Gitano Jesus."

*

I sucked Friedman in his new loft, third floor, River Way, overlooking the almost lake. Regular's discount. I was shy about taking the whole organ in my mouth: I call his penis "diasporic" because it leaves my mind's Levant when I stop loving it. He claims to be Middle Eastern, from several broken homes. I licked the balls, failed to come: he held me at the brink for an hour. When I told him I was writing about him in my Aigues-Mortes notebooks, he seemed offended. I admire his earned muscles, not merely his inherited hirsuteness. Animation left my body. Discuss Hollywood royalty's unkind treatment of Moira Orfei after release of *Terror of the Steppes*.

*

Available on the Internet: a memorial Xenia Lamont bootleg CD: her 1955 Hollywood Bowl performance (with unnamed orchestra) of Franck's Symphonic Variations, Liszt's Hungarian Fantasia, and Chopin's Fantasia on Polish Airs. I ordered ten copies, gifts for students, to show dynamic gradations (a mile of nuance, between mezzo piano and mezzo forte) Xenia Lamont could coax from a Steinway. Her finger went to the key's bottom.

*

Moira Orfei hasn't responded to my letter. Perhaps she considers Xenia's death irrelevant to the Aigues-Mortes reunion. Death shouldn't obstruct my zealous preparations. I elevate zeal above every human art. Snow burdens Mechanical Street's elm tree branches. I am learning three Busoni elegies: "Turandot's Room," "Apparition," and "After the Turning." Practicing, I exist in a metaphorical cubicle. The closer I come to performance, the more invaded the cubicle, the more naked its walls. I pretend to crave performance but secretly I would rather retire forever. Moira Orfei, too, is weary of what my muse calls "circuit," which means "dreary repetition of the same." Need gloom be the center of the Aigues-Mortes notebooks?

*

Irene Fitts, nurse, on Long Island, called. Alma's mother hangs on the verge of death, in a Cutchogue hospice, her pain eased by a morphine drip. Sometimes the patient is coherent (so says Irene) and at other times sees apparitions in her room. Tonight, Gertrude asked for applesauce instead of her usual hospice dinner.

*

I consider going to Cutchogue. Alma on the phone says the trip would be futile; she doesn't plan to visit. She is playing Villa-Lobos's "The Little Rubber Doll," "The Little Paper Doll," "Native Planting Song," and "Joy in the Garden" in Buenos Aires at Sinagoga Central de la Congregación Israelita de la República Argentina. She cannot cancel the concert and fly to Cutchogue to supervise a treatment that, she says, "could go on for weeks, months, years. There's no hurry." Despising myself can't elevate me to the position of "Alma's favorite." How "inner"—Xenia's word—the notebooks have become, to their detriment.

She taught me how to stage-whisper: play the melody loud enough, even when it's marked pianissimo, for drunks in the balcony to hear.

*

Gertrude, dying, is over one hundred years old. I recall she wore a Murano glass bead necklace and called me "foolish time-waster." Her long white hair, piled in a bun, seemed heavy as a fat angry cat I once locked in the bathroom all night.

One person at a time, the unspeakable departs. I am a new location of muteness, which hasn't been cleansed from the Mangroves. My blood and conduct may be polluted, but at least I'm speaking.

Only in retrospect may we call a body masculine or feminine. Xenia Lamont's body had masculine as well as feminine aspects. Now that she is dead, she hardens, in memory, as "woman." She becomes absolutely that. When the circus departs is a bitter day in New England. I should move to Boston, to be near Matilda. Her hand-me-down transcendentalism could correct my failures. I'll invite Friedman over to make a Super 8 film tonight. His nudity always cheers me up, if I punish it, pay him for it, or film it.

*

Alma has not wasted her life. I may be wasting mine. Xenia Lamont has two grown sons, handsome—a criminal lawyer, an anesthesiologist. What have I accomplished, playing Falla's "Dance of Terror" on cruise ships to Barbados and the Virgin Islands? This morning Friedman shaved my body: sacrilegious, to indulge in erotic grooming while Gertrude Guadalquivar expires in a Cutchogue hospice.

*

I was wrong to play two Vincent Persichetti sonatas at Derva's Trinity Church recital, upstaging her rendition of Rachmaninoff's "Dans le silence de la nuit mystérieuse." Last year Hector Arens criticized my performance of the Leon Kirchner sonata as "implausible" and "infantile." I never congratulated Derva on divorcing moody Morris Nile. If

Alma were to read my Aigues-Mortes notebooks, she'd think me misogynist and hypercritical. I never mentioned her work on behalf of civil rights in the 1960s: memorial concert after the death of Dr. King. Recall the photos of Alma hugging Coretta, widow.

*

Tanaquil, skeptical about Aigues-Mortes, wears lederhosen. Every Guadalquivar has a tongueless disposition, however talkative we appear on the surface. Thom had almost no family. I do not consider myself a Mangrove; my melancholy is 100% Guadalquivar. I will destroy my notebooks, page by page. What will decimation prove? I can't appear in Aigues-Mortes unless I have described, in advance, the preparations. My secret economy: (a) describe; (b) disappear. Tanaquil never grew to full height. Who determines maturity?

*

Yesterday afternoon I played Mompou preludes and *Suburbis* to an inattentive audience at Trinity Church, half of them homeless. This unwise gig will not afford me national exposure. Breakdown was a boon: a chance to hibernate in East Kill, apart from limelight. After the concert I met the first man Alma ever kissed. Artie Rann introduced himself. A linguistics teacher at East Kill Community College, unattractive, with a grizzled, unkempt beard (Alma hates facial hair), he said that my mother was "the love of his life." Arnie led me out of the church, to the corner of Lavinia Way and Stream Drive, and said, "I've often stood here, thinking of your mother." Afterward I called a new escort, Alejo, Argentinian. We partied at Empire Motel. His pectorals are more pronounced than Franco Idol's. Alejo noticed, after sex, my bleeding ass. Many of his bottoms have been bleeders. I need to revise my conduct.

*

Gertrude Guadalquivar is in a coma. Irene Fitts says that Gertrude, supported by machines, could last for months.

My grandmother had many loves. She loved colored cheap glass, crowded paintings, naked spankings, and cling peaches. My merely sporadic masculinity bored her: her eyes glazed over as she watched me not be a he-man. I memorize womanly looseness and tautness.

Gertrude loved paintings when they were crowded: she enjoyed a profusion of rendered objects, no separation. She loved "things of this world," as she called them, repeating the phrase as if it were "Jingle Bells." She will donate her art collection to the East Kill Museum. Last year she bought a Brice Marden. She said to me, during one of her last lucid moments, "In Brice's painting, I love the way the lasso hugs the edge." When I repeated this comment to Alma last night, she said, "That's why she can't understand my playing. There are no lassos in my work, not even in my *Goyescas*. Music is abstract. Mother was stuck in the representational moment." But then Alma mentioned her mother's cling peaches. Sickness helps performance, bolsters its claim to be real. Cling peaches.

Notebook Sixteen

Dear Moira Orfei,

Alma's mother—Gertrude Guadalquivar—died yesterday. She never told us her exact age. We surmise it was 101.

In Marseilles, accompanying your cream pony stunt, I played an assortment of my grandfather Ricardo Guadalquivar's piano nothings: waltz, improvisation, prelude, etude, caprice, tango. Did you meet him in Tangier? His compositions are minor, but his "Alleluia Rag Waltz" has an afterlife.

Please do not forget Aigues-Mortes!

Love,

Theo Mangrove

*

Gertrude Guadalquivar died yesterday morning at 11:15 AM. (after a "valiant struggle," said Irene Fitts), in Cutchogue, near corn fields and the Long Island Sound. She died in winter. No panorama. No last luxury. Alma's face will look slack and fallen at the funeral, and afterward I will rent a water-district escort: amoral antidote.

At least Gertrude didn't die slowly of cancer; she died in a coma after no particular disease. The organs failed.

Her husband Ricardo died long ago. In recent years I have not played his nothings with sufficient passion.

Gertrude's surviving sister Ruby is handling post-mortem secretarial tasks. (No one cares about Ruby, the family drudge, ninety-five-year-old workhorse.) Gertrude prepared carefully for death; the papers are in order. She had no connection to my butter inheritance, purely Mangrove. How I keep my dairy money separate from Alma is a confusing topic.

Gertrude Guadalquivar's ghost has entered my studio; she hangs, a trapeze artist, from the chandelier. I am an amateur spiritualist. Why did I not repair Alma's amorality and push her in an ethical direction? Now Gertrude's spirit crouches atop the plaster bust of Brahms and enters my spinal cord. Her doctrinal ghost is warm, like a down sleeping bag, and wet, like a deep sea fishing trip, or an essay.

*

Matilda refuses to attend the funeral.

The last thing Gertrude said to me, in her extreme sickness: "I can't talk to you now." And then she hung up.

I never slept with anyone underage, though I misled an impressionable fourteen-year-old pupil, Marcie. I held her hand in the *conservatoire* elevator. She considered me her "boyfriend," though I was twenty years older, and married.

I dusted off the green Aigues-Mortes notebook and read it, with displeasure. At present I am writing in a silver notebook. Type these fragments after my death, Anita, if you wish. Or destroy them.

*

I repeat: Gertrude died at 11:15 AM. In our last conversations, she was weak, so I avoided mentioning Aigues-Mortes. She died without hearing my ambitious plans for a comeback, Moira Orfei proving to crowds that I can excite a response if I have corybantic assistance. "Moira" is Greek for "fate." I pronounce "Moira" correctly: "Moy Ra." *Moy* as in *boy*.

*

I performed Chopin's B Minor Sonata at Gertrude's funeral. I doubt my memorial gesture's moral probity. Gertrude told me that I am a finer teacher than pianist but that it is horrible to be forgotten and that it is better to be remembered as a teacher than not to be remembered at all. At forty-three, I still lack method. After the funeral I went to the water district; at Camera Baths, I met a man with a micro-penis. I didn't catch his name. He'd come to East Kill from Lansing, Michigan, because he wanted to "make it in the arts": découpage. He complained of mood swings. His sister recently died in a train crash. Out of pity I blew him; my teeth nicked his cockhead. Men with micro-penises shouldn't be picky. Sycophant, he asked whether I'd appeared in porn.

When I came home, Alma was still awake, sitting in the kitchen, eating canned peaches over vanilla ice cream. She might have been drunk: she started talking about my bowels. They were problematic during the first two weeks of my existence: my movements had an odd color. The discoloration "devastated" her. She sent me back to the hospital for supervision; after the doctors assured her that I was intact, she brought me home again.

*

The night after the funeral, Tanaquil and I rented a disappointing video, *Copulation,* about policemen and reincarnation. It had no frontal nudity. I don't like being forced to imagine things. I'm hung over, this morning, from Forteto della Luja.

*

In the mail from Alma's subscription list: dismal sales report for my Poulenc CD. Twelve sold. I won't fill Aigues-Mortes seats. Anita, recovering from the funeral ordeal, has boycotted Mechanical Street: all day she walked aimlessly through gorges surrounding East Kill. I spent the afternoon doing laundry. Sorting, folding, ironing: activities like Poulenc's delicate mismanagement of the ordinary.

*

Mourning period over, Alma leaves for South America: a midnight concert, next week, in Iglesia Nuestra Señora de la Merced, and then a screening, in the Museo Etnográfico Juan Bautista Ambrosetti, of a special silent version of Lolita Torres's 1944 film, *The Dance of Fortune,* directed by Luis Bayón Herrera. As live piano accompaniment, Alma will play José María Castro's *Sonata de Primavera.* Anita baked a bitter greens pie for dinner. My sexual life, aside from Friedman, is at a standstill: I've lost whatever minor attractiveness I once possessed. Anita, home from gorge-wandering, served me chocolate ice cream in bed, where I convalesced after the vertigo attack I suffered during the ten o'clock news. We're bombing another country.

Xenia taught me to imitate portamento through rhythmic crookedness. I'm no longer attracted to Mozart, but I must pretend to love his music, for the sake of my students. I'd rather everyone learn the Berg sonata.

I stayed up until dawn, making piano transcriptions of Webern string quartets and trios: Anita calls my ardor "naïve."

Tomorrow is Tanaquil's forty-first birthday. I will pick up a cake from Lesquel Bakery. Pink boxes dress up the lackluster pastries inside. Lesquel's strawberry cake is adequate. Birthday dinner will be small: Tanaquil and I. Anita is away, pursuing pedestrian experiments, walking through drought-cracked riverbeds. Alma is hobnobbing with Lolita Torres in Buenos Aires. I'll heat up a chicken pot pie from Lucky. I'll give Tanaquil one thousand dollars, from the "butter" holdings. I paid for the abortion, five years ago. Tanaquil may have wanted to keep the baby, but she had no independent means to care for it. With Alma's cooperation I arranged for the abortion with Dr. Crick. Quick procedure. No complications.

Notebook Seventeen

Dear Moira Orfei,

Again I write. I haven't heard from you. Did you receive my letter? Two deaths: Xenia Lamont, Gertrude Guadalquivar. I stumble. Excuse my forwardness. Circus detains you, and I'm detained by waiting for May, for Aigues-Mortes, when we'll work together again, after abstinence and retreat. Trapani was our last performance. I played a Steinway in the center of the ring, below the trapeze, beside juggler and clown: Poulenc's *Mouvements perpétuels,* three times in a row, between your Preliminary Parade, when you led troops around the ring, and the Final Grand Parade, when the gang at first dematerialized in clouds of your making and then returned to substance. The evening ended with your galliard on the back of a cream pony. Supine Bengal tiger, jumping llama, and rearing zebra encircled you and formed your primary audience. After the performance you mentioned that my services would not be required next season.

I worry about my wife, who shows signs of unpredictable, independent action: she moves through gorges to document them. She has the grace to mention her adventures afterward, but not the wit to describe them comprehensibly.

My house has historical consequence. I directly descend from East Kill's founding father, who slept in this very room, sired my ancestors on a bed that stood exactly here. On Mechanical Street we are quiet and artful. We enjoy our lack of drama, though the town's economy, spiralling downward, depresses business. The psychic, Mrs. Clemovitz, still does a thriving trade. She helps me keep track of you.

Love,

Theo Mangrove

*

Anita wants to commit me to an asylum. I sat next to a dwarf on the bus to New York City last week when I went to check out strippers at the Gaiety, but I didn't talk to him. Moira Orfei never fired me; she only suggested I retire. She'd seen me tremble, faint, forget. But then, after Viterbo, didn't she write me, and encourage me to plan a comeback? After Aigues-Mortes I may have the confidence to play *Goyescas* in Madrid and Bilbao, and then in Seville and Cádiz.

*

Anita escapes my control. She adopted a stray kitten. It urinated on our vestibule's Persian runner. Building a wooden birdhouse, Anita cut her arm, lightly, on a power saw. I dressed the wound. I publicly acknowledged Anita when I played pieces by Mario Castelnuovo-Tedesco at the East Kill Public Library, but Anita wasn't in the audience to hear: "I'd like to dedicate the next piece, *La Sirenetta e il Pesce Turchino*, from 1920, to my wife." Now she is off to Aruba for a weekend of snorkeling. I try to ignore her lies and her racism.

*

Yesterday, when Anita returned from Aruba, we crossed Mechanical Street to offer condolences to our ratty-haired neighbor, Charlotte, who has cervical cancer and ulcerative colitis. She lives with a houseful of grandsons: hoods. Five cars in disrepair are parked outside their house. Arnie, a redhead, sat nearest the door, always open, even in winter; with a lazy eye, he seemed half-dead, mouth agape, brooding, I suppose, on Charlotte's Ma Barker aspects—skinniness, permissiveness. Maybe Arnie was reminiscing about his years as model, posing for his father, Moe, a sanitation engineer and part-time pornographer. He was the first corpse I'd ever seen; at his wake, in a bad tux, he seemed still a pornographer, posing this time rather than snapping the picture, a docile husband, because dead, to Charlotte of the open-door policy and the freshbaked tea cakes always on offer to neighbors.

Mechanical Street mixes classes: Mangroves are rich, Santes are not. Economic gulfs draw Italian audiences to Moira Orfei—she is "the princess," but also one of the earth's legendary "wretched."

*

Alma called from Buenos Aires, after a concert at the Basílica Nuestra Señora del Pilar. She asked about my upcoming Copland recitals. Gently I said, "No, Alma, these are the Frank Bridge concerts." She told me that I lack the large *duende* eyes of the Guadalquivars. I plan to play Frank Bridge's "The Dew Fairy" and "The Midnight Tide" in Aigues-Mortes, but I did not tell her. I hid my desire for grilled cheese sandwiches, bread generously buttered, boys in their camp bunks, no longer afraid of the deep end or the lines they must memorize for tonight's performance of *William Tell*. Over-practicing Rachmaninoff's *Études-Tableaux*, I damaged my wrists. Abstinence and repentance may repair the tendons. What if you always thought your name was spelled a certain way and then one day you realized you were mistaken, there was an "i" before the "e," and no one had ever told you?

*

Two scrawny cats—owned by Charlotte Sante, dying of cervical cancer—walked down Mechanical Street this afternoon. I regret that Anita and I have no children, that Tanaquil will probably have none, and that Alma's line of succession shall have reached a miserable dead end, unlike the hamburger stand, with its promises, that once operated in the water district, at a time when it was still possible I might not turn into "that pianist who fainted and lost his memory on the stage in Aix-en-Provence and other cities less significant on the international circuit, and was fired by Moira Orfei." Her recent letters imply that I've been admitted back into the fold. I did nothing to damage her ex-husband's reputation. I never publicly said that he was bi. The Guadalquivar-Mangroves, though not reactionary, prefer the past to the future: the determining events have already occurred, but we can't picture them.

*

Joyce Sante's, Charlotte's daughter, a redhead with buckteeth, overcame her speech impediment by turning it into a charming feature; she wanted French fries with every dish, whether or not fries were appropriate.

Between ages five and ten, we were fellow nudists, scientific partners. Intellectually slow, she kept up with me in sexual action but couldn't analyze it afterward. Her mother, Mrs. Sante, hair a cap of red curls, was a cat-keeper, disciplinarian, and waterer, never content to let Joyce out of her sight. Joyce and I stripped within Mrs. Sante's watering purview: on the lawn she'd stand, holding a garden hose, and in her deadened eyes (not immediately recognizing me) I'd detect insult. She hated Mangrove wealth, airs, fame—perpetual music out our open windows in summer. Alma, suspecting that Mrs. Sante wanted to poison us, never ate the doughnuts and tea cakes that she offered on snooping visits. Mrs. Sante once showed me photos that her husband Moe took of their son Arnie. Some appeared on the covers of pocket-sized porno novelettes, stored in a cabinet in the tool shed where Mr. Sante parked his racing green Sprite convertible. I told Mrs. Sante that Arnie's legs had a precocious allotment of hair, and she said, "That's why we hire him." Standing in the tool shed with Mrs. Sante, talking about Arnie's masculine legs, I learned to sap the vitality out of my surroundings, so they could match my desiccation. The tool shed, after I vanquished it, became a blank cardboard box without images or inscriptions; the Santes, standing beside me, were no longer people, but fellow obelisks who could make no demands and accept no offers.

*

I held a small dinner party at a local Chinese restaurant. Bloated, Mrs. Sante came. She brought her twin sister, equally bloated. I invited five of my most promising students, including Rabbi Gershon. Even at eighty, he improves. I introduced my students to Mrs. Sante and her twin. Pointing to the twin, I said, "Here is Ayesha, she doesn't speak." Ayesha, a factory worker from North Kill, a poor satellite of our town, was an elective mute, though Mrs. Sante insisted on taking her to parties. Mrs. Sante told me that her brother Cappy had been kidnapped in El Salvador: she said, "The C.I.A. got Cappy." I spent most of the banquet staring at Mrs. Sante's forearms, muscular despite cancer.

Later, when Alma telephoned, I was at a loss to defend the party's legitimacy. She said, "If Charlotte Sante has cervical cancer, why are you taking her out for Chinese?" Alma said that her penthouse was drafty, and that she could hear violent lovemaking in the apartment below. After our conversation she will knock on their door and tell them to hush. Alma's performance of *Gaspard de la nuit* and *Estampes* went well, she said, but she felt empty when she contemplated her accomplishments. Dr. Helen Jole, her psychoanalyst, is retiring. I fear the repercussions: a Jole-free Alma could be dangerous.

*

In Aigues-Mortes I want to program Morton Feldman's "Last Pieces," with Moira Orfei's non-genuflecting circus commentary. She should wear a black gown with demarcated zones of her famous spangles. I forgive her for not responding to my last two letters. Circus eminences have the right to remain in perpetual trance, without responsibility to fact. She hired me back; I am not forcing my services on her. In fact, I'm doing her a favor: Aigues-Mortes never before invited Moira Orfei, and now, thanks to me, she'll find a new audience for her glittering tricks. Moira Orfei and Theo Mangrove are a two-way street. I'm no interloper, no drain on a great circus artiste's resources.

Last night Tanaquil paced the hall outside my studio. I peered out the door and saw that she was nude. I have not seen Tanaquil's breasts for several years. Despite her beauty, she shouldn't parade naked through the house. When Alma dies, if Tanaquil and I survive her, we'll have won. What's the point of victory? There'll be no recumbent, apologetic Alma left to gloat over.

*

East Kill's leading music critic has accused me of limiting my emotional range, especially in Liszt, to "exclamation." Xenia Lamont called my playing too "inner" but Hector Arens finds it ostentatious. He says I project every phrase on the same level, despite my link to the Tobias Matthay tradition of exacting, suicidal nuance. The question is not (*pace* Hector Arens) whether I fail, in my programs, by overzealous devotion to "exclamation," but whether I care about this putative failure, or whether I am indifferent to it, and to Arens's well-publicized, repeated aspersions. I must obliterate futurity by constant performance and constant, grueling, ecstatic preparation, regardless of whether Mr. Arens approves. In Aigues-Mortes, I will exhibit fruitless enthusiasm, under the punished sign of what Arens calls my "cult of exclamation." (I wrote this sentence long ago, by moonlight, on a ripped paper bag, with a failing pen.)

This morning I blew Friedman in his loft—gratis—and he came plenteously within four minutes. Abstinence yellows the cum. He put two, three fingers in my ass. I felt a wave of reminiscence, of layaway. I was being price-slashed. New merchandise will replace me. Friedman said, "You've apologized to everyone else, but you've never apologized to me." More gray hairs on his chest. He's only twenty-eight: premature aging will force him to retire from hustling and go back into the more legitimate professions that his mother Samantha long ago urged him to take up—law, gardening, spying. He has worked for a detective agency. He did time in Marseilles's skin industry: I've seen film stills. Arnie Sante's efforts can't compare. Arnie was an amateur, Moe Sante's porno novelettes a mere home industry, while Friedman appeared in major, forgotten productions.

Did Alma whisper *il miglior fabbro* over my cradle? And did she surround me, as she claims, with geraniums in ceramic pots "thrown" by Gertrude Guadalquivar? Milhaud wrote difficult, esoteric, unpublished bagatelles for Gertrude. When Alma performed them, public response was lukewarm. She donated the manuscripts to the East Kill Conservatory Library, which lost them in the fire that destroyed a wing of their archive. No one should entrust precious cargo to the Conservatory, and yet Alma has bequeathed them her papers, to be deposited posthumously. I am her half-unwilling executor. When I die, my executor is Dr. Crick, good at figures.

*

On the phone, Alma told me that, in Buenos Aires's ice rink, the Palais de Glace, she played a program of Fanny Mendelssohn-Hensel, Clara Wieck, and Amy Beach—conservative fare, with a laudable feminist slant. Alma did not tell the audience that the concert was a memorial for Gertrude Guadalquivar; the commemorative aspect remained secret. As encore, Alma played Liszt's "Fantasia on Themes from Bellini's *La*

Sonnambula." On the phone, I talked about my spiritual evolution: I used the phrase "the compost heap of the unheard." She called me "prissy." After talking to Alma, I paid an emergency visit to Dr. Crick. I don't want Anita to see the bruises on my arms so for a few days I am wearing long-sleeved oxford-cloth shirts.

Notebook Eighteen

Dear Moira Orfei,

Thanks for your condolences. Yesterday I saw Dr. Crick. Resolutions: no more drinking, no more water-district nights, no more East Kill recitals. And I must no longer throw out the medicine Dr. Crick prescribes.

Please ask your ex-husband to videotape our Aigues-Mortes appearances for later release.

How is Chloe? The animals? Is the winter palace cold? How are your sinuses? Have you found the missing scrapbooks? Are contracts in order for Aigues-Mortes? Do you understand the game plan? Are you comfortable with "winging it," or would you like more explicit directions? We'll set up your circus tent in the Place Saint-Louis. The town has agreed to take down temporarily the statue of the armed king ready to embark for the Crusade. We'll begin the Grand Parade at La Tour de Constance. Don't be afraid of the marshy ground. Before the show begins, we can climb the tower together and blow a trumpet of doom out the grilled lookout post, the "Farot." Drums and tambourines will supplement my numbers, your flotilla of dancers, your hoops and mirages.

You should lead your Grand Parade along the sentry-walk, upon the town's southwest ramparts. We could meet up again in the Place d'Armes, the circus tent set up in the esplanade, where troops once gathered. There, I could play bits from *Années de pèlerinage*. Or, if you wish, something lighter. You could banter with clowns and jugglers, introduce and tame the seals, somersault, let your dancer protégée do her upside-down blindfolded tango. Will you merely be emceeing, or will you attempt strenuous stunts? When we last spoke—in Viterbo—you told me that you were eager to segue from stunts into emceeing. Perhaps you said that merely to comfort me. At the time, I was segueing from piano into electroshock.

I will play a few of Rachmaninoff's *Études-Tableaux* as centerpiece of the Saturday night program. The études, like anything real, make incompatible demands: stillness and motion, recollection and amnesia. We discussed those paradoxes in Ajaccio, at the Hotel de Anza. We found a snake curled (dead or alive?) outside the hotel entrance. We stayed a week in Ajaccio. For the final night, we did our "unconsciousness" program. Your performance received delirious, salacious praise—references to your breasts implicit in the critics' prose. That was six years ago. Why did Ajaccio never invite me back?

Love,

Theo Mangrove

*

Last night, I fainted while attending an amateurish performance of Verdi's *Nabucco* at the East Kill Lyric Opera. I faint twice a day, after urinating: my pulse feels slow. Blood pressure problems, warns Dr. Crick. Weakness overcame me midway through Abigaille's first furious cabaletta. During the stretto, I saw black spots. When I regained sense, the opera had moved on to the next scene. Derva Nile, when her voice recovers, should be cast in an East Kill Lyric Opera revival of Charpentier's *Louise*. Derva's "Depuis le jour" has a pathos that proves Alma, who criticizes Derva as "voiceless and debauched," wrong.

*

Alma complimented my virility, the few times she saw it in action, because she considered it the most rigorous exercise of sloppiness in East Kill musical history. Originally I wanted to be a singer, but Alma discouraged me: she recognized that my only register was falsetto. Tanaquil hoped for an acting career; Alma's realism intervened. In our house, ruined dreams have a precise location. Tanaquil's ambitions, or their vestiges, live in the upstairs hallway connecting our bedrooms. Anita lacks her own bathroom; itinerant, she shuttles between mine and

Tanaquil's, but finds widest berth in Alma's—Diorissimo bottle on the glass shelf above the john a beacon.

*

Matilda finds my foreplay too rough and anally centered. She said to me, yesterday, when I visited Clarendon Street, "Put your hand there. Stop scheming about repertoire. You spend too much time giving free concerts at the East Kill Home for the Blind. My backyard garden is flooded." I changed my angle. About my hardness, she said, "At least we have something to be thankful for." Then she switched: "Stop acting. Don't imitate Tanaquil's dreams—aren't yours unreachable enough? As a child, you bought me a bottle of Charlie by Revlon. Did Alma tell you it was my scent? She forbade me to visit, after your father died." Post-sex, Matilda and I ate chicken sandwiches. I expect to be lacerated in Aigues-Mortes for artistic liberties. Matilda described my pianism as too "autochthonous." She praised me as "the only beatnik classical pianist in the western hemisphere." Reclining on her Sarouk rug, she told me that she was keeping a detailed journal of responses to my visits. She read aloud an entry: "He fails as a person and a pianist because he can't tell the difference between reality and dream." Listening, I realized that Matilda had psychological acumen, though the journal made too frequent mention of her property. It was marvelous that she could see the ocean from her apartment in Miami, where she planned to spend her old age; but did her sea view need to appear in every sentence?

*

Logan Airport: in the Delta Shuttle bathroom a man in the next stall smelled like my father. Suddenly I recognized that odor, as if from the Portbou hotel corridor—mélange of tobacco, rose petals, dung, and ash. Did his father smell the same? For such genetic legacies, there is no proper way to express gratitude, except by practicing good hygiene and good posture, and by paying a call on bygone grade-school teachers when the year is up and we pretend to have transcended former instructors but secretly want to visit them and are also afraid to advertise our longing, lest we become known as "the one who wants to visit his sixth grade teacher," or, worse, "the one who visited his sixth grade teacher, unannounced, after class, when she was erasing the blackboard." I knew I'd be laughed at for visiting a teacher who was no longer my current flame, and so I never went back to see Mrs. Campion, she of the wide Australian need, she who'd accused me of plagiarism. Did she ever show up at one of my concerts, unannounced, in the back row? Mrs. Campion claimed to have had polio as a girl—a sympathy ploy, to dress up her dull, disorganized lessons. Instructing us to build a dodecahedron from plastic drinking straws, Mrs. Campion made art seem a matter of blindly following complicated directions.

*

Vance Brown, a nerdy twenty-three-year-old from Queens, devoted to Schoenberg and the Frankfurt School philosophers, never sucked my cock. (He had a strange "finky" smell—halfway between "funky" and "sink." Bacon lodged in his smell—maybe because the plumbing company Fink and Bacon services Mechanical Street.) The night after hearing Vance play Ernst Krenek's *Little Suite*, I saw him suck off a Scarlatti specialist in Space Bar's backroom. I tried to enter their scene, but Vance scowled. (In an earlier notebook, I described my love for him. That description didn't suffice.) Since then, I have never seen his name in *Musical America*. I wonder if he died of AIDS. That can happen.

*

Perhaps I should stage Satie's *Socrate* in Aigues-Mortes. First, do a dry run in East Kill. Use Derva Nile as the singer. Derva isn't up to Aigues-Mortes standards. Moira Orfei will upstage her. Derva will insist on doing her *inutile* Lana Turner imitation. Derva in a blonde wig gilds the lily. The Jews will despise Derva Nile's Lana impersonation, nested within (and ruining) Satie's hemlock scene. Shall we ask Merce Cunningham to choreograph Moira Orfei, or shall we leave her alone? Who is the ideal witness to Moira Orfei's *Socrate*, as sung by Derva Nile, with piano accompaniment by Theo Mangrove?

*

Perhaps in Aigues-Mortes I should play the anti-ecstatic *Cheap Imitation* by John Cage, while Moira Orfei tames a seal, tap-dances on a hat, and other odd, spontaneous tricks, each a tribute to her mother. Moira rarely talks about her father, and yet his madness explains her commitment to circus. Aristocratic Moira Orfei pretends to be bohemian but dines at Le Grand Véfour on the rue de Beaujolais and travels without me to circus festivals in County Cork and Singapore. Once, when we got drunk together, and argued, over bouillabaisse, at the Hotel de Anza in Nice, she called me "passive," and accused me of never initiating circus arrangements. I am afraid of Moira Orfei's temper—afraid that she will lash out at me on the Aigues-Mortes festival stage. Beforehand, she will pretend to be a happy, polite collaborator, but then, unforewarned, in the ring, she will accuse me of under-preparation.

Time for rehearsal is running out. Unkind, to expect Moira Orfei to improvise in Aigues-Mortes. She is waiting for explicit instructions. Tomorrow I will prepare the battle-plan.

*

I drank two bottles of Côtes du Rhône Villages and fell into a stupor at the kitchen table, then summoned spirit to drive to Jacob's Ladder, the new men's clothing boutique in downtown East Kill. For Aigues-Mortes, I bought pink sandals.

Define *musical ecology*. East Kill considers me confusing, despite my decades of effort to be clear. "No phrase truly ends on the downbeat," Xenia Lamont used to say. "Outwit coarse public expectations. Play loud warhorses quietly. Play Mozart like Rachmaninoff, Rachmaninoff like Mozart."

*

Visions of dead women's hair, exiled Guadalquivar aunts I never met, accumulate in my notebooks. I plan to be kinder to Alma in the future. I have a creeping suspicion that my European breakdown was the spitting image of Alma's 1964 catastrophe, when critics implored, "Return Alma Guadalquivar Mangrove to her rightful place as ruler of the piano world!" I shall put an ad in *Musical America* (under Derva Nile's name), seeking a videotape—does one exist?—of Alma's onstage collapse, when she fainted (and more) during Liszt's "Mazeppa." I can use the tape as blackmail, should Alma cross the line; I can use it in Aigues-Mortes as visual counterpoint (sound turned off) to Moira Orfei's Maltese Cross maneuver, and my performance of Poulenc's "Valse-Improvisation sur le nom de Bach."

*

Tanaquil is coming into her own. In consultation with Dr. Gaston Lair she has upped her dosage of Thorazine and has befriended Derva Nile's younger brother, Jon, a dissolute ex-hippie with permanent brain damage from LSD. Now, on her invitation, he sleeps in our backyard shed, which Tanaquil has converted into a small guest cottage. Fearing tarantulas, I haven't entered it for years. Yesterday she took me into it. Lo and behold, Jon was sitting at a Knabe grand, an old practice piano of Alma's. I noted Jon's pigtail and his oily, pimply forehead; he showed me the gun under his pillow. Tanaquil said to him, "You look ten years younger now that you've lost the beard." She'd been nagging him to shave it. Tanaquil and Jon are having a sexual relationship—her first love affair (to my knowledge) since the abortion. Tanaquil wants Jon to gift her with Nile seed. Jon said "faggot" under his breath, referring to me; considering the shotgun, I ignored the insult. I don't keep close enough watch over Tanaquil's movements. She has reason to avoid me: she knows that an atmosphere of Theo-as-rapist surrounds me when I give master classes. The rapist nimbus originates with my father; his cheekbones (genetically he was a pan-European amalgam) are vivid to me, today, as I weigh the likelihood of Schoenberg conscripting Aigues-Mortes audiences to my cause, whatever it may be. With Moira Orfei, I want to rehabilitate piano-circus art, to show Ajaccio, Trapani, Montepulciano, and Marseilles—cities where I have failed—that I can rise to her level. We'll test-drive our act in Aigues-Mortes.

*

Emergency phone call from Buenos Aires: Alma worries that audiences no longer vibrate to her art. Former fans gathered to complain at the

Mausoleo de los Caídos en la Revolución de 1890. I wonder why I don't spend more time with her in Latin America before she dies. She would be happy for her agent to book me concerts there. Maybe she has male company; she has not mentioned a steady partner, but she must have Argentine admirers. We have only rarely discussed sexuality. In Alma's opinion, I suppress erotics on the altar of recherché musical tastes—as if Auric and Honegger were not genital profiteers! Alma concertizes exclusively in South America to flee my barnyard sensibility's limits; I owe her a pathway back into New York State musical life. Absent, she dominates East Kill. On the phone, she complained about Buenos Aires light: it falls on building cornices in the Palermo Viejo and brings on melancholy fits. Psychotropic drugs paradoxically intensify her paranoia.

*

Derva Nile and I rehearsed music that others call trivial, that we call meat: Chaminade, Chabrier, Hahn. Because I had a 102-degree fever, she agreed to stay the whole afternoon and answer the phone: "Mangrove household, Derva speaking." When my fever descends, I will help repair the bad break between her vocal registers. A long-ago dropped anvil left a welt on her right forearm, a triangular gouge I caress in passing. Today she chatted about her big, dead sister, Minerva, slain years ago, on a religion-and-drugs retreat in the Santa Cruz mountains, by a fellow tripper, who, like Minerva, spoke in tongues: cat language. Derva carries in her purse a photo of the murdered sister, a year before the breakdown that precipitated a flight westward, a personality disintegration—from cheerleader to born-again druggie.

Thoughts of Minerva's glossolalia, a magnetized dust cloth, wipe clean my delirium. I miss my former gloom, which Moira Orfei appreciated. She wouldn't want me to cheer up. In Viterbo she said, "You've never been more promising as a circus partner." Lunacy gave me, onstage, a gibbous glow. She held my hand in Viterbo and we planned a tour that never occurred. Without a piano in the asylum, nothing could distract me from her hands, with their glittering rings; from her arms, with their snake-charmer silver bangles; from her hair, with its permanent, paralyzed demeanor, like cuisine or immortality; from her eyes, with their heavily painted outlines; from her lips, with their plump yet flattened appeal to my good nature; from her lips, with their appearance of owning more property than a pair of lips could legally claim; from her nose, with its serene, perfect coating of makeup; from her body, what one could see, in outline and suggestion, through a Pucci dress. Her body, greeting me, held itself inside the Pucci fabric with a stoic, normal reserve. No one would ask her body to do anything. Circus star, she overpowered every echelon of freak, contortionist, and clown. During those few, charmed, scattered days in which I functioned as her pianist, in Ajaccio, Montepulciano, Marseilles, Trapani, and other well-placed but evanescent locales, I had the opportunity of being mastered by her, but she did not exercise the iron glove with malice or rage; though I was securely and permanently "under" her, as Beelzebub is under Lucifer, her purposes were not nefarious. Under her training and command, the seals spoke, the lions danced, the jaguars behaved. In Viterbo, during her visit to the asylum, her chest rose and fell as she sighed, in the electroshock chamber, the Pucci fabric seeming to alter and deepen with every respiration. She bore the weight of circus history on her shoulders without complaint. That we ceased to communicate for five years is not a fact I can hold against her. I am equally to blame. I retreated to East Kill, cancelled all European performances; and no more continental offers came, until Alfonso Reyes called, with the good news from Aigues-Mortes. I contacted Moira again; and, when she did not respond, I continued to write, once a week, then once a day, each letter sent to the winter palace in Montecatini, a copy sent to Chloe in her Luccan palazzo. Moira Orfei's letters, evasive though passionate, indicate willingness to work with me in Aigues-Mortes, though Alfonso tells me that no contracts have been signed. Aigues-Mortes is a small town; arrangements can be last-minute. No one else is booked for May: only Moira Orfei and Theo Mangrove. According to Alfonso, we are the only participants in the Aigues-Mortes festival.

*

When I saw Friedman at the Statute of Limitations he babbled about the fire that robbed him of possessions, including his mother's rag doll. He is developing the lion face of HIV-positive men: protease inhibitors. I have never developed side-effects. Dr. Crick calls me a wonder. I dwell in a fairy tale. And yet everything I say here is true. If it were false, I would not need to waste hours, weeks, on these notebooks—time stolen from the piano, my real art. And yet I enjoy squandering time on the Aigues-Mortes notebooks, indulging a substitute practice. I will donate the notebooks to the Moira Orfei Living Museum, once I organize it. Aigues-Mortes plans take precedence over museum schemes. Moira Orfei has not yet agreed to be a museum, or to lend her name to it, or to donate her film and circus costumes. Without a full collection of her bangles, rings, tiaras, and skirts, the museum will fail to attract visitors. Moira Orfei has not informed me whether she will contribute scrapbooks, posters, and correspondence. She has not stated where she wants the museum located. In a letter, I suggested East Kill. Given her Italian renown, perhaps the museum should be in Montecatini.

*

When I spoke to Alma in Buenos Aires last night, after her grueling weekend of concerts at Museo Xul Solar, Hospital Fernandez, Basílica Nuestra Señora del Pilar, and a midnight appearance at the Tangoteca, she mentioned a Sunday morning, long ago, when we had bathed together, or she had observed (*déjà vu*) me taking a bath. I didn't sit down in the Easter tub; I half-stood, so I could converse with her while she observed (*déjà vu*) me. Last night she spoke enviously of Matilda's big lips, "like a woman in a Gauguin painting": the lips brought Matilda many marriage offers when she was in her teens. Long ago in her Clarendon Street townhouse bedroom she took my virginity, good riddance. Twenty was a fine age to lose it. Matilda's Christian Dior pumps and Deco cigarette holders make her a family *précieuse*, our Dietrich. My tendency (following Alma's lead) to criticize Matilda must be checked; she never said one negative word to me in my entire life.

*

I will not return to East Kill after Aigues-Mortes. I will relocate to that city of salt, ramparts, and arcades. I will buy a house near the Chapel des Pénitents Gris and ask Moira Orfei to move in with me. My lumpish loyalty to East Kill flustered her, when we drank negronis in Ajaccio's Hotel

de Anza, with its atmosphere of the V.I.P lounge but also of the primor-
dial hut, lizards crawling under the door, and small Paul-Klee-like
designs of random antic journeys frescoed on the walls. She asked, "Do
you want to leave East Kill behind? Are you ready to leap into circus?"
She blinked rapidly. An important fence of mascara surrounded her
eyes. I nodded. She took a slow breath, as if preparing to chant, and said,
"Then you must give me control of the situation." My hands sweated,
trembled, like a bank-robber's. She leaned closer, held out a cigarette. I
lit it. She blew smoke over her shoulder. I thought, but did not say aloud,
"You are my demiurge." The word "demiurge" took my attention, for a
crucial instant, away from Moira Orfei. She said, "We can continue our
work. Circus is large. Circus includes all kinds." Pride, within me,
swelled, at the thought that she was stretching the word "circus" to include
me, despite her doubts. She said, "My family hated Mussolini." She
described her father's war-time sufferings, his mind's decay. A sparkling
tiara upheld her hairdo. Did the hair keep itself aloft without the tiara's
assistance? I felt privileged to be seated at a table with Moira Orfei, in
public. Other guests noticed us. A swarthy gentleman, hair wrapped in a
turban, asked to take her picture. Moira politely refused.

*

Yesterday I did not memorize the Webern Variations, as planned.
Instead, I let Friedman's new boyfriend, Jacques, finger my ass at the
Space Bar urinal. Jacques's nipples were overly long; his chest hair was
not well-organized (I prefer the Louisiana pattern). If you are reading
this notebook, Anita, don't be alarmed. The Ives *Concord* sonata awaits
me. I have not abandoned recalcitrant American masters. I will export
my crotchety East Kill temperament to Aigues-Mortes. Alma has played
almost everything decent written for the piano, but she has never played
Ives. I will accept Alma's Lord; I won't demand one of my own making.
Take no shortcuts to the truth, unless Moira Orfei, princess of dovetail-
ing and compression, commands.

  Alfonso Reyes called. He has moved temporarily to Aigues-Mortes,
to handle festival arrangements; he occupies the entertainment office at
5 boulevard Gambetta. Moira Orfei has contacted him. He said, "Moira

Orfei seems to be taking Aigues-Mortes more seriously than you are. You'd better settle down to work." I need a new European agent.

*

Gertrude Guadalquivar was not a Marxist but she sent utopia into my bloodstream. Rich, she taught me to despise the market. Alma, too, taught me that commerce was whoredom. Aigues-Mortes is not the market. Moira Orfei is not the market. Thom Mangrove was a practicing socialist. Alma said of him, "Whenever we went on vacation, he had dental emergencies." I'm sick of lies. I've spent my life trusting Alma's tales of Thom. If I start disbelieving now, I will be forced to reconstruct his entire past. Alma has shown me pictures of their trip to the Golfo dei Poeti—Thom standing upright in a tottering boat. I don't remember anything of the weeks immediately before or after his death. I don't remember being told of his death; I remember *remembering being told* by Alma that my father was dead; that he had died several weeks ago; and that the circumstances of his death could not be precisely determined.

Gertrude Guadalquivar's possessions are mine, if I desire. Alma said, on the phone, "Gertrude had fine antiques. She wanted *you* to have them, not Tanaquil." Wrong. Tanaquil, the more ingratiating grandchild, deserves love seat, pier table, console, étagère, and schoolhouse globe.

I remember Gertrude's nineteenth-century Venetian glass candelabra, now lost. I never saw it in person—only in a photograph of Alma, taken forty years ago. In those days, Gertrude plied ailing Alma with botanical poultices from Florentine labs: herbs to cure a wayward daughter's melancholy. Alma's former cheerfulness (so I hypothesized) was the place in my pianism where I stored cardinal treasures, as, in a church, one hides the bones of saints in a crypt; I could not conceive of the relation between melody and accompaniment in romantic music without recalling the photo of cheerful Alma standing beside the Venetian candelabra that might, if I can find it, become my property and prove that Alma was once not miserable. Perhaps I could program Poulenc trivia on my Aigues-Mortes concert as a way to wing this corrective to Alma—making it actual, even if in another hemisphere, even if Alma never hears my performance, in the Aigues-Mortes bandstand, amid smell of burning tar and coal, of Poulenc's *Mouvements perpétuels* accompanying Moira Orfei's glacial whirling-dervish dance, her spinning body encircled by a corps of camels. Moira Orfei complained to me, in Trapani, of the tumblers. She said they made passes at her. I will never make a pass at Moira. She stood outside my hotel room, in the Trapani Hotel de Anza, after midnight, in a white dress, knocking. I answered, and she remained, holding an ice bucket, in the hall. I thought of inviting her into my room, but she said that she was just passing through and wanted to know if I needed to refresh my own ice bucket. I brought my ice bucket into the hallway and she took a pair of tongs and removed a dozen or so cubes from her ice bucket and put them in mine. Then we said goodnight and I closed the door. The next morning, at rehearsal, we didn't discuss the ice-bucket incident. I may be wrong to see significance in it. She knows I like to drink whisky on the rocks in the Hotel de Anza alone in my room at night while I am writing in my notebooks about performances and rehearsals. At the time, I was keeping a series of notebooks I called the Hotel de Anza Notebooks, which I never showed Moira Orfei, though she appeared in nearly every paragraph. I will donate the Hotel de Anza Notebooks to the Moira Orfei Living Museum, and after my death, she can read them. She will be flattered by most of the references. I discuss in detail the time she came to my hotel room dressed in a white gown and a white coat over it; we sat on the couch and talked about her desire to retire from circus. I urged her never to quit, though circus exhausted her. Her eyes were ambivalent; eyelashes moved slowly up and down, never coarsely, always with refulgence and weight. I looked into her eyes but was unable to speak. That day my paralysis began. The Moira Orfei Living Museum is taking my attention away from Aigues-Mortes. I must concentrate on the future.

PART THREE
Retrenchment

Notebook Nineteen

News bulletin: after a long period of hearing sporadically from Moira Orfei, I am receiving daily postcards, in Italian. Why the sudden regularity? Today, my birthday, I will begin translating Moira Orfei's postcards and transcribing them in notebooks. Responsibility for errors is mine.

*

Theo:
Do you ever hear voices? Do you answer them, or leave them be?
Eavesdropping on Vesuvius, I fainted during my Napoli circus.
Here begins the slow, difficult trip to Aigues-Mortes, against Chloe's warnings.
Please rescue me.
M. Orfei

*

Am I capable of rescuing her? Who has kidnapped her? Managers? Rivals? The Wanda Osiris clan? Orfei cousins? Settled onto the train, riding to Boston, I lie in what the sages call "the lap of contentment," but to what end? I was a complainer at birth, Alma says, and I've never stopped. Out the window I see defunct farm, hayrick, stilt-propped barn, red church, white church, apple orchard, harbor, gorge, college, golf course, marsh, cranberry bog. I wish I'd brought my Super 8 Bolex camera. I've passed these same vistas many times, but I've never noticed the sublimity. "Sublimity" is the nonsense I idealized ten years ago, before I rediscovered Moira Orfei's magic powers, before I met

Friedman and penetrated the water district's secrets. Time to destroy some local reputations, including my own.

*

I am sick of Matilda's wealth: she flaunt her rubies, Gertrude's leavings. I sat on Matilda's bed while we watched the long-lost, recently-surfaced video of Alma's 1964 breakdown. Alma sat at the piano, eyes closed; she stopped playing. I shouted at the screen, "Wake up!" Alma is a sorceress, even in her slump. I dozed, trying to defend magic, trying to picture the insignificant, undignified ridges that surround East Kill. At five o'clock Matilda nudged me awake by encircling my erect penis with her mouth, but not bringing me within a mile of orgasm. We don't consider the mouth a likely source of transmission. I returned home to a phone message from Alfonso Reyes: to print the program, he needs my final repertoire list.

*

Aigues-Mortes is France's most defended town—ancient ramparts intact. Some of Moira Orfei's postcards show parapets, while others come from St-Rémy-de-Provence, Les Baux, Orléans, Passy . . . Each image offers an assignment: picture of the road leading to Rocamadour (pilgrims walking up the hill on their knees) tells me to think about humiliation as I prepare Poulenc's *Mouvements perpétuels*. Poulenc insists that his music be performed *sans nuances*; if I omit nuance, Moira Orfei will compensate with a double load.

*

I may not live long enough to finish my notebooks. Closure depends on Moira Orfei cooperating, our performances proceeding as planned; they have not yet been organized. I am scheduled to appear for a full week of recitals in Aigues-Mortes, with the guest-starring collaboration of renowned and ephemeral circus artiste Moira Orfei, but we have not nailed down a single program; she has neither agreed to appear nor specified her manifestations. She may contribute fireworks, aquatic dives, animal-tamings, ordinary nostalgic ballet movements, interpretive dances—or postures of stillness, sculptural, bodhisattva-like, to wow the crowd. When fever descends, I'll get practical. Problem: it's difficult to telephone Moira Orfei directly. If I began to tell the truth about my relation with Moira Orfei, the likely reason for her decision to "bump" me from her routine, then Alma, reading these notebooks, would close off my communications with the outside world. It is not always possible to turn one's life into a movie. Some existences must be slow, dull, without women.

*

Dear Theo:

En route to Aigues-Mortes. I fear the loss of reputation, the "stain" you attributed to me, years ago, in Positano, before you understood circus eminence, the "misterioso" mood I cast over you as you sat beneath the lemon bower.

Moira Orfei

*

I sat beneath the lemon bower

under Moira Orfei's power:

I remember Positano with Moira Orfei—starched Hotel de Anza linen. She demanded more hand towels. Tonight I'll forego Aigues-Mortes preparations and escape to the water district—Space Bar, Statute of Limitations, Camera Baths, Fortune 500—and try to memorize a few faces so I can describe them tomorrow. I want to caress the notebook itself, but I have called an end to the human; I use notebooks not to "liberate the expressive potential of dissonance" but to avoid the hard work of listening to intervals. There is no time to gauge each phrase before I produce it; I cannot plan Aigues-Mortes, I must let it occur, explode without premeditation, even if calamities ensue and Moira Orfei never forgives me for involving her in a colossal embarrassment, an epic disaster, like Airport or The Adventurers. Moira Orfei, not an appropriationist, is a fabulist; circus is the least realistic art, therefore the most despised. Gypsies, in May, gather in Stes-Maries-de-la-Mer. Alma suggests I include them in my festival. I'm planning a Super 8 film called *The Water District.* The Aigues-Mortes concerts, tape-recorded, will be the soundtrack.

*

At Jacob's Ladder yesterday I bought a pair of checked trousers to wear as "rehearsal pants" in Aigues-Mortes. There may be no rehearsals, only performances. If I start treating Moira Orfei as a principle of realism, then I jinx Aigues-Mortes. Long ago, a ballet dancer, Cyndie Val, embraced me and offered her breasts, though she was sexually my superior. I could see asscrack above her stretch pants when she bent down. Later in the Berkshires she opened the door of a moving car, fell out, and died. She was trying to escape the predator who'd picked her up: she'd been thumbing a ride. Her mother sent me Cyndie's obituary; scheduled to perform at the memorial, I cancelled. To me she was mostly optimism, breasts, buttcrack, and a willingness to eat Baked Alaska and to consider it (the organic vanilla ice cream rather gray) a treat, which it is not, because no one loves Baked Alaska or understands its identity, despite the name's saloon atmosphere.

*

Anita read me the riot act—no more gay sex—and then she fixed me a Brandy Alexander. I may agree to intercourse tonight. Reading Tsvetaeva, Anita is trying to reach transcendence: Guadalquivar territory. Perhaps I lack the strength to perform Liszt in Aigues-Mortes. My *Mephisto Waltz* octaves don't puncture or bite. Though I play the sentimental middle section adequately, Aigues-Mortes audiences will think me a whiner.

*

Theo,
   I write to you from Belgrade. Quick detour, unforeseen, unwanted. I am taping a pathetic TV show. On it, I must pretend to be drunk: an insult to circus. My earlier appearances on Belgrade TV were lovely work. I can't justify my eleventh-hour return.
   Moira Orfei

*

I faxed Moira, via Chloe ("Please Forward to Belgrade"): I told Moira not to worry about TV humiliations. Complaining about weight loss and failing vision, I asked why she didn't mention Aigues-Mortes in her last postcard, and whether she'd sue me for embarrassing her. I visited East Kill Cemetery's Mangrove plot, larger than the Guadalquivar. The world has deference for Moira Orfei, but not enough. My Toulon palpitations, Nice memory lapse, Ferrara fainting spell, Carcassonne absence: Aigues-Mortes will be my final, unforgiveable bewilderment.

In Atrani's Hotel de Anza I drank espresso macchiato and Moira Orfei drank lemon verbena tea. Before a circus, she'd get the bends. Everyone in the café was staring at Moira Orfei, her makeup vermeil. I wanted to be her identical twin: if I moved slowly enough, without bump or discontinuity, I might match her frozen poise.

On the phone Alma discussed her recital at Sala Leopoldo Marechal in Biblioteca Nacional. I mentioned the Aigues-Mortes notebooks. She approved. She said that they are "adequately Guadalquivar." My bone structure and blood type are Guadalquivar. Although she hates the Guadalquivar genotype, she uses it as cudgel. I will bring the notebooks to Aigues-Mortes, so Moira Orfei—her judgment impeccable, terminal—can embrace or reject them.

*

Tanaquil wastes her mind on *Dragnet* reruns. Our family contract has an immortality clause: we observe no temporal limits. Has Moira Orfei arrived in Aigues-Mortes? Her last postcard was ambiguous. Alfonso Reyes, when I called, withheld specifics. We speculate that she has rented a flat in Aigues-Mortes, rather than a hotel suite. Trying to forget Moira Orfei's alarming plea that I rescue her (from what kidnappers?), I follow Matilda's advice and reread Simone Weil. Weil's witty. European martyrs lubricate my path to Aigues-Mortes, home of the first Crusaders.

*

Anita wants to star in the East Kill Lyric Opera *South Pacific.* Her audition piece is "Do-re-mi." I hear her practicing it softly at night, downstairs, while I, upstairs, am reading Weil and perusing the *Années de pèlerinage* score. Anita's voice was never properly trained, though she has modest natural abilities. Tanaquil, too, harbors operetta ambitions: she yearned for a role in *Li'l Abner,* years ago, before Alma discouraged her. She still wants to appear on soaps. She has a library of great plays (from Sophocles through Strindberg), potential parts optimistically highlighted. Tanaquil's theatrical cravings complicate the family scene and pay no respects to our dead father, who hated illusion. If Anita comes home in tears from the "grocery store" (her euphemism for the East Kill Lyric Opera headquarters), the solution is Ambien, a private stockpile in my porn drawer. Dr. Crick, careless prescriber, pushes legal boundaries.

*

Anita returned triumphant from the "grocery store." She won the role of Nellie. Apparently at the auditions there was a "buzz" about my Aigues-Mortes recitals, though I've made no local announcement. Ross Sachs, an East Kill Lyric Opera coach, is planning a tour package—flying twenty East Kill folks to Aigues-Mortes to hear my concerts and then wander the Camargue. Ross doesn't know beans about the *étangs*, my inexplicable ponds. Seeing a gaggle of East Kill loyalists in the audience might unnerve me. Moira Orfei has never come to East Kill, its residents blind to circus.

*

Matilda telephoned to accuse me of "slapdash compartmentalization." She said that until I came to terms with "the nature of the vagina," I'd never make musical progress. She suggested that Moira Orfei do Aigues-Mortes in the nude. Matilda misinterprets circus. Moira's filmed nude scenes don't betoken live striptease.

*

"Crisis is a Hair," Emily Dickinson wrote, but it is also true that Crisis is my student Rabbi Gershon, who wrote, several years back, an article in the *East Kill Times* trashing the Mangroves, suggesting that we had too much influence. Contemplating conversion, I once visited East Kill Synagogue to convene with Rabbi Gershon. An old grumpy man with a messy beard and a perpetually unzipped fly, he kept a skateboard in his office. He asked about my conjugal relations: was I sufficiently pleasing to my wife in our "intimate traffic"? I assured Rabbi Gershon that erection with her was never a problem, although I preferred impromptu water-district sojourns. The rabbi's face brightened.

*

Yesterday's pianistic revelation involved the simple phrase *cash box*. If I say "cash box" while playing Ravel's *Sonatine* (1905), then its melodies speak, no longer sullen, closed. *Cash Box*. The word "cash" is higher in pitch than "box." Each vowel's length—a, o—is equal, though I tend to hold the *a* of *cash* longer than the *o* of *box*. *Cash box* matches Ravel's primary rhythmic module! Two equal notes, the first accented, the second unaccented. We call this sad phenomenon an appoggiatura. Alma asked me to drop Ravel in favor of Frank Bridge's forgotten character-piece, "Fragrance." Matilda called "cash box" a nonsense phrase. She thought I meant "whore's vagina." She said, "I've asked my Boston friends how far they'd travel to see Moira Orfei perform. Most wouldn't drive to Medford."

*

Dear Theo,
I want to fill your holes.
Call.
M. Orfei

*

Problem: Chloe will not give me Moira's number. A circus artiste's location changes daily. I overheard Alma say to Tanaquil, "Your brother does exactly what he wants, and *only* what he wants, and only *when* he wants." Alma laughed as she offered this character analysis; my whimsy—my weather—originally wounded her, but she learned to respect it. I worry about our country's aggressions. Today we're dropping bombs. Tanaquil started a magazine bonfire, destroying my porn back-issues.

*

Phone message from Buenos Aires: "Emergency. Ring me immediately." I delayed. When I finally called, Alma said, "Moira Orfei is unreliable." Wrong. Alma means her own 1964 breakdown. Moira Orfei has never cancelled a booking, though she occasionally faints in the ring.

Moira's circus master class dominates June. She admits students via grueling auditions. Five winners are flown to Montecatini. I've seen photos of apprentices sitting on Moira's white leather couch (the very couch I accidentally vomited on). Moira, I want to sit on your sofa and understand your ankles, your secret sloppiness, your housedresses, your scrapbooks, your fights with Chloe.

If I were to ask Moira Orfei about her body, the Aigues-Mortes notebooks would become a replica of an earlier set, called *False Flowers*, detailing my first visits to the water district, and the men I found there: unlikeable confessions, in a void. Years ago I read them aloud to Tanaquil, in an unattractive whisper. Last night after dinner, she sat on my lap. We occupied the third-from-the-bottom stair. The longer I held her, the smaller she seemed to grow, the less capable of living without my warlock genitals. Someone (Alma?) watched me fail; the failure continued, while she watched. I tried to explain the failure and her watching of it, but she watched me explain the failure, too, on a step outside the living room, where den met kitchen, and where a lamp composed of three clown-hat cones bought my patience.

*

Theo,

I have arrived in Aigues-Mortes to prepare circus groundwork. I won't stay long. Stop sending me fantasies. Chloe has forwarded several. The town is surrounded by towers! Quaint. I give you them: Tour de Constance, Tour du Sel, Tour de la Mèche, Tour de

Villeneuve, Tour de la Poudrière, Tour des Bourguignons.

Each tower must inspire a tribute. You may use them to salute anything you wish. Warn me beforehand.

Moira Orfei

*

Towers! Panicked, I called Alma in Buenos Aires to complain about mouth cankers. She loves my distress, as if she were discovering it for the first time: "Sweetie, you have no memory. You forget birthdays, and yet you are always so worried—and have been, since a tot—about the need to complete projects. Why not leave them unfinished? We must get rid of the word 'project.' Walt Whitman said (according to my good, late friend Edward Steuermann, one of my links to Schoenberg), 'We must march my darlings,' and I'm in 100% agreement. Theo, we must march. But toward what destination? Into a rose garden? A lilac bush? Do we avail ourselves of every allusion, or leave some fields fallow? Have crocuses appeared yet on Mechanical Street lawns?"

She complained about her leased Pontiac: "I can't drive a dirty car." A birth-damaged body can never be repaired. Her voice sounded like a computerized automated help line, vowel intonations inhuman. How much candy does she keep in her desk drawer when she stays at the elegant Hotel Panorama in Córdoba? Are there fruit cocktail jars in her mini-bar? She sees lightning flashes, a Guadalquivar affliction, in the corners of her eyes. She dyes her hair black, to distinguish it from her late mother's.

Chance encounters in East Kill bathhouses resemble chance procedures in John Cage, who dedicated one piece to Alma: "Sexual Practices in Indochina in the 1960s," for solo piano and television set, a difficult, prurient work she was ashamed to perform. She favors musical zoning: keep X-rated shops out of residential neighborhoods. I favor musical mixing. Also slashing and burning.

*

Theo,
Belated one! I wait in Aigues-Mortes.
Moira Orfei

*

Shame on me. Lazy in East Kill, I let a world-class circus star do my prep-
work. My mouth sores ache. Falling asleep, I see Moira Orfei's horses
performing tricks—the Levade, the Courbet, the Capriole, the Cupada,
the Ballatade, the Perotte, the Piaffe. I can't live without the 1962 Levade,
in Castelfranco, a wound, a video, better than anyone believed possible,
not frequently enough credited, never praised enough, a clear high step,
an innocent leg and arm. No one said, "Moira Orfei, do the Levade."
Her soul instructed. Moira Orfei's relation to the horse brings transcendence and wakefulness to the circus tent. In Aigues-Mortes I will tell
Moira Orfei about her 1962 perfection.

Notebook Twenty

Theo,

I write to you from Aigues–Mortes. Sardines. Chloe took a photo of me standing outside a yellow house I could imagine buying. The town's charms wane. Each gateway has an appalling likeness to earlier gateways I have seen and fled. I give you them: Porte de la Gardette, Porte St-Antoine, Porte des Cordeliers, Porte de la Reine, Porte de l'Arsenal, Porte de la Marine, Porte des Galions, Porte des Moulins, Porte des l'Organeau, Porte des Remblais.

Each gateway must host an entrance: mine or yours. We will enter together and reverse the exit of the Crusaders, heading East. We feel guilty about the Crusades and wish to expiate French guilt?

I am not just an idea you are entertaining. Chloe told me that you called. She described your progress toward circus.

Moira Orfei

*

I called every hotel in Aigues-Mortes; not one has a guest named Moira Orfei. She may be registered incognito, or she may be staying at a private home.

I believe her. Moira Orfei knows my sordid pastimes. As surety we hold between us the memory of that fine restaurant in the lobby of St. Sebastian's Hotel de Anza, The Branding Iron, where we ate fried chicken and orange sherbet and discussed future tours, future visits to churches, future trips on which we would climb towers and look past city walls at surrounding marshes and wonder together about wildlife (horses, flamingos) and contemplate our distance from early tribulation.

*

Theo,

Still in Aigues-Mortes, still commemorating, at breakneck speed. I wrote out directions to my house in Montecatini, as if it were a compound I was forced to flee at gunpoint.

I have visited each of the churches. I give you them: Église des Sablons, Chapelle des Pénitents Gris, Chapelle des Cordeliers, Chapelle des Pénitents Blancs—from which the crusade began. "The slain," Chloe said, "are really slain." Here are no plaques, no memorials. Next to the crimes of Aigues-Mortes crusaders, yours are nothing. Forget our Cyprus argument.

Moira Orfei

*

Alma said that I ruined Tanaquil, years ago, in childhood, by flashing her. Last night Tanaquil sat on my lap again. I had room enough in my heart, after cold beef supper. I regretted my generosity: kindness might dilute Aigues-Mortes preparations. We sat in my studio, beside the two Bösendorfers. Low-grade fever intensified my love. Anita was rehearsing *South Pacific* at the "grocery store."

I tried to explain away Tanaquil's wounds. She is at least six inches shorter than I. (Not as small as Alma.) Tanaquil asked me to face westward so she could look out the window onto Mechanical Street. Every time a person passed on the sidewalk, Tanaquil waved. "I'm no longer a shut-in!" she exclaimed, bouncing on my lap. And yet I wished, unkindly, to say, "You're becoming a miniature."

When Mrs. Sante, pretending not to pry, peered in the window, Tanaquil waved and shouted, "When do I get my doughnuts?" (Mrs. Sante occasionally brought us bags of homemade greasy crullers dipped in powdered sugar.) Mrs. Sante couldn't hear what Tanaquil said. My sister was blocking circulation in my legs, so I pushed her off my lap and followed her into the diningroom, where she sat on a normal chair. She agreed that Aigues-Mortes has its own virtue, as ancient Israel had its single god. I nearly wept to hear Tanaquil say "Aigues-Mortes": by uttering it, she countenanced and forgave my potential glory. I didn't name a city that pleased her. What is Tanaquil's Aigues-Mortes?

My Tanaquil regrets are circular. I hurt her, I hurt her again. I watch her being hurt, I watch the apology. I hurt her again, I watch the apology. As a child, she didn't mind bending her life to fit Alma's keyhole, a decent vision, not a punishment: Alma wanted a docile daughter, white on white. I played a record of Venezuelan nationalist lullabies, sung in French translation by Yvonne Printemps. To Tanaquil I explained the differences between Yvonne Printemps singing "Mon rêve s'achève" from the film *Je suis avec toi*, and the Algerian chanteuse Marie-José (originally Mauricette Lhuillier) singing "Peut-être" from the film *Rappel Immédiat*.

*

Dear Theo,

I remain in Aigues-Mortes, in debt. I don't like the Camargue's flimsy sand wines. Let's pour Muscadet de Sèvre-et-Maine Sur Lie, free, during our festival, to insure an inebriated audience. Circus requires intoxication. Afternoons, I visit Alfonso. If I answered, when you called his office, my reality would destroy you.

M. Orfei

*

I've given up believing that the phrase "cash box" is the key to the proper execution of Ravel's deceptively simple *Sonatine*. Its secret is automation, lack of tone. Ravel hewed his *Sonatine* out of insensitive pylons, not Alma-based chimeras.

Anita's moist hard groin pushed into my upper thigh last night in bed. I didn't reciprocate. The next morning at breakfast, neither of us mentioned the rebuffed advance. We let her crotch drift into the unexpressed.

*

Theo,

I promise to send you a videotape of my Arena di Verona performance, 1978. But first I must find a copy. Where? I have asked Chloe, the disconsolate, preoccupied with planning her upcoming leukemia benefit. I can't firm up repertoire for Aigues-Mortes until we review what went wrong in 1978. It was a debacle: all Verona trembled.

I don't mind repeating my mistakes. I'd be happy to re-enact what went wrong in Verona, if I could only remember.

We could turn Aigues-Mortes into an homage. Homage to 1978. Homage to what went wrong.

Moira Orfei

*

"Sick," says Anita, when I show her Moira Orfei's latest postcard. Trusting Dr. Crick, Anita thinks me psychotic. She can't understand why arts crossbreed: "If you're a pianist, why fiddle around with a circus artiste?" "Leave her to heaven" is Anita's philosophy, but I mustn't be passive about Moira Orfei's salvation or damnation. Aigues-Mortes approaches; Moira Orfei and I have not yet scheduled rehearsal times. Serendipity may create scandal—our reputations compromised, my vaunted "neatness of execution" (*Corriere della Sera*) dashed on the rocks of Duchampian *déshabillé*.

*

Theo,

Chaos must henceforth be my calling-card: an Aigues-Mortes disorder, typified by a performance that has not yet taken place.

We will take the stage together and lift the movement arts to a new plateau. I pray your parochial critics will not fly to Aigues-Mortes to check out this final installment in a strange career, or two careers, yours and mine, and, by extension, Mother's, since my every movement implies a movement she did not live to make.

Moira Orfei

*

If I fail in Aigues-Mortes then I will never again have a chance to redeem the coupon that Moira Orfei offered that first time she invited me to Montecatini (she had seen me play *Carnaval* on Italian TV); though I spilled Brunello on her white leather sofa she immediately initiated me into her cult, of which I was already an avid, invisible member. Her couch is in five sections: a modular modern piece. How documentary must I become in recounting my sad affair with Moira Orfei? Should the reader—Alma, Anita, Tanaquil—fill in the sordid details? Should I describe the time Moira found me lying drunk in my own vomit on her white leather sofa? She consented to perform with me a week later in Marseilles, by which time I had dried out and was in top form, playing *Gaspard de la Nuit* for the first time to a skeptical yet sympathetic audience of fishermen, pimps, gamblers, impresarios, aristocrats, gunrunners, terrorists, and thieves. Time for a morning purgative. Stomach upset is the figure in my carpet. Dr. Crick doesn't respect my sturdy Guadalquivar physique. He should scan Alma's brain and compare it to mine. Is it a surprise when someone who is slowly dying finally dies? To regain concentration for Aigues-Mortes, I need to find a medication that will prevent blackouts. And yet Moira Orfei always found a way to work blackouts into her routine, to justify collapse.

*

Dear Theo,

If only I had uninterrupted weeks to prepare for Aigues-Mortes, without needing to consider the public! I am your morphine, but I need morphine, too, and who among my circus brethren can offer it? In Aigues-Mortes I find no Hotel de Anza. Its absence explains the town's silence, siestas always underway, mules wandering noon streets, clip-clop of indolent hooves. Fork tines sound the mid-day clash of needs, mother and children wanting opposite respites. Mother in Montecatini had no peace. We exhausted her with rehearsals and tour. And then she died. She was five years older than my father.

Moira Orfei

*

Since my European breakdown I have chosen to ignore the listener. On the phone last night from Buenos Aires, Alma mentioned my "early graves"—my childhood habit of burying dead insects in the backyard and marking their resting places with toothpicks and tiny handwritten memorial pennants.

*

Theo,
Yes to the tigers. Yes to Ravel.
Moira Orfei

*

Expiation of European guilt must begin in Aigues-Mortes; only a circus artiste, and a pianist who loves her, can initiate interrogation.

In my next notebook, I must flesh out the connection between body odor and ethics: why good people sometimes stink.

*

At Jacob's Ladder I bought orange leather moccasins, for our first night, when Moira will dance with tigers and I will play the Ravel *Sonatine*.

Since Alma is away on tour I can hide my notebooks anywhere I wish—including her underwear drawer.

*

I telephone the Aigues-Mortes festival office, at 5 boulevard Gambetta. Alfonso Reyes says that absolutely my letters are being forwarded to Miss Orfei, who wants to keep her address a secret. Confidentially he tells me that she is staying at the Hotel Constance, beside the Tour de Constance, on the edge of Aigues-Mortes, beneath the encircling medieval stone rampart. The circus tent has not been assembled. The truck from Montecatini, carrying supplies, is stalled: Italian labor-union strike, roads closed. He is worried that I won't show. Moira is staking her reputation on my appearance. At least I'm insured.

*

Alma, on the phone last night, described her affair with Leonard Bernstein in the 1960s, during one of his "straight" phases. She said, "I could give you quite a list!" She meant a list of her body's favorite parts, from Bernstein's point of view. She began the blazon. When she litanizes, and I listen, her voice becomes a heldentenor's, and my temperature lowers, like East Kill under snowfall when I was a *conservatoire* impostor, pretending to be Alma's heir, when in fact I deviated from her noble line.

Orchestras these days rarely invite me as soloist. Moira Orfei alluded to the cause, when we argued after the Atrani performance: my love of bent time. Delaying the beat, I confused her; her hunky juggler faltered, dropped a torch. Moira Orfei's emceeing faltered, too; her eyebrows rose.

*

Dear Theo,

Coincidental one, I'll marry you—

For God's sake don't take me literally!

Aigues-Mortes is nature morte, as if painted by Chardin.

Perhaps you misunderstand.

I must stop writing postcards. Words eclipse my warm-ups, daily, with tigers. My legs are sore from splints; the anchovies, good; the sand wine, flaccid.

Moira Orfei

*

By delaying arrival, I help Moira Orfei, give her freedom, privacy. Practicing Ravel, I separate each note from its enclosing phrase. I try to apply Arturo Benedetti Michelangeli's advice: it is wasteful to accelerate and crescendo simultaneously. Thinking of Michelangeli, that peasant, I find myself re-occupying a moment from 1975, an instant, hard to specify, of moral uprightness, self-control, and a sexual abstinence separate from my current lax state. Battista, who works the towel desk at Camera Baths, experimentally spanks me. Stripped in my cubicle, he shows off hairy upper thighs, flax changing texture and thickness when it reaches the tan line, the contrast between white buttock and dark leg as absolute as a "slant of light" in Georges de La Tour.

Battista tells me that authorities threatened to close the baths. East Kill elected Mayor Dreyfus on a platform of moral crackdown, and our water district, our pseudo-water district, was his first scapegoat. Bombing raids continue; Dreyfus approves. Political unrest never enters Moira Orfei's performances. I hope protesters won't interrupt Aigues-Mortes.

*

Yesterday I visited the East Kill Conservatory, where I am on probation. The elevator smelled, inexplicably, of Gertrude Guadalquivar's hair spray, Secure.

*

Some medical material leaks into the Aigues-Mortes notebooks, but I have tried to keep them free of sickness-and-health questions.

Dr. Crick—histrionic, fallible—trusts phone consultation. No matter what I tell him, he prescribes Jell-O. He is planting a dream garden outside his office window. When I next come to give blood, he'll show me the regraded rock slopes. He has seen me erect; once during a prostate exam I fell into the error of arousal, and the occasional testicular palpation excites response. His paunch comforts me. A fat doctor can't lie.

Dr. Crick asked if I'm still taking my pills. I said yes, though often I skip a dose: they cause vertigo. My condition improves, despite what he has trained me to call the nightly "blood in the bowl," startling, picturesque. Dr. Gaston Lair recently removed Tanaquil's fibroid tumor, she said. Why didn't you tell me about the surgery, I asked. She said, you're barely alive. We were standing in Alma's bathroom. Alma was in Buenos Aires; her absence permitted liberties.

Notebook Twenty-One

I should be putting all my eggs in the Aigues-Mortes basket, but I can't help wasting time remembering that Xenia Lamont never liked me to go down on her. She wanted to get intercourse, a trill etude, over with. Tanaquil's fibroid tumor: benign. I hope I showed concern.

*

Dear Theo,

Italy's truck-driver strike rages; the sets are stalled in Montecatini. I can't begin work until they arrive.

Here in Aigues-Mortes I met a lovely West Indian woman. "My daughter, my daughter!" she screamed, disturbing my prayers; I helped her out of the Chapelle des Pénitents Gris. We walked through the arcades. Wind picked up. "My name is Moon," she repeated. "Mrs. Moon. And I thank you." We found her daughter huddled by the Tour de Constance. Alive but crying.

Mrs. Moon knew nothing of my career!
Moira Orfei

*

I took Tanaquil to East Kill Lyceum; we saw *Kitten with a Whip*, starring Ann-Margret and John Forsythe. On the walk home Tanaquil discussed poetry. She has a theory about Hart Crane: a Key West male prostitute knifed him, and the wound entered the poems. I telephoned Alfonso Reyes in the Aigues-Mortes entertainment office. No answer. Tanaquil agrees: remedies secretly poison. Mangroves must practice circumspection.

*

Theo,

I'm planning our performance while I wait for the truck strike to end.

Let's project a video of me thirty years ago. I'll sit in the front row, watching, and then I'll come onstage and join you. Treat the audience first to video Moira, then to real Moira.

After the video, I'll pretend to sink into stupor, meanwhile waiting for my cue.

Moira Orfei

*

The story I tell, on the piano, is self-mutilation. Hector Arens wrote: "What is Theo Mangrove's motive?" I'm sexually attracted to suicides. My *conservatoire* friend Risa, harpsichordist, had a breakdown when we were twenty. She ran up to me, in the practice-room hallway, shouting "Grandfather!" Then at lunch in the *conservatoire* cafeteria she sat with asylum staff. Fake jollity: psychiatric nurses pretended to be her friends, but then took her away.

One day it was ornaments; the next, sanatorium. And then she hanged herself. In Aigues-Mortes my Liszt "Orage" will embody the rope.

*

Theo—

I have returned to Montecatini. As always on Sunday mornings I am depressed because I remember Mother's death and her disappointment that I was not the sort of circus artiste she had dreamt of me becoming, though I wore the pink sweater set she sewed for me and I did not mock schoolgirls with obvious public illnesses ("Never make fun of a sick person," Mother told me, and I, listening, would lose track of time, so entranced was I by her compassion). If I can drown in my late Mother's warnings, why can't you collapse in mine? I don't predict a long life for you. Witness the dreary world of all that is not circus.

Moira Orfei

*

Conservatoire dean Gustavo Clemens requested my resignation because of on-the-job fainting spells and missed recitals. I wept in his office and refused to quit. Is it a mistake to write down incriminating incidents that Alma and other saboteurs might later read?

*

Theo,

Hello from Verona. Eros Ramazzotti and I performed at the Arena. Newspapers printed false sexual rumors.

Consider Messiaen's "Petites esquisses d'oiseaux." Why not schedule an all-bird evening? I'll gladly improvise a robin redbreast twirl and take last-minute requests from the audience: choose your bird, I'll dance to it.

Moira Orfei

*

Yes to Messaien. Matilda, wearing Joy parfum (no more Charlie), held my cock in her hand and said, quoting Alma, "You are raw ingredients I could never shape into a decent meal." Then Matilda told me about the time she threw an infant across the room. Babysitting, Matilda imagined herself Mary Magdalene. She said, "I know my meds need to be adjusted when I start thinking about the Lord." Instead of hitting the wall, the baby boy landed on a beanbag chair. Years later she apologized to him, a stockbroker. She stopped holding my cock. She said, If you don't want to climax, why bother visiting me? I said, I like build-up for its own sake. I never properly explain Moira Orfei's grandeur.

Afterward I climaxed in a stall of the Boston airport bathroom (Delta Shuttle) with a tall young black guy wearing sweatpants: mutual hand jobs. Traffic prevented intricacies. When cum left my system, I regretted the venue and remembered dissonance, my new fad: I am modernizing my ear, removing its anti-Semitism. Also I am boning up on dialectical materialism. When I returned home, I pleased Anita by saying that she resembled Mitzi Gaynor.

*

Theo,

Still in Verona, with Eros Ramazzotti.

Do you understand CIRCUS? My echelon? Circus largesse enfolds me, when, in the wings, I wait, ready to emcee.

Moira Orfei

*

Rainy afternoon alone at home. Mechanical Street deserted. Drunk on a bottle of Chinon, I wrote Moira Orfei a letter defending my understanding of things circus, rebutting her imputation that I was ignorant, unfit to appear beside her. For our performance, I require a stage; Moira requires a ring. Horses surround Aigues-Mortes. I didn't tell Moira Orfei, in my letter, that I lack the tonal precision of her illustrious compatriot, Arturo Benedetti Michelangeli, who tried, Lord knows, to teach me "secrets of the line," those he didn't already communicate in pillow talk to Alma, if I believe her philandering tales.

*

A wandering bum threatened Charlotte's daughter, Joyce Sante, my fellow childhood nudist. He had inscrutable hobo reasons to know and haunt Mechanical Street among equivalent local thoroughfares housing world-class musicians who'd give up their careers for love. Joyce is pregnant again; maybe she'll miscarry. She continues to get knocked up, though the fetuses are never viable. Charlotte is still sick with cervical cancer and ulcerative colitis. Mechanical Street grows seedy; a trannie hustler, Edna du Pré, formerly a regular in the water district, now works our sidewalk.

*

Theo,
Back in Aigues-Mortes. Consider the plight of the world's forsaken infants, dying from malnutrition, without circus stars to rescue them. I stayed up late last night, depressed, drinking scotch in my hotel lobby. Circus brings me up and down.
Moira Orfei

*

Derva Nile suffered a vocal breakdown last night, at a "performance" of Nuits d'été in my living room (we called it a performance, though only

Anita and Tanaquil were present). On the second syllable of "*reviens*" (come back) in the song "Absence," her voice broke; a fissure—incapacity—split the pitch, and I travelled miles down it. I called Buenos Aires to ask Alma about tunnels in missed notes. She'd once heard Jussi Björling's voice crack at the climax of "Di quella pira": time, a caged lion, shook. Then she told me about her urethra infection, imperiling *Goyescas*, and about her concert at Museo de Arte Hispanoamericano Isaac Fernández Blanco, and about Gertrude Guadalquivar's final incontinence. Stoppage, not leakage, worries me. Alma relishes illness, the surrounding talk. I have a melancholy relation to words. They fall away the moment I try to use them. Decline on the pianistic front is all I can foresee.

*

Theo,

I have briefly returned to Montecatini, where they are filming a documentary about me. It is a costume picture. In one scene, I wear a pink bunny outfit. In another, I dress as Clytemnestra and slay a circus Agamemnon. Finally, I occupy a ticket booth. Horny pathetic men wearing anoraks wait in line. The movie is an elegy for Mother.

The crew will follow me to Aigues-Mortes. The documentary, which I fear will remain unfinished, culminates in our performance.

When we first greet each other and embrace, in the Place Saint-Louis, the camera will record the great moment, beneath the king's statue. It is crucial that we not meet until the director is ready to film our reunion.

My performance will be impromptu. I don't want to give the public a canned Moira. I have always given them the real Moira, even if it hurts them.

Moira Orfei

*

I saw Dr. Crick yesterday for a physical. He asked if I was still seeing blood in the bowl. I said yes, every night, blood in the bowl. We agreed to speed up treatment. I don't know if my sex is "safe"—no one told me absolute rules. Tricks can be mum about fine points. When Dr. Crick asked me to lower my shorts so he could feel my genitals, I repressed a boner by thinking of Derva Nile's vocal failure. Dr. Crick knows everything about my condition but he has only seen me hard a few times and I would like to keep it that way.

*

Today I enter East Kill Hospital for treatment, registering under an alias: Thom Murdoch. Question: does Aigues-Mortes contain a Hotel de Anza?

Notebook Twenty-Two

When I woke in the hospital after surgery I remembered languidly swimming in the Hotel Flora pool, in Portbou, while my father, sitting on the balcony, watched; and I remembered seeing Charlotte Sante's crotch, across the street, accidentally, while passing her house at night, the bedroom shade momentarily opened, Charlotte standing on a bureau to lower the pull. Facts: loss of circulation, skin discoloration, numbness.

*

I left the hospital and returned to Mechanical Street. Then I rimmed Sing, at Statute of Limitations, in the water district, and called Alma in Buenos Aires to ask whether she sleeps with ex-Nazis or their children. Her answer was evasive, but she told me about her special afternoon concert in the Andalucian patio of the Jardín de los Poetas. My family keeps quiet about its sexual practices. Tanaquil never tells me her dreams anymore. Not for years have I shown her my genitals, or she shown me hers. Flashing was equilateral, though I instigated it.

*

Dear Theo,
Back in Aigues-Mortes. Its tiny red-light district won't sully our festival. Trucks from Montecatini have arrived: ring, tent.
Moira Orfei

*

I saw on the *East Kill Times* art page a small informational article, just an inch, announcing the Aigues-Mortes festival, and yet no exact description of what Moira Orfei planned to do. I was distressed to see Beethoven's *Tempest* Sonata mentioned. My bulemic student Devorah played it at her botched debut; she vomited on the keyboard. My friendship with words is over. Friedman called from Guadalajara, collect. Stranded, he wanted me to wire him money. He said, "Trust me, I'll pay you back," his voice gruff with the lie, the badinage, rings of deceit pulling him down. I can't save him. Through Western Union I wired him $500. Anita, overhearing, mentioned divorce, not for the first time. Fascist wife, she calls me incomprehensible. I thought she enjoyed confusion. Now she goes to Sunday mass: her Ackroyd roots are showing.

*

Theo,
Greetings from Aigues-Mortes. My circus act will resemble opium and will revive nine-teenth-century Paris. I suggested to the Aigues-Mortes town fathers that they rechristen their central arcade "Galerie Vivienne Retrouvée."
Moira Orfei

*

I'm lost: I should be thinking about Moira Orfei's Galerie Vivienne Retrouvée, olive-oil soap in the arcades, mille-feuilles she is eating at the Hotel Constance café, increasing racket of the bandstand hammered into place in the town plaza. Instead I spend afternoons lying in bed with Friedman, back from Guadalajara, where a wealthy oil man kept him prisoner for a week. Friedman's chest hair has begun to go grey, though he is not yet thirty. The Guadalajara oil man was "abusive," Friedman said, in a drugged tone, as if he were singing Fauré's "Après un rêve," and were limited to that song for the rest of his life.

In Paris, the impasse Maubert, near the former house of a revolutionary poisoner, I learned the news of my ill health, details I promptly forgot. I concealed from Alma my trip's diagnostic purpose. I told her that I was performing Chopin at the Polish embassy.

*

Theo,

What happened to your "regime of pleasure"? Your two-hour naps on the white sofa in Montecatini?

Chloe borrowed my green chiffon for her leukemia benefit and hasn't returned it.

My spine is sore—lingering after-effect of a road accident in Rome.

Moira Orfei

*

Moira Orfei's postcards confuse me. An Agrigento postcard is postmarked Barcelona. A Bruges postcard is postmarked Atrani. A Montecatini postcard is postmarked Monte Carlo.

Moira Orfei must be counterfeiting the postmarks. The international circus cartel has its own mail machinery, protecting Moira Orfei from detection. She can postmark as she pleases. Soon I fly to Nice.

*

After reading (without my permission) the Aigues-Mortes notebooks, Anita filed for legal separation. She left the house, and will call later for her possessions. Let's leave legal quandaries for another notebook. I will give Anita generous alimony, from my "butter" holdings; she can build a new life, as a musical comedy actress on local stages. I'll miss the occasional good day's rear entry. Anita once said, "You and A. E. Housman. You and the other boy-lovers. Fine. Just give me an evening's peace, my TV programs undisturbed." She considers me a "rape victim, minus the rape." I tell her not to take the name of rape in vain. She blames her miscarriages on my concert schedule. I was not present to ease her load: in my absence, she moved a refrigerator. I don't mourn those two fetuses. It's difficult to mourn a figment, without a career to back it up.

*

Friedman brought his mother, Samantha, to an after-hours bar, Destiny, a white stucco cottage in the water district. She looks like Hope

Lange, tall, blonde, eyelifts, elite jaw. She put her arm around Friedman and seemed his erotic buddy. Suddenly she wept. I assured her that infection was no longer fatal. She said, "Oh, as long as he uses sunblock, I'm not worried about his skin." I suggested that his medical problems were complicated. She repeated her sunscreen injunction and pointed to a place on her nose where pre-cancer had been removed. She was educated at Salt Manor, a finishing school. She mentioned a daughter, a debutante in Redwood City. Samantha split her time between California and Corfu. She said that I should fly to Corfu and give a concert: "Bring Friedman. If I can drag you boys to Corfu, I'm gonna set you up in a beach hut. Forget the main house. I want you boys in a hut." I could picture the trail leading from her cottage on Corfu to an impoverished beach shack—without running water or septic system—where Friedman and I would fornicate all day, repairing at night to Samantha's house for elaborate catered dinners. I could picture her sending a servant in the evenings to fetch us from our hut, and I could imagine her tearfulness, when we arrived at the house. Weeping at the after-hours bar, she said, "I see Friedman as an anthologist, collecting moments in other people's lives, never his own."

*

I bought a performance outfit for Aigues-Mortes: blue leather moccasins and purple velvet suit. Velvet might be too heavy for spring in the Camargue. If I appear feminine on the Aigues-Mortes festival stage, Moira might get bored in the middle of our act and break off the alliance.

*

Theo,

The world may call you "fortune hunter" but pay no heed.

At the Hotel de Anza without you I remembered your insistence on being yourself and I could not bear to rue that insistence, though the world regretted it, that "world" you declare your enemy, and mine.

Moira Orfei

*

I am known for delicate touch, but is it any great shakes? When was the
last time a reviewer praised it? My playing, as a critic in Nice once wrote,
"lacks imagination." I'm preserved only by Alma's charity, and her
coterie's. I lack proof that my New York debut was not a disaster. My students don't win international competitions. As sexual dynamo I have a
claim to fame, though in Aigues-Mortes I must prove my pianism once
more.

At least I'm not as desperate as Tanaquil, who, late in her reproduc-
tive cycle, now wants a baby. I can't imagine Tanaquil holding an infant,
or helping it bloom into a toddler. Thinking aloud, Tanaquil said to me
last night, "Would Alma attend the christening? She'd ruin it. I'll time
the baby's birth so it occurs while Alma tours."

Tanaquil and I used to talk about murdering Charlotte across the
street—how convenient, we decided, to have a crime under our belts.
Murder, a cleansing thought, bleached ambiguities, like the time that
Joyce Sante, nude, poured Clorox over my scheming head.

*

Theo,
Your room is booked. I will wear a sari for my final prestidigitation.
Moira Orfei

*

Even though Aigues-Mortes approaches, and even though it hurt, I let
Friedman enter me—with one condom. He went more deeply than any
escort. As he bumped repeatedly against my insides, I thought about
courses I had failed in college. (After the *conservatoire*, I studied pre-med
at East Kill University, to rebel against Guadalquivar tastes.) Chemistry.
Calculus. Biology. Perhaps if Friedman regularly humiliated me, my
Ravel would improve.

The next day, I visited Matilda in Boston. While she knitted a ski
sweater for Lu, I talked about Anita's departure. Matilda, relieved,

changed the subject: "Some of my anally centered friends are dead, but that's no reason to starve yourself."

Later that afternoon she put her finger up me: Matilda seemed to be expressing Alma's will, a message from Buenos Aires. (I had indigestion for a few hours afterward.) At this enjoyable, intimate moment, Matilda did not emphasize that she was my aunt—she posed as a neutral helper, a woman with technique. Her finger imitated the pedagogy I was trying to spread through East Kill's musical circles, an emphasis on initiation. When students play for conservatory juries, they should focus on a melody's beginning: the first note is the most difficult. At least we pianists don't have to worry about intonation. I wonder about Aigues-Mortes weather. How many sweaters should I bring?

*

Theo,

While waiting for you, I plan a future without circus. I'll circulate a brochure: "Psychic Reading by Moira Orfei. You owe it to yourself to consult this gifted lady. Come today to Montecatini." Why advance?

Moira Orfei

*

I once played the Liszt Sonnambula transcription while Moira Orfei did an act celebrating "The Real." I understand Moira Orfei's beauty, so I needn't sweat over Aigues-Mortes. I can count on her Jean Marais act, trapeze feats timed to film clips. Our performances never include sex, though I played a fellatio recital in Troy, New York: Beethoven's second piano sonata, its opening theme's chiming thirds sodomitic.

*

Theo,

I will spin in synchrony with your first memory of the possibility that you were a reincarnation of a former, more humiliated person, whose shame you would reverse in your own hard-working life.

Moira Orfei

*

In high school I had a crush on my geometry teacher, Mr. Leopold Brash, with a French nose. Rosicrucian, he told the class that he was the descendant—nay, the reincarnation—of a man who once owned East Kill's water district. I started going to clubs when I was fifteen. I must stop relying on Alfonso Reyes as go-between. If I were practical, I would e-mail Moira Orfei, but she has chosen postcards instead, a more passionate route. She, too, fears technology. Friedman once asked why I don't call Moira Orfei directly. Answer: I don't have her telephone number. My conversation upsets her. And the documentary filmmaker forbids Moira and me to speak before we actually meet.

*

Theo,
  I write to you from the hotel. I can't say which—not yet. Aigues-Mortes natives don't understand history. Our performance will help them remember what you called our "imbrication," our helpless—yet engagé—relation to emergencies, like Montecatini air raids my family endured. Chloe, who has become my manager, wants to begin planning the fall season, but first I must live through Aigues-Mortes, slowly. Chloe has never imbibed circus. She has no eye for the sacrosanct. She demotes my act to "dream."
  Moira Orfei

*

I've never used the word "imbrication" in my life. I'd never say "imbrication" in Atrani's Hotel de Anza while drinking negronis and cheering up Moira Orfei. I know what she means by history, however. I bear its brunt. My father was a small man, and yet my mother believed in his seed's latent greatness. "I never had a problem getting pregnant with Thom," she often said. Her lazy eggs could sit around for days, and eventually admit one adequate tadpole. That is the "history" that Moira and I, in performance, will revisit.

*

Again I enter the hospital for what Dr. Crick says resembles shock treatment but is not precisely that. He wants to shake up water-logged habits.
He is also worried about my blood: "We have entered the unreasonable."
Giving blood, I used to be frightened, until I found a doctor with whom
I was half-comfortable being erect. These are not the health and sickness notebooks but I take the liberty of mentioning shock treatment. I
wake up afterward dazed but refreshed, ready for Aigues-Mortes.

Notebook Twenty-Three

Dear Moira Orfei,

Dr. Crick gave me shock treatment, but don't be alarmed. I'm ready for rendezvous. I speed this medical bulletin to Aigues-Mortes with every expectation that you might not receive it before you see me in May, though our postal life, these months, has been charmed, fleet, immediate.

Slowly,
Theo Mangrove

*

I feel guilty that I haven't mentioned Moira Orfei's gladiator films. Listing them might help me behave like a more subservient associate to Moira's trapeze antics, which she has called, in an earlier postcard, "our circus of memory."

The Two Gladiators
Ursus
Terror of the Steppes
Totò and Cleopatra
Rocco and His Sisters
Hercules Returns
The Triumph of Hercules
The Birds, the Bees, and the Italians
Samson and the Slave Queen

In *Triumph of Hercules*, playing sorceress Pasiphae, mother of evil Prince Milo, Moira materializes, ageless, out of a red smoke cloud, and says, "I am Pasiphae, sorceress. I come to you from a cloud, and give you the magic sword."

*

On top of everything I'm coping with (shock treatment, bad blood, dis-ordered stomach, numb extremities), I must take a train to New York City to meet my "butter" executors on Fifty-Seventh Street, to ensure that they keep my accounts liquid. The Aigues-Mortes notebooks need a detailed cash-flow chart.

*

Theo,

I posed on a rock yesterday, outside Aigues-Mortes walls, for a local photographer. The photo will be a study in difference, how I can look like three separate women, how I can face in disparate directions and yet still remain unitary. First (following his instructions) I turned my back to the camera. Then I looked down at the rock. Then I stared up at the sky. I wore a backless dress. Modest, it obliterated my personality. The shoot was a huge production—we spent hours on hair and makeup, three girls helping. I am an old-fashioned star, afraid of haphazard preparations. I arrived in Aigues-Mortes before necessity called—to absorb the view from the parapets, to see where the Crusaders walked, on the verge of inflicting cruelty.

History slows me down. Tigers, not yet tamed, are quick: they know your tempo.

Moira Orfei

*

From the Guadalquivars I inherited euphemism: I can mingle with all echelons, from café society to the destitute, and can drift in and out of realism with the deftness of Dr. Crick's tongue depressor. Moira thinks I love her simply because she is famous, but I, child of a musical star, am indifferent to celebrity. I hope the reader (if there is ever a reader) will forgive my occasional use of well-known names, which I include for documentary reasons; real names pacify. Here I give you a semi-public record of how a musician, avoiding and approaching a destination, exists in time.

"Your tragic months," Alma calls my current interstice—awaiting Aigues-Mortes. Blank time immobilizes happy me.

*

Theo,

If you find me weeping in the Aigues-Mortes arcades, you will understand how history hunkers down on the circus-affiliated.

Moira Orfei

*

The last time Alma called, she said, "Critics here give me a bum rap." She said that if I treated Aigues-Mortes as a task, then I would certainly fail. She should record a boxed set of Beethoven's thirty-two sonatas, to rival Barenboim's and Schnabel's. A going-haywire desire for immortality upsets her platform poise. She has sex-addict tendencies, too. She wants a museum of her own; she is jealous of my plans for a Moira Orfei Living Museum in Montecatini. On the phone I didn't mention shock treatment, trembling hands, dehydration. Alma had hoped that the Pablo Casals Museum in San Juan would commemorate her—shadow box, vitrine, or wax mannequin, illustrating her sonata work with the cellist. Marta Casals, the widow, nixed the Alma diorama.

*

Theo,

In Aigues-Mortes, I begin to flower, behind your back, though I don't mean to deceive or precede you, or commence performance without your in-person assistance, ambiguous friend.

Moira Orfei

*

Despite dehydration, I visited Matilda: philanthropist, cultural leader, erotic chameleon. Practicing mime, she wore all-white makeup. As we took off her kimono, she murmured, "I want a vacation." I remembered, with an unpleasant flash, the first time I caressed her breasts beneath her Louise Brooks hairdo. My foreplay bored her. She said, "Lu thinks I've had a face lift." Indeed, her forehead had lost its frown lines. We began our sporadic, sacrosanct liaison soon after I turned twenty. Yesterday her breasts seemed to melt: guttering-candle hallucination. Xenia Lamont's breasts also melted in my hands. Dissolving breasts might ruin my Liszt performance in Aigues-Mortes. Moroccan fabrics cloaked Matilda's walls and floors. She said, "I'm not a gay man, Theo," but turned over anyway. I committed the usual desecration. Suddenly she played the incest card, calling our behavior indecent. I told her that I am above the age of discretion. Ritual heals. I pointed to the parlor, which she calls the masturbation shack. Each room in her house is consecrated to a separate function: a room for studying, a room for screwing, a room for designing.

If I have ruined my relation with Matilda, then I will memorize Rachmaninoff's First Piano Concerto tomorrow: expanded repertoire equals ethical bulimia.

*

Theo,

Aigues-Mortes, soon to occur, is life or death, not casual, not incidental, not a mere stop on a tour. Its largeness appalls me when I sit on my hotel balcony and look at the tower, the marshes—toward Spain and other confusions.

Please verify my vision.

Moira Orfei

*

I wrote back to verify. The town walls of Aigues-Mortes are fortified and composed of towers, so there are no ambiguities about being *in* Aigues-Mortes. Aigues-Mortes is like a hotel room; you have either checked in, or you have checked out. There is no middle ground. I lack a complete list of Aigues-Mortes hotels. A Hotel de Anza in Aigues-Mortes would rescue me from this dismal situation.

*

Tanaquil and I drove to Long Island and visited Gertrude Guadalquivar's house, recently sold. Her furniture was still there. Pain medications on a Bauhaus bedside table. Her own paintings—André Derain imitations. On a prie-dieu, books mentioning her: novelettes by Salvador Dalí, Darius Milhaud, Simone de Beauvoir. Gertrude liked leaflets: they moved quickly. As I looked out her bedroom's window onto the park, its fruit trees unblooming (the coldest winter in decades), I recalled my ungenerous distaste for Gertrude's final incontinence.

Downstairs, on the way out, Tanaquil and I found the Venetian glass candelabra that appears in the photograph where Alma seems happy. I took the contentment candelabra back to East Kill.

Gertrude's death-hallowed chamber moved me, but I will be unable to explain this experience to Moira Orfei. Fatigue eats away at my feeble, undemonstrative playing. My recent Scriabin run-through at Trinity Church gave pleasure (so Derva said) to AIDS sufferers and their compatriots, gathered in the church, by arrangement with the hospital, to hear the effeminate Russian's excursion beyond the tonal pale. For encore, I played Liszt's "Au lac de Wallenstadt." During passagework, a catastrophe occurred, just as in Monte Carlo six years ago: I felt a spasm of immobilizing panic, and for a fraction of a second—no more—my fingers stopped mid-air, uncertain where next to proceed. I regained control, but the lapse haunts me; when I mentioned it to Tanaquil, as we stood in our late grandmother's bedroom, she said, with uncharacteristic seriousness, "What Jews went through in World War Two keeps repeating, throughout the world, onstage and off, and will never cease its repetitions until the sins of the perpetrators have been expiated." Tanaquil rarely mentions Jews; I didn't know that she cared about destroyed people. She said that my lapse, during Liszt, was not an accident. God planned it.

When, later, I told Alma about the lapse, she said, "How like you," and mentioned her planned trip to Iguazú Falls. I vow to restrain my effusions.

*

Theo,

Mystery!

Your last letter was illegible.

I never wanted to mention this to you before: you appear to me as a blur, more often than as a person.

Where "person" should be, sometimes I find mist.

Moira Orfei

*

Dr. Crick wants me to fast. I ignored the tray of breakfast dainties that Derva Nile brought to my bed, where I am convalescing. Black tea will satisfy, and a Fleet Phospho-soda purge at 5:00. Aigues-Mortes demands austerity. Derva has become aesthetically opinionated. Tonight, her face seems divided, one half smiling, the other frowning, like schizophrenic patients attending my Trinity Church concerts. Derva says that pastiche is our time's reigning artform. I disagree. Pastiche is tresses caught in your mouth when you air-kiss a great lady at a cocktail party.

*

Theo,

Aigues-Mortes is "on"—alive with wonders and visitors.

I am sitting in a nightclub, Passé Composé, outside the walls of Aigues-Mortes, in the new development: sometimes I need to breathe recent, other air.

Genius has been re-bestowed to me, under the aegis of downfall. Call it rage, fear, premonition: it rushes back into my hands and legs, as I see trapeze artists warm up and elephants circle the ring, dancers upon them—a rehearsal so rigorous it seems our final performance.

A storm knocked down Aigues-Mortes telephone lines for a few days but that did not matter, because I have not used the phone in a full year. Can you imagine my peace of mind? The quiet, in which to contemplate what went wrong!

Moira Orfei

*

I demonstrated spectacular competence in my Aigues-Mortes run-through (the Liszt program) at a church in Springs, a memorial concert for Gertrude Guadalquivar. Few attended. Tanaquil made the trip. Her presence was enough. Though I began life loving the baroque, near the end I prefer Liszt's sick insincerity. Music is acoustics, not willpower: music exists in space only because time already gave its retractable blessing.

*

Theo,

Do you remember the first "splash" we made—how noisy and unheralded it was, and how it threatened to overhaul our past and send it in an opposite, painful direction, as at the road-side restaurant you took me to, outside Catania, after we played the opera house, shocking the Catanese with our conflation of opera and circus, our theft of Britten's "Rape of Lucretia"?

May I occupy your ear?

The longer I spend here, alone, preparing, the more my old spirit emerges, and I become the flame, not merely its witness.

Moira Orfei

*

Moira Orfei won't be offended if I discuss erotic grooming rituals. Working with Kirk Morris, Dan Vadis, and other gladiator he-men, she witnessed shiny oiled male smoothness. At his loft, Friedman shaved off most of my body hair; we are eager to see me resemble a boy. Now his masculinity exceeds mine, as Alma's recording of Milhaud's *Cinq études* outshines mine. I don't wish to overpraise Friedman's penis size and semi-Semitic features, or to take seriously his claims to be a healer. He said that I looked fatigued, after my recent "shock treatment," to use Dr. Crick's phrase. My last exam showed micropolyps and abrasions. I blew Friedman, while, in a cubbyhole, his mother slept off her hangover.

*

Dear Theo,

The other evening at the Aigues-Mortes Cinémathèque I saw René Clair's 1930 film "Sous les toits de Paris," starring Albert Préjean in the role of Albert, and Pola Somebody in the role of Pola. I remembered a Europe ruined by war, and my family's connection to Albert Préjean's music-hall artistry and to such forgotten trifles (they nourish me!) as Reynaldo Hahn's operetta "Ciboulette."

I finally understand my fatherland. Europe was torn apart, made wintry, at the end of WWII; each family, including mine, saw its edges frayed.

Thank you for the Satie morceaux. I will devise movements—war-torn leaps—to accompany them.

Moira Orfei

*

The early pin-up stars of *Mandate*—Max Jordan, Lee Ryder, Miles O'Keefe, Bob Free—could not have helped my career or saved me from disease. Illness taught me how to play Chopin. Reading Moira Orfei's letter, thinking of war as our *modus operandi*, I remembered that pianism equals epilepsy—not mine, but Wendy's, the sheet-pale girl who fell on the *conservatoire* lawn in an unchecked fit because she had worked too hard preparing Beethoven sonatas for junior-year juries. Rumor: she miscarried. I, her teacher, had demonstrated the *Appassionata* Sonata's last movement; after the lesson she convulsed on the lawn. Looking out my studio window, I saw her contortions. My tyrannical approach to the *Appassionata* was to blame. It inflicted Guadalquivar standards on an innocent junior not ready to play three sonatas, the *Appassionata*, the *Pastoral*, and op. 110. A *conservatoire* nurse put a dowel between Wendy's teeth so she would not bite off her tongue.

The next week, Wendy returned for a lesson. We replaced op. 110 with Chopin's First Impromptu, which she had learned over the summer. Surveillance destroys artistry: unsupervised students do best work. Wendy's boyfriend was a large-limbed trombonist, Manfred. I'd seen them necking in the Navajo hut, a refreshment stand in the conservatory atrium, while I snacked on sweet coconut shavings.

*

Theo,

Only Aigues-Mortes—city we must face, never turning away—is the properly austere backdrop to what Chloe calls our lewdness. What riposte can I give the precipice? Let lewdness be the fins of our transit through Aigues-Mortes's blue, dead, salt waters.

Moira Orfei

*

Sinus headache. Alma called yesterday from Buenos Aires. She told me that she played a disappointing concert of Haydn sonatas at Nunciatura Apostólica. Charlie Chaplin's death was, for her, a fresh wound; he attended her recital at Wigmore Hall, and, afterward, at dinner, groped her under the table, despite Oona's presence. I told Alma I was diligently preparing Aigues-Mortes, and she said, "Diligence won't help. Rely on lightning bolts." She never properly trained me to use thumb as impersonal masculine lever rather than as sensitive girl-digit. Although she must guess that I have squandered my Guadalquivar mind, she mentioned Milhaud's opus 295 piano concerto as a possibility for Aigues-Mortes; I told her that opus 295, a staple of her repertoire, was not part of mine. I would make do with the catchy Poulenc, its first movement suggesting a Citroën I will never drive, a nude race-car-driver I will never lie beside. Perhaps I will attempt the piano solo role in Messiaen's *Turangalîla-Symphonie*, with pick-up band, and Moira Orfei's trapeze oscillations and interpretive tamings.

I reminded Alma of my multiple infections: bad blood and nerve decay might impede my return to the European concert stage, even with a circus star shielding me from critique. Sage Alma said, "Reality never stopped a Guadalquivar," her voice low and sultry, below the *bel canto* "break," the tightrope of shame. She called me "naïve" (was she drunk?) for loving reality.

Alma, don't vanish forever into Argentina's pampas. When you describe your blissful isolation, I picture tundra. Let me join you. Do you notice how I spring to life when I hear your advice, how I return to what you kindly (delusionally) call my "gift"? You make me wish that Tanaquil and I had installed a spiral staircase on Mechanical Street, in your absence, to inspire you, upon return, with a wish to overcome vertigo, a syndrome you acquired as a girl in Paris, atop the Tour Eiffel, before the first time you played the Fauré Ballade (solo version) for Nadia Boulanger. Henceforth Fauré's spiralling passagework numbed your masculine wish for outcome, samba, tango—a rhythm you impose on any piece, even Mozart or Caplet. "Let it *seem* a tango," you told me, when I played the Webern Variations.

Alma, the azaleas on Mechanical Street are in bloom. When you played Rachmaninoff's First Concerto with the Baltimore Symphony, I stood, a schoolchild on vacation, mesmerized, watching in the wings. Touring Appalachia, you brought piano to the underprivileged and the bored.

*

Theo,

I reign over circus, whose ring divides my heart. Trapped in trapeze, I long to imitate your free rendition (in Marseilles) of a Liszt Hungarian Rhapsody, its trumped-up patriotism. Dispossession's anthem: Father taught me to forget the country one hates to love.

In Aigues-Mortes, please play the piano fantasy based on Georges Auric's score to "Lola Montès," the movie that describes my situation, that paints Father, Mother, Chloe, me. Auric's piped-in music, my Muzak, confines me in things circus.

Moira Orfei

*

I spent my evenings this week in Friedman's loft, getting sucked off by his friend Manny, an HIV-positive stud sleeping there for a few nights while waiting for side effects of his latest medications to calm down. I fear him and his devoted mother, Ada, staying in Friedman's loft to supervise her ill son. Once a top-flight modern dancer, she retains a good figure; she walks around the apartment naked. I barged into the bathroom and caught her *in medias res.* She is a good friend of Friedman's mother, Samantha, also in temporary residence. Too many mothers crashed in the loft: must I please them all? After I intruded on Ada's bathroom repose, Manny said, "Let me suck your cock"—within Ada's hearing!—but I said no, it was irritated, I need to return home to work on the *Lola Montès* medley. My forearms are rigid with tendinitis, a paralysis recalling my breakdown five years ago in Carpentras, where mauraders desecrated Jewish graves; playing Liszt's Second Piano Concerto with the Carpentras Chamber Orchestra, I lost my place in a *vivamente* cadenza. Years ago, at a Fontainebleau memorial concert for Wanda Landowska and her loyal girlfriend, whose name I can't recall, my teacher Nadia Boulanger warned me against the repertoire of excess. She also said, "Didn't you sometimes want to spank Wanda, despite her greatness?" How right Nadia was; I should have followed her advice and avoided Carpentras.

*

Theo,

Yes to the Ravel "Sonatine"! I seek indifferent fields, wet Cádiz, penal Seville, specious Bruges, anywhere but France, any outposts where crusaders could forget their pledge not to dwell on the past. I'm a women felled by "religioso" swords. Are trances good for my career, Chloe wonders, but I have stepped beyond "career," beyond audience, hoop, elephant, and trapeze; I now reach toward flames I long ago vowed to stop swallowing, and toward baubles encircling my neck—gems not paste, not real.

Moira Orfei

*

A Russian pianist I once loved, Peter Razumovsky, who looked like Rudolf Nureyev, died on the rue de Seine two years ago; Peter's Slavic face (shaped like the marriage of parallelogram and egg), his Czerny-won finger independence, and his shirt opened to the waist—fashionable then—"slayed" me, though he was just an *American Gigolo* likeness, not an original, not a husband. He called my sexual style "immature." To Alma, I described Peter Razumovsky's charms, but they failed to interest her. Now I find, on www.internationalescort.com, an Aix-en-Provence stud (Fabien) resembling the Peter Razumovsky who wore Knize Ten cologne and called me "Ice Princess," the Peter Razumovsky I've failed to render in decades of notebooks: before the Aigues-Mortes notebooks, I kept Marseilles notebooks, Trapani notebooks, Nice notebooks, Montecatini notebooks, Portbou notebooks.

Notebook Twenty-Four

Theo:
One word.
Barcelona.
M. Orfei

*

The Orfei cartel dominates the Barcelona circus underground. Perhaps Moira's been kidnapped. She may have already returned to Aigues-Mortes or Montecatini. I'm hemorrhaging. Given my recent paralysis at the Liszt run-through in Springs, Long Island, should I cancel Aigues-Mortes? Absolutely not. Cancellation would be career suicide. Aigues-Mortes, swallow me with adulation. Moira Orfei has spent weeks there, preparing clowns, mules, tumblers, elephants, horses, midgets, zebras, dogs, sea lions, monkeys, Brazilian mules, brown and black bears, jumping llamas, cream ponies, and white doves.

*

Theo,

I keep a publicity photo of myself on my hotel's bedside table, to remind me of the past. But I think of you, not only of myself: I get choked up when I remember your Viareggio "Carnaval." In Aigues-Mortes you'll regain that level.

Why isn't a Nobel Prize awarded for circus? Swedes shortchange acrobatic sublimity. Didn't the Flying Concellos deserve lauds? Babette? Agube Gudzow? May Wirth?

People falsely assume I'm jealous of Wanda Osiris.

When I enter, a flock of white doves surrounds me, their feathers a cloud.

Moira Orfei

*

From Buenos Aires, Alma described a potential ulcer and a miserable afternoon spent wandering the cemetery, La Recoleta, seeking Guadalquivars. Gaining weight, she may be barred from concert stages. Untrustworthy Buenos Aires physicians find her ailments psychosomatic, and so she wants to return to East Kill to see Dr. Crick; she tires of Helen Jole's psychoanalytic listmaking, despite the bougainvillea-clad office near Plaza Güemes. Alma mentioned her upcoming concert at the Musée Saint-John Perse in Guadeloupe. A louche branch of the Guadalquivars settled in Basse-Terre and remained ne'er-do-wells, prostitutes. If Alma had moved us to Basse-Terre, she said, I'd be selling underwear, not playing piano.

She asked about illness and Aigues-Mortes: is it forthcoming? Have you adequately prepared? I told her that though Moira sends postcards nearly every day, she never indicates precise whereabouts. Alma insisted I quickly fly to Aigues-Mortes: "Why dilly-dally? Are you overdoing the Cabernet?" Truth is, I'm abusing Percocet. She called me "catatonic schizophrenic." She finally understands Aigues-Mortes, realizes I'm warden of Moira Orfei's public ecstasies. Alma mentioned the seamy Aigues-Mortes underbelly: arms-traders, mercenaries, smugglers, drug-dealers, money-launderers, pimps. Perhaps the Mafia has imprisoned Moira.

Friedman massaged my prostate; over Mechanical Street, a sickle moon shone. He asked me to clarify the performance that Moira Orfei and I plan to give. I'll coordinate Ravel's *Sonatine* with Moira's horses doing the Levade and the Capriole; I'll match Messiaen's *Petites esquisses d'oiseaux* to Moira's bird-dance on the wire; I'll play Liszt's "Orage" while Moira manages the sea-lions' anger. "Ark-ark-ark," I cried, imitating her underlings, while Friedman repeatedly brought me toward orgasm and away: I paved a tantra route, recirculating heat into my Crick-opiated chakras, enjoying gelatinous *interruptus* in thighs, testicles, and rectum, like wanting to dynamite a neighbor's house or a concert hall, and leaving me this morning with a bad case of blue balls. With my remaining days before Aigues-Mortes I will abstain from prostate massages and from all drugs not prescribed by Dr. Crick. My virtuosity will appall Alma, unflappable mistress of the "Lugubrious Gondola." Moira Orfei understands that my hands, though not huge, are powerful. Wrongly I've forced piano to imitate violin, bird, gunshot, and waterfall, but have avoided innate gruesome "Tarantella" sounds. Guilty, I flee the present: didn't a great American conductor say that waltzes were kaput? Why agree with that racist maestro? Follow Moira Orfei's example. Waltz—Moira Orfei's famous Andalusian surrender to three-quarter time—is why the Aigues-Mortes committee invited me to dominate.

*

Sultry Derva Nile—ally, subordinate, love—has reserved me two flights: Barcelona, Nice. Meanwhile Brad Olney has promised to compose me a piano concerto based on the lives of Jeffrey Dahmer and Joseph Cornell. Maybe Brad wrote Alma a concerto, which she's performing behind my back at a Buenos Aires *tanguería*. Today I bought a plastic see-through tux shirt at Jacob's Ladder: performance outfit.

When a local heiress, Arletty, who resembles the young Elizabeth Taylor in *Rhapsody,* and who runs a publishing house, Slumber Press, heard that I was keeping notebooks (twenty-four, so far) on Aigues-Mortes preparations, in the event that my reunion with Moira Orfei becomes historic, Arletty offered to print a facsimile limited edition. Slumber Press recently published Artur Schnabel's appointment calendar. Arletty can do good business with my notebooks, which represent, she says, "the situation of fallen boy." I will donate the original notebooks to the Moira Orfei Living Museum, once I found it.

*

Theo,

You never told me about your family. I regret their tenuousness: they are difficult to hold in the mind. Was not "confusion," from that first rendezvous at the Montecatini bandstand, our rapport's rivet? Did not "confusion" follow us to Catania? Has not "confusion"—and its antidote, "love"—been the slow path leading us directly to tomorrow, to Aigues-Mortes, where I remain, prepared, stunned, anticipating? Elephants, monkeys, dogs, ponies, tigers, and seals have been trained; trapeze artists, clowns, midgets and magicians hold themselves aloft. Afternoons in my hotel, I nap away nervousness. I grow to tolerate the sand wines.

Moira Orfei

*

For morning warm-up I played a *Per Aspera* Moszkowski virtuosity study, and then said farewell to Tanaquil. Shivering, she refused to see Dr. Crick; her own disreputable physician, Gaston Lair, says that she does not have a relapse of "red brain." She suffers from anemia, vertigo, vaginismus, and agoraphobia. Dr. Crick praises my fugue states: all great pianists have dissociative amnesia. I lack nerve to try Liszt's Second Concerto with the Aigues-Mortes festival orchestra; in Carpentras, the *vivamente* cadenza paralyzed me. To erase coma, I must re-enter it.

*

Theo,

You and I will be Aigues-Mortes headliners together and redeem the past, our separate pasts, each flawed, and the new, present past we are piecemeal constructing together.

I won't address your mistakes, only your successes—the time you played the Mephisto Waltz in La Spezia's public gardens, near the gulf. I nearly fainted as you began, but I recovered spirit, and entered the ring, with midgets, for my biased act.

Moira Orfei

*

Unspecified time has passed—"nervous breakdown days," Tanaquil calls them. I won't discuss my hospitalization, aphasia, hand paralysis, urinary incontinence, pregnancy hallucinations, "borderline" diagnosis, subsequent rescinding of hasty diagnosis, cancellation of my appearance as headliner at the Aigues-Mortes festival and then re-instatement, postcards from Moira Orfei *not* forwarded to me at the East Kill Hospital, my failed attempts (from the back ward) to contact Moira via Alfonso Reyes, Dr. Crick's refusal to let me call Chloe, hours of television in the rec room with the other morons, Tanaquil's refusal to visit (hospitals, like funeral parlors, upset her), Friedman's visit . . .

"You never initiate social arrangements," Friedman told me at the hospital. East Kill society has dropped me. Men in the water district are dying. Friedman noticed my disappearing voice and told me not to overuse it. He quoted his mother: "Remember Corfu." She counts on our visit.

The hospital gave me a single bed (as if I weren't famous enough for a double), and a blanket the color of our Mechanical Street house: Dreamsicle.

Alma telephoned once. She described her performance of the Joaquín Nin-Culmell *Tonadas* at Palacio San Martín and told me to keep open the pipeline to madness. She named two of her yearly hospitalizations: the 1965 nervous exhaustion after playing César Franck's *Les Djinns* in Kyoto; the 1966 nervous exhaustion after playing Ernst von Dohnányi's *Variations on a Nursery Song* in Lima. She plans to appraise the Guadalquivar jewels—Gertrude's. Who owns them? My glans burns.

*

Theo,
Where are you?
Remember: mist is our modus operandi.
Moira Orfei

*

This afternoon, an unseasonably warm early spring day, I played Liszt's B Minor Sonata at the East Kill Hospital, a concert in the central courtyard garden. I wanted to tell the crocuses that they would die in a fortnight, and that during their brief existence they would not universally delight staff and patients. I wanted to tell the crocuses that I was cruel to use them as scapegoats, but my attention drifted to the audience, waiting for me to begin the Liszt, which turned into another display of what Alma calls my "egregious athleticism." Liszt emigrates from melody into noise. Tanaquil visited the hospital to say goodbye.

Derva Nile has cancelled my flight to Barcelona but not my flight to Nice. I will show up in Aigues-Mortes when I show up.

*

Theo,

Climbing the Tour de Constance, its walls twenty feet thick, I remember Protestants imprisoned here for thirty years; outside the town walls, heaps of salt await.

My languid camels will echo the Revocation of the Edict of Nantes.

1248, 1270: in a trance, I see St. Louis, in Aigues-Mortes, sending forth Crusaders, and embarking, himself, on the fruitless expedition of extermination, from which he never returned . . .

Moira Orfei

*

I left the hospital, returned home to Mechanical Street. My left ear doesn't work. Dr. Crick came this afternoon to set up the care situation. Derva Nile drops in to nurse. Soon I'll fly to Nice and drive a rented car to Aigues-Mortes. I may choose not to mention Moira Orfei in the following notebooks. Will I find her in Aigues-Mortes, or will she have already departed? Certain dreams have lapsed, Alma said, on the phone, and yet she was referring only to her final performance of Xavier Montsalvatge's *Tres Divertimentos* and *Sonatine pour Yvette* at the Teatro Coliseo in Buenos Aires, a city whose musical community, she fears, has turned against her, as if against every consummation.

Did the remembered, corrugated fabric of Alma's maternity blouse (when pregnant with Tanaquil) provoke my return to Fauré's preludes, as if no time had elapsed, and as if my reunion with Moira Orfei were not hopelessly compromised? Would there be a memorial service, in Aigues-Mortes, for the Aigues-Mortes festival that never transpired, or would the comeback take place, an impromptu execution, without premeditation? I will ask Moira Orfei, when I see her in Aigues-Mortes, what acrobatics she has planned to accompany my performance of the preludes.

Notebook Twenty-Five

Theo,

My hotel room is equipped with a video monitor, and I have been reseeing my films, with disappointment. They are not as great as I had remembered. I envy the career of Brigitte Bardot, lucky enough to work with better directors. Of course I had Visconti and Godard, among others, but not always, and sometimes the director was powerless to save the production. Watching the gladiator picture I made with Eric Rohmer gives me no pleasure.

And yet I would not exchange my career with Brigitte Bardot's. In "Contempt," her longest film, she reveals her buttocks. In this scene, as I recall, she is lying on her stomach, waiting for something or someone—waiting, as you once put it, "for meaning to arrive." It never showed up. Brigitte may not have been happy to expose her buttocks but lo and behold they appear. I will ask her, the next time we meet, whether she was pleased to exhibit them, and whether she wishes she could eradicate her earlier mistakes.

Moira Orfei

*

Theo,

Resurrection is not too much to hope for. Healing, contemplating my errors, I wait in Aigues-Mortes. I look down at my body and see, beneath the beauty, scars. Traumatized by circus, I remember you watching me tap-dance on a straw hat in Seville. The whip cracks! The show begins!

Moira Orfei

*

Moira Orfei gives no forwarding address. It is her nature never to mention an address. If I were able reliably to write to her, she would not be Moira Orfei, circus eminence. Today is her birthday and I have no method of reaching her. Am I perhaps the one person from whom she genuinely wants to hear? Mechanical Street: I lie in bed. Tanaquil is a patient nurse. More details later. Tanaquil helps transcribe Moira's letters in the Aigues-Mortes notebook. I dictate translations, and she writes them down.

*

Theo,

I have not forgotten you. Nor, I trust, have you forgotten me. Your regular messages are a boon.

Sometimes I am disconsolate, as I sit in my room in the Hotel Constance, staring out, beyond the Aigues-Mortes walls, at the salt heaps, and thinking of the unfinished work ahead. In my act, the mother elephant guides the baby elephant; the baby's tricks surpass the mother's.

Moira Orfei

*

The Hotel Constance! At last, Moira has admitted her address. (Of course, Alfonso Reyes had already spilled the beans.) I recall sitting beside my Guadalquivar grandfather—Ricardo—in a Chevrolet, while he coughed. A mechanical device, installed in his lungs to help him breathe, made the sound of a circus artiste climbing, with bare hands, a rope-ladder. I patted helpless Ricardo on the back to clear his congestion. Aigues-Mortes approaches. If only I could convince Moira Orfei that she is Brigitte Bardot's superior! Tanaquil agrees: Orfei in *Triumph of Hercules* is more beautiful than Bardot in *Contempt*. In my bedroom, Tanaquil and I watch the *Triumph* video. In Moira's first scene, she emerges, sorceress, from a red cloud that clears only to form a denser, more enveloping fog.

*

Theo,

In the Hotel Constance, I dream. Late in the day, reality dawns; I push it aside. We perform not as ourselves, but as replicas. The incongruity drove Father mad.

In the Hotel Constance, I remember Father, asylum-committed (I see Lucca's ramparts); again circus insists I enter its séance.

Moira Orfei

*

Theo,

Fasting, I remember what Marguerite Duras told me, soon before her death: never hesitate. Was Marguerite wrong?

I'd like to destroy all my circus programs from the past twenty years, to forget.

The Spanish Inquisition and the Spanish Civil War enter my sleep. Long-ago mistakes, re-erupting, shatter Europe. Reparation is performance's point. In our act, Europe will finally cohere, even if unity is horror.

Please appear to perform these truths within the ring, beside trapeze and Indian leopard.

Moira Orfei

*

Theo,

I spend my days napping in the Hotel Constance, waiting, dreaming. I wake, and suddenly remember that we were to meet tomorrow, at six p.m., under the arcades, within view of the Constance Tower. And then I fall back asleep.

Six turns into seven, but then, seven turns back into six.

Moira Orfei

*

Theo,

Afraid of vibrations in the Hotel Constance walls; afraid of towers, parapets; afraid of the Middle Ages, returning; afraid of dying lagoons surrounding Aigues-Mortes walls; afraid of the four canals leading to the town, and what the canals have carried; afraid of seriousness and of levity; afraid of the work awaiting us, and the unfinished nature of circus; afraid of Aigues-Mortes—

Afraid, I left Aigues-Mortes, though I will soon return—

Afraid, I fled, for Portbou. You told me that you vacationed there, as a child. Now I learn that Portbou was where Walter Benjamin took his life. I had not realized until today. The information sinks deep into me, as I nap, in the hotel. I remember Father telling me that

Walter Benjamin (known to my family not as a philosopher but as a circus connoisseur) was a follower of the great Grimaldi, the clown; that Walter rode a Liberty Horse in the Grand Parade of the circus of the Fratellini Frères; that he idolized the immortal Paul Cinquevalli, juggler . . . Father's information may be wrong. Though not a circus artiste, Father walked on wires, the crossbars of lunacy . . .

I enclose a photo of Portbou's Hotel de Anza, recently opened. If you hurry, you may find me there, before I return to Aigues-Mortes.

My tone is cold but my heart is warm.

In the graveyard, I met a young man, Paolo, a handsome young Italian, from Monterosso al Mare; for a living, he leads tours of Portbou, but no one these days wants a tour. He told me details of Walter's suicide, which I forget. Did he shoot himself or drown? Paolo took me to the memorial, a staircase that leads down—almost—into the ocean. Right before you fall into the sea, a plexiglass plate with a mysterious inscription stops you. Then you walk back up the passageway, returning to the light. Ascent is more melancholy than descent; return, more horrifying than departure.

Circus has not given me time for philosophy, though there are more profundities in the elephant trunk swaying, the artiste somersaulting over seven horses, than in entire libraries.

I am learning my lesson, traveling, dissolving former mendacities in the Golfe du Lion, the Côte Vermeille, the Costa Brava, even if I never visit them, even if these coasts are chimeras.

Moira Orfei

*

Theo,

Profane, I wait in Portbou, preparing for return to Aigues-Mortes, where I will meet you, upon your tardy—never too late—arrival.

Paolo put me in touch with a Portbou psychic, a gypsy who told me that I would soon contemplate a religious vocation, and that I am Spanish, not Italian. I sank into trance, Paolo said, when I sat in the gypsy's parlor (her necklace the color of amontillado), and I began to speak of continental slaughter, of Europeans destroying their neighbors, of carnage that we can never erase or rectify. And when I woke from my trance, I felt again entrapped in circus, and I knew what it meant to be lost in Portbou; to fear return; to wait for rescue; to ignore the sea view; to descend a staircase into Stygian waters; to have no art, or too much art; to wonder about the existence of palm trees in the North.

Moira Orfei

*

Theo,

Indefinitely I remain in Portbou, so quiet I imagine that Europe has collapsed and that only I remain. The postal system is about to break down: a strike. I must mail this letter, before communication fails.

Moira Orfei

*

Friedman came by. He will fly tomorrow to Corfu, joining his mother. She promises to nurse him back to health, though I doubt that Corfu doctors are sophisticated enough to finesse his case, and I doubt that Samantha will tolerate Friedman's violent tantrums. Will he hustle in Corfu, or will that vocational chapter close? I said farewell to Friedman, our eyes moist as the red cloud from which Moira Orfei, playing Pasiphae in *Triumph of Hercules,* emerges.

*

Theo,

At the risk of endangering our act (I am a circus artiste, not an historian), I remain in Portbou, at the Hotel de Anza, absorbing exile's frequencies. Each day I wander with Paolo, who is obsessed with Walter Benjamin. I understand the preoccupation: Father trained me to forgive men's monomanias. Aloud, Paolo speculates about what manuscript Walter carried in his heavy black briefcase over the border from France to Spain. These speculations mean more to Paolo than to me, and yet, sensing their urgency, I listen, as if hearing Chloe's sick cat cry. No one knows what happened to Walter's briefcase, or the manuscript inside. Paolo thinks it was an unfinished autobiography. According to Paolo, Walter died by overdosing on morphine in Portbou; the Spanish authorities had threatened to send him back to France, and the thought of the return journey over the difficult mountains, with his weak heart, made him choose death. I understand. I would take morphine, if I were forced to leave Montecatini forever, and never lay eyes again on the huts and palaces of my forefathers.

According to Paolo, Walter said, "This manuscript is more important than I am." I understand. My circus is more important than I am. Paolo is very handsome! He is only twenty-five, but already a scholar. I may conscript him into circus. He tells me that Walter could be cruel, ruthlessly dropping friends when he tired of them, or when they interfered with his work. I understand. When I am deep in circus preparations, all I can think is trapeze, ring, elephant, tiger, bauble, wire hawser, crossbar, midget, monkey, flame. I cannot think "friend." I can only consider the passages that link slumber to circus. Each night I need ten hours of unconsciousness. Paolo provides tranquillizing draughts.

Moira Orfei

*

On Mechanical Street, I lie in bed, and fail to recover. Dr. Crick visits daily. Tanaquil takes dictation. I translate Moira Orfei's nearly daily letters. She writes on handmade paper, neatly folded, her tiny penmanship difficult to decipher. Her Italian is ornate, archaic. I consult an Italian-English dictionary, extrapolate meaning from context. Between bouts of translation, intervals of stupor, I study my score of Liszt's Second Piano Concerto, hoping to undo the Carpentras memory lapse. Rereading Moira Orfei's letters and postcards, reciting their translations to Tanaquil, I picture Moira Orfei, in Portbou, in Aigues-Mortes, sleeping in her hotel and then rising and walking onto the balcony to watch a small white sailboat cross the Mediterranean. I know that she is falling in love with Paolo, as is her wont, and I am glad. If only I could stretch the Aigues-Mortes notebook page into a movie screen and project onto it the complete films of Moira Orfei . . .

*

Theo,

Infidel, I left Portbou, bringing Paolo with me. I write to you from Nice, after visiting the Israelite cemetery. A stone marks the spot where soap made from the fat of Jews was buried.

I went to a psychic near the Hotel Negresco. She told me that in my heart I am a Jew from Spain. Perhaps that is what the Portbou psychic meant, when she said that I was on the verge of contemplating a religious vocation. I have asked Chloe for corroboration. She agrees with the Portbou psychic: the early Orfeis, orphic and wandering, were Sephardic Jews. Mother's deathbed mumblings lead to this conclusion.

In the Israelite cemetery, in Nice, I saw familiar names: Derida, Aline, Klein, Picard. These are women and men I have loved and entertained with circus feats.

Chloe finds Paolo simpatico, for now.

Moira Orfei

*

Theo,

In Nice, at a street fair this morning I bought Hugo's "Hernani" and poèmes by A. de Musset. Did you know that Nice (Nizza), until one hundred years ago, was Italian property? So much of Europe has been stolen! She robbed herself and others, as I, in circus, have stolen from earlier circuses, from Erich Hagenbeck and his sea lions, from the Medrano sisters and their rosin-backs, their Percherons.

Fish don't have sphincters, Chloe told me today, as we sat in the lobby of the Hotel de Anza, watching tropical fish swim languidly in their aquarium. The Egyptian mouthbrooder and the pink-tailed chalceus may be dying.

Walking along the Promenade des Anglais, I realized that I am a victim of my own excesses. But to be in error is simply to be in circus.

Reading my letters, you enter my ring. As Bertha Burleigh, writer, artiste, know-it-all, who coached me in circus trickery, used to say, "Moira, let the act begin! Stop hesitating!"

Moira Orfei

*

Theo,

I remain in Nice, uncanny city. A woman selling socca at the marche des fleurs looked exactly like me! I introduced myself. Her name was Therese. She refreshed her makeup between arrivals of batches of socca, wheeled in, on a cart, by a handsome man (I think he was her son); each time she put on a fresh coat of makeup, she looked more like me.

Near Therese, I found a small booth selling spices and healing spirits. I bought a bottle of eau de bluet, which, Chloe tells me, has medicinal properties: it clears vision. This evening, preparing for reunion, I applied the salve to my eyelids. Paolo looked twice-born, refashioned, in hotel-room mood-light.

This afternoon Paolo and I wandered again through the Israelite cemetery, looking for Orfeis, finding none. Tomorrow I'll try again.

Your letters have been forwarded to me at the Hotel de Anza in Nice. I am glad that, in your sickness, you have had the strength to concentrate on me, to focus on my invisibility, my mourning.

Do you remember, once you recited a poem by Mayakovsky, as we ate pomegranates? Yesterday, when a pomegranate stared at me from a table in a Matisse painting, I thought of our conversation. Sometimes the objects inspiring a painting are more inspiring than the painting itself.

Moira Orfei

*

Theo,

In Aigues-Mortes. I have made the resolution to devote myself full-time, without reservation, to pursuing my ancestors. Paolo and Chloe concur.

Have you discovered the meaning of Aigues-Mortes? The moon remains half-empty, half-full, over the Tour de Constance.

Moira Orfei

*

Theo,

In Aigues-Mortes. Chloe departed this morning for Montecatini, Paolo slept in, and, I, alone, went on a tour of a salt-making plant. I will incorporate, in the Aigues-Mortes performance, a sequence of acrobatic movements devoted to the secret history of salt, a mineral substance that leads to profane ecstasy as surely as it leads to the Lord.

As a circus child, I never had time for Sunday school. Religious education was subordinated to excess; Father and Mother delighted in overtaxing my body and imagination, for the good of the ring. Thus I understand Sodom. Some magnetic, wicked cities you must turn your back on; other, blessed cities you must travel to—places of anesthesia, amputation, correction.

Playing Fauré in Aigues-Mortes, as you will soon do, cannot lead us down the staircase, in Portbou, into the ocean, but it can lead us back up the staircase, to the level ground, the earth on which the Hotel de Anza, recently built in Portbou, reigns.

Don't worry about the unpopularity of piano recitals. Yours, imaginatively augmented by a circus artiste, will be a treat.

I trust that you have not destroyed my postcards, but that you are keeping them in a safe and permanent place. I fear their disappearance, as I fear the evaporation of the meanings of Aigues-Mortes, residing in me today, as I rest in the hotel, waiting for Paolo to awake.

Moira Orfei

P.S. I do not wish you to be humiliated when you enter my ring and play your pieces, but do not fear disaster! When you appear this year in Aigues-Mortes you will be the strangest artiste in the festival. I have prepared carefully, as have you, and we need not be cautious about reunion. Consider the performance a rest cure, a vacation. DO NOT POSTPONE AIGUES-MORTES.

*

I would like to write Moira Orfei a truthful letter, but I am afraid to disappoint her. I have not asked Tanaquil to transcribe my recent missives to Moira Orfei, because they deceitfully avoid mentioning my physical state.

"Moira Orfei, I am in no shape to travel," the honest letter would begin; it would describe my sickness. Certainly she would forgive fatigue? Here I lie, in East Kill, in Alma's bed; she is away on tour, and would not mind that, in her absence, I occupy her room, large and quiet enough for convalescence. I have brought into her bedroom Gertrude's Venetian candelabra, and placed it on the armoire. Alma is in Buenos Aires. She called last night. I used the speaker phone. She said that she is happy, being lauded. Her voice had a new simplicity, after decades of complications. Her career, she said, will last for many more years. Contentment, or a stasis that misrecognizes itself as happiness, filled her Mechanical Street bedroom, where I lie in indeterminate convalescence, translating Moira Orfei's daily letters, and seeing them transcribed, with Tanaquil's assistance, in the Aigues-Mortes notebooks. Tanaquil asked permission to marry Jon Nile, who still lives in our guest cottage. I wonder if he has proposed, or if Tanaquil is exaggerating their bond. In any case, I gave Tanaquil my blessing. Jon stays in the barn, and doesn't bother me in my decline. Matilda has stopped telephoning. My sickness frightens her. She, too, will die; someone, not me, will read her obituary in a Boston newspaper, and will notice that she is described as the sister of Alma Guadalquivar Mangrove.

*

Dear Theo,

I write to you from the Hotel Constance, in Aigues-Mortes. The town is ready for you. Everything is in place: my ostrich feather costume, the Liberty Horses, the bears on their bicycles, the hanging iron hoops for the upside-down tango, the cobra and its fakir. You and I have worked together so carefully in the past, that I am confident we can proceed, after your arrival, without rehearsal; we can skip preliminary steps, and speed directly into the white heat of performance.

Last night as I was wandering the arcades, a dog (a greyhound, Paolo guesses) bit me lightly on the leg. No infection.

Moira Orfei

*

The house on Mechanical Street will be Tanaquil's. Much of my "butter" money will go to Tanaquil. The *conservatoire* will get nothing. Anita will continue to receive alimony until she remarries. The Aigues-Mortes notebooks, the health and sickness notebooks, the divorce notebooks, the Portbou notebooks, and all the other notebooks, go to the Moira Orfei Living Museum, which doesn't yet exist. Some of the "butter" money goes to the Moira Orfei Living Museum, as a seed fund, hoping to attract other investors.

*

Theo,

That you are not yet here is an absence that fills me with sadness, as does your recent silence. Your disappearance disturbs Paolo, too, though he has never met you. I can only wonder about your health, whether you have been faithfully seeing your doctor and following his regimen. You and I have spoken about the pleasure of rejecting doctors. But there is also solace in obeying.

Is the blankness you feel, waiting to depart for Aigues-Mortes, equal to the absence I feel, waiting for you to arrive? Have you forgotten that we'd planned to meet? I keep before me, on the hotel bureau, your many letters, attesting to your fidelity, your bankable truth, the certainty of your imminent arrival.

The idea for our reunion was mine. I extended to you an open invitation: a late spring co-performance in Aigues-Mortes, the town best suited to host our reminiscences. Alfonso Reyes tendered the invitation, never mentioning me. I came into the picture later, unforeshadowed. You wrote to me. You wrote to me again. I took my time responding. And then I answered in floods. You and I spent months communicating, preparing separately. We did not fail to coordinate our visions. Wanda Osiris, mistress of variety spectacle (you are too young to remember her prime), always told Father that the most haunting part of a performance is the moment before.

My serious friend, together we create a circle: in circles, circus secrets dwell. Enjoying circuitousness, I peacefully dwell in the dead center of a ring of special effects; around me, particles circulate, like a flock of white doves, and I remain motionless. My job is not to imitate a bird but to greet, domesticate, and pacify the birds: to turn the birds into cloudy image, a froth of feathers.

I may have given you the impression that circus was forced on me, as a child. Perhaps I was unwilling, at the start. But by the time that Father was locked in the madhouse, and Mother had died, I was committed to circus—a life of commemorating Mother, patient and credulous, watching me. She never saw me perform with you, and yet to her I will dedicate Aigues-Mortes, as I dedicate every circus. My mother is buried in Montecatini, but she is also buried in Aigues-Mortes; she is entombed wherever I travel to commemorate her delight in seeing me perform, even if, at the time of that first, death-dealing spectacular, I was only half-willing to be watched.

That your health is fragile has never been a secret from me. That we wait together, for departure and flight, is no secret from the men and women who watch our act, nervous that we will fall from our unwise height, above the ring, and die. Do I grow too abstract, in my gesture of invitation to you? Are you happier without me? That is a secret I could not bear to hear.

Have you considered a period of convalescence in Aigues-Mortes, after our perform-ance? There is no need for you to rush back to Mechanical Street. I could book you a room, on a floating, semi-permanent basis, in the Hotel Constance, overlooking the Étang de Psalmody. I would not like to give up my privacy, by suggesting that we share a suite, but we could have rooms on the same floor, and we could meet, in the morning, before rehearsal, for breakfast downstairs, as we did at the Hotel de Anza. The Hotel Constance lacks the glory and repute of the Hotel de Anza, but I have it on faith, from Alfonso Reyes, and the Aigues-Mortes festival organizers, that a Hotel de Anza will open here, beside the Tour du Sel, before next year, and we could reserve rooms, if you recover spontaneity, and arrive in Aigues-Mortes before the border closes, the threshold always about to shut down, whether or not the news-papers faithfully advertise this fact.

But I do not wish idle speculations about next year to distract you from the present moment. Paolo tells me that what made Wanda Osiris great was her attention to everyday consciousness. I am tired of circus, but I am not tired of awareness.

A circus star wearies of her travels and tricks. Exhaustion helps me understand history, how wrecked Europe is, as it waits, in the sea, for other conquerers to overtake it, as it has plundered others, in turn . . . Resting in my hotel, I recall the cemetery in Nice: I think of Picard, who enjoyed my Grand Parade, as I led the cream ponies, and, later, danced upon their backs.

Take heart. As long as there is Moira Orfei, there will be circus. As long as there is circus, there will be Aigues-Mortes. As long as there is Aigues-Mortes, there will be Mechanical Street. As long as there is Mechanical Street, there will be Moira Orfei. Perfect circulation of the parts creates circus happiness.

As long as there is Moira Orfei, there will be Theo Mangrove. As long as there is Theo Mangrove, there will be Mechanical Street. As long as there is Mechanical Street, there will be Aigues-Mortes. As long as there is Aigues-Mortes, there will be Moira Orfei.

"Much of my life has been a waste, but not this moment," you once wrote to me. Which moment did you mean?

Words. Mere words. Circus is more. That is why the public yearns for the Orfei precipice, my dive away from the known, the sayable. With me, darling, stumble away from circus, in the unbuilt Hotel de Anza: decline need not be solitary.

On carnival distractions I have wasted my life, looking away from the mystery. In my hotel room, facing enigma, I find it less frightening than I had thought, when I avoided it, in Montecatini, and in other stops on my endless, reality-deferring tour. I wish I had had the strength, years ago, to halt my life, escape to Aigues-Mortes, and here, in the Hotel Constance, witness the fall away from dream into fact. For what you will see, when you arrive in Aigues-Mortes, and greet me, is not a dream. Horses, flamingos, parapets, salt: the daily arrival of darkness, here, is as authentic—and paralyzing—as the distance between us.

Moira Orfei

Wayne Koestenbaum has published five books of nonfiction prose: *Andy Warhol*; *Cleavage: Essays on Sex, Stars, and Aesthetics*; *Jackie Under My Skin: Interpreting an Icon*; *The Queen's Throat: Opera, Homosexuality, and the Mystery of Desire* (a National Book Critics Circle Award finalist); and *Double Talk: The Erotics of Male Literary Collaboration*. His books of poetry are *Model Homes*, *The Milk of Inquiry*, *Rhapsodies of a Repeat Offender*, and *Ode to Anna Moffo and Other Poems*. He is currently a professor of English at City University of New York's Graduate Center.